THE FAT BITCH DIET

By A. R. Khan

Copyright © 2017 by Amir R. Khan

All rights reserved. This book or any portion thereof may not be reproduced or used in any manner whatsoever without the express written permission of the publisher except for the use of brief quotations in a book review.

Cover design by Suzana Stankovic
Edited by Crystal Watanabe

Arkhanbooks.com

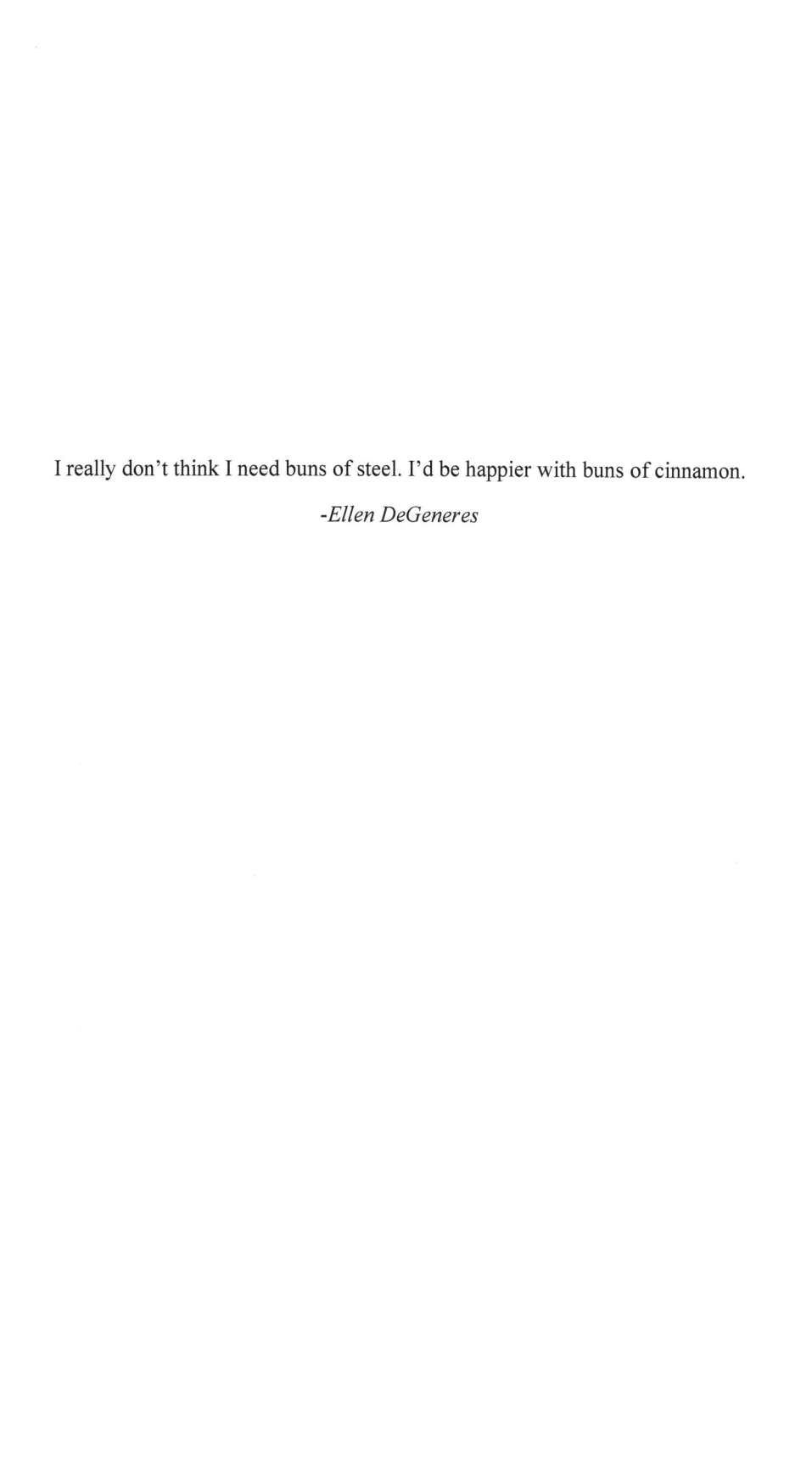

I really don't think I need buns of steel. I'd be happier with buns of cinnamon.

-Ellen DeGeneres

Chapter One

November 12, 2016

I lifted an oversized bag of brownie mix onto the kitchen counter, huffing and puffing, and not just for show.

I adjusted the camera on my laptop, then paused to caution my loyal viewers, "Always lift with your legs, I once threw out my back lifting a bag of flour."

"For those of you who are new to my channel, my name is Viola Ginamero." I spun around, showing off my five foot four, 193-pound figure. "As you can clearly see, I'll put anything in my mouth."

I tucked my long blonde hair behind my ears and held it in place with a chip clip. "Don't want my co-workers picking hair out of their teeth; they're still mad at me for the food poisoning incident."

"Quick note to my new viewers: this is no ordinary cooking channel. I like to alter my meals in adventurous ways. I'll be honest, some of the meals turn out bad. I mean, last week's chocolate chicken pot pie gave me cramps for days."

My arms shook from the weight of the bag as I poured it into a large ceramic bowl. "Let's go over the ingredients in this mix."

"See these little hard chunks over here? These are pieces of bacon, and if you look closely over here on this side of the bowl you will see a shiny texture. This is bacon fat that I captured in a shot glass this morning."

I tilted the bowl to let light bounce off the chocolate mixture. "You may have also noticed the large white lumps over here. I know what you're thinking: They look like marshmallows. Wrong! These are pieces of chicken breast I cut up last night."

I lowered the bowl and reached for a nearby spatula.

"Oh! I forgot to add something." I ran off camera towards the fridge.

"Here it is… Velveeta cheese!" I couldn't help but smile gleefully. "Ladies, don't you wish your man smelled more like cheese?"

"You know what? Let's get wild, I'm going to mix in the full block."

"As you can see, it's getting a little dense, so I'm going to pour some pancake syrup over the mixture to thin it out a bit."

"So while I stir, I just wanted to remind you all to like, comment, and subscribe below. You can also catch me on Facebook and on Twitter under @ViolaSwallows."

"So… this looks well mixed. Let's grab an 11x7-inch baking pan. Don't worry about the thickness; as the mixture slowly flows into this pan, I will flatten it out with the spatula."

I gracefully inserted the pan into the oven. "Earlier, I preheated the oven to 300 degrees Fahrenheit, so I should be okay to bake these for fifty to fifty-five minutes. Side note: last week I discovered that this oven has a self-cleaning option. I stumbled upon it after I accidentally set a lasagna on fire."

"That brings us to the end of this video. As always, I will post a follow-up video with my review of the brownies later tonight. Till next time… I'm Viola Ginamero, and this is #ViolaSwallows."

I felt great. Full of energy and eager to upload the video right away. It was exciting to think of how quickly a year had passed since I posted my first video, and now I was uploading video #29. Interesting fact: If you were to sort the videos by date you could really see how much weight I gained in a year.

I wasn't always this heavy; as a pre-teen I was really petite, it was a few years later that an event triggered my weight gain.

It was an oddly quiet night in the apartment—the usual loud music and drunk laughter from across the hall was sadly missing.

Thankfully the silence was quickly broken with the ringing of my cell phone—it was my best friend, Shaniqua.

"Viola speaking!"

"Girl, why do answer your phone like that? You know it's me."

"Hang on a sec, Shaniqua, I need to put my laptop away."

"Still makin' those videos? I think you're addicted."

"I'm addicted to two things: eating chocolate in bed and Snap chatting on the toilet."

"Whatever. Anyways, can I grab a ride with you to work tomorrow?"

"For sure. Pick you up at eight?"

"Sounds good. Honk really loud when you get here, that way Shamar's unemployed, lazy ass can wake up."

"Okay. Night, girl. Love ya." I made kissing sounds into the receiver.

Shaniqua hung up, and I could almost hear her eyes roll.

Forty minutes passed, and I couldn't resist the aromatic seduction of the brownies anymore. I raced to the oven and removed the hot pan with a hand towel, slightly burning my fingers. Then I looked at the time—it was almost midnight! Realizing that they needed time to harden, I decided to refrigerate them until tomorrow.

Chapter Two

198 Lbs

November 13, 2016

I don't remember what woke me up first, the sunlight or my bladder. Either way, I was ready for the excitement of a brand new day. In fact, I would be spinning around singing 'Oh, What a Beautiful Morning' if I didn't get motion sickness so easily.

After springing out of bed, I headed straight for the bathroom for three minutes of brushing, two minutes of nude posing, and a forty-minute shower.

Living alone had its perks. I had no issues tiptoeing naked past the living room window, unless you count that one time the landlord slipped a note under my door, requesting that I close my curtains.

I slipped into my work uniform, neurotically combed my long blonde hair ten times on each side, and headed straight for the kitchen for the usual: four eggs sunny-side up, ten pieces of bacon, five sausages, and one large chocolate milkshake. This had been my morning breakfast since I was a teenager.

After gulping down the milkshake, I was ready to pick up Shaniqua. With optimism by my side, I grabbed my car keys and headed down to the curb.

The really heavy eating began after my parents got divorced, right around when I was entering middle school. I only remember this because I was forced to see a school therapist due to what they called 'disruptive eating.'

Since when is eating a bag of chips in class disruptive?

Anyways, he diagnosed me with some sort of anxiety disorder, which ultimately caused me to eat even more.

After the divorce, my parents shifted their focus away from me and onto their new, separate lives, and I went from being their child to a bitter reminder of their former other half. After that, the closest thing I had to a mother figure was Aunt Jemima.

"Come on, you stupid thing… start!" I yelled, shaking the steering wheel. I was driving a rust bucket from the nineties and, similar to an office photocopier, had to put up with its constant failures every day.

Five minutes later, I was well on my way to Shaniqua's house. I was getting a little nervous as I was running late and even though we're besties, she's not very understanding.

Shaniqua was on the heavy side, too. We became best friends in high school and have been tied to the hip ever since.

The thing about being mocked and bullied in a school environment is that you have two choices: You can either accept it or fight it. I let people roll over me, but Shaniqua was a hard-hitting, foul-mouthed, in-your-face fighter. If you messed with Shaniqua you'd get a heavy dose of attitude and humiliation. Her protection is the only reason I made it through high school. There was only one problem: She didn't know how to turn her aggression off.

Approaching Shaniqua's house, I followed her instructions and honked multiple times.

After five minutes of waiting in the parked car, I was getting impatient. "Come on, Shan… Where are you?"

I honked a few more times just before she finally came out of the house.

Shaniqua strutted towards the car with a large designer bag in hand, a not-so subtle black curly weave, and a tight leather jacket.

I reached over and opened the passenger-side door. "Good morning, my ball of sunshine. And how are you today?"

She got in quietly, slamming the door behind her.

"Shan, I had some car trouble." She remained silent, tightly crossing her arms in front of her chest.

"Viola, you need to get yourself a new car. Don't be so cheap."

"Hey, I'm not cheap, I'm *financially strategic*."

Suddenly, a minivan pulled in in front of us, blocking our movement. Shaniqua poked her head out of the window. "Umm… what is this woman doing?"

"It looks like she has a little girl with her. Maybe she's dropping her off, sit tight."

Shaniqua leaned back into her seat. "Well, it looks like they're moving now."

The car maneuvered into the middle of the road, where it came to a stop.

Confused, I looked at Shaniqua. "What the hell? Now she's blocking the middle of the road."

Shaniqua undid her seatbelt. "Drive up close to her for a sec."

"Okay, but don't be rude, not in front of the kid."

"Viola, I'm not rude, I'm assertive." Shaniqua slid over to the driver's seat, leaned over me, and poked her head out the window. She politely got the little girl's attention.

"Excuse me, sweetie, can you please call your mom?" The little girl tapped on her mom's shoulder, she was a slender African woman with a cornrow braided hairstyle.

The woman looked nervously at Shaniqua. "Can I help you?"

"Bitch, do you know how to drive?" she yelled. "Or are your braids cutting off the blood to your head?"

Needless to say, the car quickly sped off. I never said Shaniqua's feisty attitude and anger wasn't effective—it definitely had it's benefits.

"Shan, I think you made her mom cry."

"She's lucky I didn't get out of the car and strangle her with my purse."

I looked over at her. "Umm, you're more irritable than usual today. Your IBS acting up again?"

She rolled her eyes. "I asked that numbskull Shamar to do one load of laundry yesterday when I was getting my nails done and my hair did, and that foo shrank all my clothes, including my uniform!"

"It's okay, I think we have some extras at work. So… how is Shamar?"

"He's still unemployed, annoying, and useless, even more so than usual."

I frowned. "Is he depressed?"

"How should I know? Like most men, he doesn't open up."

"Shaniqua, you need to communicate more with him."

She quickly got defensive. "I do! Just this morning I told him he's a dumbass. That's communicating, right?"

Shamar and Shaniqua had been dating for five years. Anyone would agree that they didn't look right for each other. Shamar was as skinny as a twig and Shaniqua was built like an oak. But they loved each other.

Or so they said.

The awkward drive to work was thankfully saved by the perfect timing of my favorite radio show. "Ooh! I think *Talk New York* is on!"

"Viola, I can't listen to that garbage, it gives me a headache, and if I wanted a headache I have that birdbrain Shamar for that." She rolled down her window, as my car had no air conditioning.

"Oh, shut it. I *love Talk New York*. Remember that lady who called in contemplating adultery because her husband forgot their anniversary?"

"Girl, that caller was trippin."

As we hit a commercial break, I turned down the volume. "I swear, this station is more advertising than talk."

"Doesn't matter, we're almost there. Hey, did you know there's a new personal trainer starting today?"

"Yeah, a woman named Christa." Shaniqua's cell phone began to ring, and she quickly ignored the call, which meant that it was probably Shamar.

I couldn't help but stare at her.

"Don't judge me. I ain't got time for Shamar's stupidity right now."

"You ever think about the future? Like do you see yourself marrying Shamar and having kids?"

"Yeah, sure. I just have to iron out all of his stupidity wrinkles first." She slid the phone back into her pocket. Even though their relationship was rocky, I had no doubt in my mind that Shaniqua would end up marrying Shamar, as it was her longest relationship to date.

"We're here," I said. "Ready to get your work on?" She barely heard me, as she was too distracted checking out some guy in the parking lot.

"Damn, girl. Who is that fine-looking man?"

She peeked out of her window like a dog trying to catch wind, but I couldn't get a good look due to the glare from the sun.

I got a better look once I got out of the car. He was a bearded, muscular man with a large blue duffel bag draped over his shoulder. His hair was styled high and was clearly full of product. Most women would be attracted to a man like that, but I wasn't one of them.

"He must be new to the gym," I said, watching him head in the door. I wasn't at all impressed. Shaniqua, on the other hand, was practically panting. "Well, let's get in there and open up shop."

Shaniqua and I worked at a fitness gym called The Fitness Hut. Well, actually, we worked at a juice bar, The Protein Hut, which was located inside The Fitness Hut.

We started working at The Protein Hut as part of a work experience program in high school.

She held the door open for me. "Seriously, Viola, you need to get a new car. Get something sexy, like that fine man who just walked into the Hut. Don't be afraid to splurge on yourself."

"Hey, I splurge. I splurged at Costco just last week."

"Viola, buying lubricant in bulk doesn't count as spoiling yourself."

The gym was virtually deserted; the few members I saw were gossiping around the treadmills.

I was surprised the gym lasted as long as it did with its old equipment, unenthusiastic personal trainers, and rude employees.

Aesthetically, The Protein Hut stood out from the gym with its yellow walls, brown tile flooring, and tacky signage. Like any juice bar, the mainstay sellers were protein shakes, fruit beverages, and overpriced gourmet sandwiches.

The sandwiches and wraps weren't very popular and ended up sitting behind the glass for days. If you ignored the fact that a few club members had complained about food poisoning, the sandwiches were pretty tasty.

I scanned the gym floor. "Is this place going to go belly up?"

"It better not. With Shamar's unemployed ass I would be hooped without this job."

I knew one day I would have to move on from The Protein Hut. The problem was that I had nothing to fall back on. Eating was a lot higher on the motivation scale than post-secondary education.

It was clearly another typical day at work, with the familiar sound of barbells hitting the floor and local radio on the rooftop speakers.

The hours of The Protein Hut were appetizing. Who couldn't be attracted to a shift that started at 8:00 AM and ended at 2:30 PM? That gave me the whole day to upload YouTube videos, binge-watch Netflix, and eat fried chicken.

Due to our late arrival we were behind on the opening procedures, but fortunately nobody was in line.

Smiling optimistically at Shan, I said, "Are you ready for another exciting shift at The Protein Hut?" She rolled her eyes and walked into the tiny office at the back of the Hut.

Since Shaniqua and I were the only weekday staff, we had a lot of responsibilities. The gym owners had mandated that morning cleaning and preparation procedures should last at least an hour and a half. Shaniqua and I have figured out a way to do it in a fraction of that time.

Shaniqua walked out of the office with a stopwatch. "Okay, are you ready, Viola?"

"What was your time again yesterday?" I filled the spray bottle with Clorox, praying that I could beat her time, as the loser would have to clean the disgusting bathroom.

Shaniqua replied, "The time to beat is six minutes and twenty-three seconds. Go!"

With the bottle in hand, I walked briskly along the narrow counter, spraying the cash register, blenders, and the shelves. The trick to being efficient was to only spray once from the bottle.

I quickly spun around and sprayed the few tables and chairs that were positioned by the wall. Throwing the bottle down, I folded the rag and retraced my steps backwards to wipe down everything that was sprayed.

"How am I doing?" I said, feeling breathless, like I was about to go into cardiac arrest.

"You're at... just over three minutes." Shaniqua's eyes were glued to the stopwatch. "Hurry up, girl, fruits and vegetables are next."

I could barely move. Clearly I was not in the shape I thought I was. "I'm feeling dizzy," I replied, wiping sweat off my forehead. I walked towards the back of the Hut and dragged over a mixed bucket of fruits and vegetables. "I think I am going to throw up."

"Away from the apples this time, Viola!"

I scooped up the fruit into my arms and dumped them onto the counter, followed immediately by the vegetables. Breathing heavily, I ran towards the fridge to grab the wraps and sandwiches.

With the glass display in sight, I began tossing the wraps into it.

After I threw the last sandwich in, I slammed the fridge door shut and shouted, "Done!"

"Time is... five minutes and thirty-four seconds. Ugh, I guess I have to clean the bathroom," Shaniqua said, dragging her feet towards the bathroom with a bottle of Clorox in hand.

"Oh, come on, Shaniqua, it's not that bad," I said, putting on my tacky Protein Hut apron.

"This is humiliating!"

"Shan, trust me, I know what it feels like to be humiliated. In my high-school yearbook I was voted Most Hungry."

With Shaniqua cleaning the bathroom, I found myself standing behind the cash register, staring blankly as if I was in a hypnotic state.

"I'm sooo bored," I whispered to myself. I slipped my cell phone out of my pocket. No messages or notifications. You would think I would at least have a tweet or Facebook comment to reply to. Nothing.

Whenever I was alone at the till I would daydream about the past, specifically my employment experience and high-school days.

"Excuse me," said a motherly voice, grabbing my attention. I raised my head, noticing the first customer of the day—a heavy sixty-five-year-old woman with short brown hair, wearing gray sweats and a white T-shirt. She was a regular at The Protein Hut who spent more time walking to our till than actually walking on a treadmill.

"Good morning, ma'am. How can I help you today?" I said, perking up like a peppy cheerleader. Her eyes were glued on the menu above, but I already knew what she was going to order as it rarely ever changed.

"The usual, a large strawberry mango please." I felt kind of bad. She was very sweet and had been coming to The Protein Hut every day for almost a month and I still didn't know her name.

"Great! Will that be all?"

"Yes, dear."

"Excellent, that will be $3.75. Can I get a name for your cup?" I felt a little embarrassed asking.

"Barbara-Anne," she replied, smiling warmly. "You know, dear, you're a very pretty girl."

"Aww, thank you! I don't get that a lot, actually." I shoved a handful of strawberries and mangos into the nearest blender, and when it was done, I cheerfully handed her the smoothie.

The afternoon finally arrived, and not a moment too soon. The day couldn't have dragged on any slower; it felt as though the minutes on the clock above my head were moving at a snail's pace.

"Shaniqua, I think I am gonna take my break," I said, removing my apron. She was busy helping a customer, so I wasn't even sure she heard me. I walked away from the Hut anyway.

It was a hot afternoon, and I had a craving for something greasy and fatty. A pit stop at the street meat vendor was a must. Sure, I'd had a big breakfast, but regardless of my appetite, you could always find me with something warm, soft, and slippery in hand. Sometimes I could fit two pieces of meat in my mouth simultaneously!

"Oh my God!" I said to myself, staring at a large billboard. "Shaniqua is gonna lose her mind!"

I walked back across the street to The Fitness Hut to share the life-changing news.

But Shaniqua was nowhere in sight. I checked the parking lot, the gym floor, and the office—there was no sign of her.

"Viola, where have you been?" she said from behind me. "Girl, I need you on till."

"Shan! I have amazing news… remember that dream we had? It's about to become a reality!" I was shaking with excitement.

"Girl, are you for real? You better not be trippin," Shaniqua said, heading towards the parking lot.

I followed her out the door, excited to see her reaction.

We both stood across the street, staring as if we were looking at the Mona Lisa.

"Viola... this is the single greatest thing to ever happen to us," She stared intensely at the coming soon sign.

Taking a calm deep breath, I smiled and peacefully said, "In-N-Out Burger... coming soon."

It may seem a bit ridiculous for Shaniqua and I to be so excited, but this wasn't any ordinary fast food joint.

"Viola, we can finally be a part of the trend!"

"Hey, I'm already trendy. I buy strapless bras from Target."

When we arrived back at The Protein Hut there was a line of customers. The peak hour of the gym was upon us. It was also the hour my fatigue kicked in. The day was almost over and I was more than eager to go home, as I had dinner plans with my boyfriend, Franklin. Did I mention I was in a relationship of nine years? More on that later.

Chapter Three

 Lbs

November 13, 2016

Shaniqua and I were lazing about behind the counter when I recognized a familiar man across the room.

"Hey, Shaniqua, isn't that the guy from the parking lot?" I nudged her with my elbow. He reminded me of one of those models on the cover of Men's Fitness magazine. His dark hair stood tall and still had a lot of product in it, his body muscular but not bulky. What grossed me out was his modern full beard. My educated guess was that he was in his late twenties.

"Viola, that is one fine man. If I wasn't with Shamar I would let him penetrate my mouth…"

"Shaniqua!"

"Did I just say that out loud?"

I burst out with laughter.

"*What*? like you wouldn't?"

"No, thank you, I'm with Franklin, and the only thing I allow to penetrate my mouth are hot dogs."

"Seriously, though, Viola, don't you find him attractive?"

The truth was that I didn't; he wasn't my type, and he was way out of my league.

"Not at all, and what's with the beard? Beards are like vegetables to me—they gross me out." I cringed, staring at the man.

"I think it's sexy." Shaniqua couldn't take her eyes off of him.

"Ohh no," I said, suddenly noticing something critical. "Is he wearing a name tag?"

"Umm, I think so," she said, squinting.

"I don't think he's a member; he must be the new personal trainer," I said.

I felt a little uncomfortable, there was something about him that made me feel nervous. It was a familiar feeling; the same one I had when Franklin asked me out in high school—part butterflies, part nausea.

Our obsessive staring was quickly interrupted by an angry female customer.

"Excuse me!" She violently dropped a plate with a wrap on it in front of Shaniqua.

"I'll let you handle this," I said to Shaniqua, quickly walking away. I didn't like confrontations. I wasn't a pushover but I didn't know how to be assertive, either. For that reason, Franklin won all of our battles. Truth be told, we didn't argue much, but when we did the focus was always on our long-term future goals.

Franklin was the kind of guy who always wanted to change things up, while I was okay with the status quo. He was like this in high school as well, always trying to keep up with the latest fashion trends and technology, constantly trying to get me to dress a particular way or use a specific cell phone. To tell you the truth, even though it was annoying at times, he did always know what was best for me.

You would think that in a relationship spanning over nine years nothing would be missing, but something was—a ring on my finger. Sure, I would always hint at it, at one point I even sung along loudly to Beyoncé's "Single Ladies" whenever he was in the room. Either he was playing dumb after all these years or he had no interest in marrying me. Who would date somebody for over nine years and not propose? It just didn't make sense.

I think all the stress of trying to be a good girlfriend added to the rapid weight gain. I have to admit I did envy Franklin a bit. He'd had his professional future planned out since high school. The one thing he longed for the most in life was being a doctor by age thirty, and in a few months it would become a reality.

The two things I longed for the most in life was a marriage proposal and extra cheese.

Maybe his wealthy parents guided his success. It certainly pays to have parents with a lot of dough, or at least ones who encourage you. I think I would have been able to fit in a pair of skinny jeans had I had motivated parents.

I admit that I had some uncertainties about my relationship with Franklin, but I was also 100% certain that I couldn't imagine spending my life with anyone else.

You see: we had an unbreakable bond. In high school, I discovered that his parents divorced before he hit puberty. Our lengthy discussions about our family issues brought us closer and closer together until he finally worked up the courage to ask me out. It was a day I'll never forget because it was the same day I asked my mom about birth control… big mistake. My mom called my dad and lo and behold another argument erupted, which somehow ended up with me living with my dad by the end of the week.

It didn't bother me much. I was used to being a Ping-Pong ball. In the end, I was happy because I had a boyfriend, and I vowed to never let him go and never argue.

"Earth to Viola!" Shaniqua said, bringing me back to reality. I walked towards the cash register after seeing the long line that awaited my service.

"Sorry, I got lost in my thoughts." I flipped my long blonde hair over my shoulders. She was still helping out the angry woman.

"Grab the till for a sec; I need to check up on something," she said. That was code for 'I need to get out of here before I lose it.'

"Welcome to The Protein Hut, how can I help you?" I said, cheerfully hoping to disarm the angry customer. She was a short, overweight, middle-aged woman who was clearly looking to yell at somebody for sport.

The woman pointed at the plate and yelled, "This wrap is dented and it tastes like bleach! I demand to talk to the manager!" Suddenly I realized that I may have accidentally sprayed a few wraps with Clorox earlier.

"Umm... Shaniqua?" I waved her back into the ring. My stomach was in knots, and I could feel the woman's anger. "The manager will be with you in a few moments. I'm sorry you didn't enjoy your wrap." With Shaniqua back behind the till, I quietly moved to the side to observe.

"What's your problem?" Shaniqua said, trying to be professional and failing miserably. As you can guess, Shaniqua didn't shy away from telling customers off.

The woman pointed at me. "That girl told me she was getting the manager, where is he?"

"I'm the manager. Can I help you?" Shaniqua ground her teeth while trying to keep a friendly smile.

"Not only did you sell me a wrap that tastes like bleach, but you also gave me a protein-based smoothie when I asked for soy!" She opened the lid of her smoothie and held it out to Shaniqua. "I'm allergic to protein!"

"Listen you cherry-ass lookin' she-womp," Shaniqua yelled back, "if you're allergic to protein, why the hell would you order something from a place called The Protein Hut. Bitch, use your head!"

Suddenly the line behind the angry woman thinned out as frightened customers walked away.

"How dare you talk to me like that! This isn't over," the woman said in a threatening tone. As I watched the woman storm off, I couldn't help but get a bad feeling.

"Shaniqua, you don't think she is going to actually do something, do you?"

She shook her head. "Forget about her. So what do you have planned for Franklin tonight?"

"Well, I was thinking of fried chicken and mashed potatoes." I felt a bit embarrassed, as we both knew I was going to buy a bucket of chicken from the nearest KFC.

"Seriously, Viola, a little creativity won't hurt you," Shaniqua said as she wiped down the counter. Cleaning was a stress reliever for her, as long as it wasn't the bathroom.

"Hey, I have a creative side! It comes out during the Doritos Name Your Chip contest."

Shaniqua rolled her eyes. "You know, despite Shamar's dumbass antics, I still cook nice meals for him."

I puckered my chapped lips. "Now that I think about it, I usually only focus on desserts for #ViolaSwallows. Maybe I should make dinner."

"Girl, you need to change that name. #ViolaSwallows isn't doing you any favors."

(I eventually changed it, but more on that later.)

"So what do you think I should make for Franklin tonight?" I was always eager to receive advice from Shaniqua. She knew me better than myself.

"Well, first of all, what's the occasion?"

"He has something important to tell me. I assume it's about his residency. I think he'll be starting this month." I jumped up and down, clapping in excitement. "I'm so proud of him!"

"Viola, you don't know how lucky you are to have a doctor as a boyfriend. I'd be lucky if Shamar became a barista."

"So what should I make?" I said, refocusing the conversation.

"Girl, I got you. You can have my recipe for fried lasagna."

"Seriously?" My mouth was watering just thinking about her secret fried lasagna recipe. "Did I ever tell you how I had to wash my bedsheets after eating your last batch in bed?"

Shaniqua pulled out her phone. "I'll forward the recipe to you right now."

"You're the best, Shan!" I squealed in excitement. "Tonight is going to be a special night, I feel it."

She gently pushed my shoulder. "You know what? What if Franklin has something big to ask you?"

"You don't think?"

"Girl, what if tonight's the night Franklin *proposes* to you?"

"Oh my God, what if you're right? I'll lose my mind." I felt nervous and excited at the same time. It wasn't too far of a stretch that he would plan a proposal dinner close to the day he was officially becoming a doctor.

"Girl, I think it's gonna happen." Shaniqua smiled as if she knew something secretive.

"Oh, I hope it's true. I saw a beautiful wedding dress on Craigslist the other night, and after I get the blood out of the veil, it will be perfect!"

"Girl, are you for real?"

"Yup. Actually, I have several wedding ideas planned."

"Really? We pretended to work, fiddling with the fruits and moving the blenders around.

I may not have been a life planner like Franklin, but I did have our wedding day planned out in my head. It wouldn't be a typical wedding, either, as I wasn't a fan of the copy-paste church and hotel wedding. I liked the idea of doing something different.

I would have the ceremony on a long pier and the reception on a large boat. It would have to be docked, of course, as motion sickness was like second nature to me. I'm not joking; when I was eight, I once filled an entire paddleboat with vomit. It wasn't embarrassing until the girl next me started screaming as if someone had dumped acid on her feet.

I started organizing the chairs, still talking to her as I worked. "Well, if Franklin does propose tonight, I doubt we'll be staying here in New York."

"Girl, if that's true you better visit. Don't think for one second that I won't drag your ass back here."

"Aww, are you gonna miss me?" I wrapped my arms around her from behind. "I love you, too, Shan."

Shaniqua pushed my arms off of her. "Girl, don't be trippin, I'm serious."

"Don't worry, I'm not going anywhere. I've done too much damage to my apartment to get out of the lease. Besides, I'm sure Franklin will work in a hospital here in New York."

"Girl, I'm warning you, if you leave me and I'm stuck with that dumbass Shamar, there might be another homicide on the news."

"Shan, you're overreacting again."

"What? I'm just saying you help me stay calm, that's all."

Time began to crawl as we approached the end of our shift, with still an hour to go, I couldn't help but think about Shaniqua and her future with Shamar.

"Hey, Shaniqua… can I ask your opinion on something?" I tossed fruit slices into my mouth.

She turned to me and said, "You're not thinking about buying Spanx off Amazon again, are you?"

"No, I learned my lesson. The last time I wore Spanx I made a baby cry."

"Okay, then what's on your mind?"

"Have you and Shamar ever discussed the idea having children?" I felt the subject was a little touchy, but I was bored out of my mind.

"What, with each other?" Shaniqua said in disgust. "The only thing that foo should produce is another source of income. He ain't ready for no baby."

"But what about you? Do you want to be a mother?"

"Viola, the two things in life that turn me off the most are hard work and poop, what do you think?"

Baby talk was always a sensitive area for her; I never really knew why. I knew her better than she did but in this area I couldn't help but think that I was missing a piece of the Shaniqua puzzle.

"I can't wait to have a little monster of my own," I said, cheerfully looking up at the rickety ceiling fans. "Maybe I'll talk to Franklin tonight about going off the pill. I mean, I am almost thirty; if it's going to happen it needs to happen now." The more I thought about it the more fruit I kept stuffing in my mouth.

"Girl, you're getting baby fever again. Relax! You'll get your fairy-tale wedding and a cute baby boy or girl. But for now stop touching the fruit with your nasty-ass fingers!"

Maybe Shaniqua was right, I needed to relax and just let everything unravel on it's own. I'd already found the love of my life and if he proposed tonight, the stars would finally align.

I couldn't help but feel excited, as there was only half an hour left until home time.

"Hey, Shaniqua, guess what fabulous radio talk show is about to start?" I said in a devious tone.

"Viola, I am not in the mood for hearing more people problems."

"Oh, come on, it's the best way to end our work day." I turned towards the reception desk and shouted, "Hey, Janette! Can you turn the volume up?"

She slowly turned to me ever so graciously and gave me the middle finger. Shaniqua saw and immediately hollered from across the gym. "Hey! I missed lunch and I'm hungry for some skinny bitch, so don't think I won't bite that finger off!"

Shaniqua's bark put enough scare in Janette as she quickly scurried off to increase the radio volume.

"Ah, my knight in shining armor." I grabbed her shoulders like a damsel in distress. "Always there to defend my honor. The perfect companion—if only you had a penis."

We were just in time as we caught the host of *Talk New York* announcing today's topic.

"For those of you who are just joining us, today we are letting our listeners give advice to our callers, so if you have a dilemma or need help with an important decision, give us a call and let the Talk New York *family advise you."*

I clapped cheerfully. "Oh my God, I love when the callers give advice!"

"It's aight," Shaniqua said. "It can go too far sometimes."

"Are you referring to the caller who wanted advice on how to address her boyfriend's bad breath? The advice wasn't *that* bad."

"Sometimes cruel advice should be left in silence."

"People are cruel, Shaniqua. In middle-school, for three years I was led to believe that there was a fat tax." Shaniqua started laughing. "It's not funny! I actually saved my allowance for it."

"Girl, let's clean this place up so we can get out of here on time." I nodded, completely distracted by the radio chatter.

"Our next caller's name is Sherry. Are you still there, Sherry?"

"Yes, I'm here."

I turned to Shaniqua and said, "I knew a girl named Sherry in high school. She was so full of energy and confidence. I've never met a more optimistic person in my life."

"What happened to her?" Shaniqua began emptying the cash register.

"She committed suicide," I said bluntly.

"Girl, that is cold."

The host continued to talk. *"Sherry, tell us what advice you are seeking from our listeners."*

"Okay... well... my boyfriend is a germaphobe who doesn't know that I have been using his toothbrush for a few months now. It wasn't an issue until he found a cold sore around his upper lip one day. Now he refuses to let anything touch his mouth until he finds out what caused the sore. Should I tell him it was me and I was using his brush?"

Shaniqua and I looked at each other, clearly thinking the same thing.

"Well, Sherry, how would he react if he knew you were using his brush?"

"He... he would lose his fucking mind."

Shaniqua quickly looked in my direction. "Did that bitch just swear on live radio?"

"Shhh!" I said, listening attentively.

"Sherry, we are live, so please watch the language. Okay, so what do you think, listeners? Should Sherry tell her germaphobic boyfriend that she has been using his toothbrush for the last few months and passed a cold sore on to him? Or should she keep it to herself? We will be back in a few moments to discuss."

Shaniqua yelled, "See, this is why people should not share a toothbrush—it's nasty!"

I rolled my eyes. "A penis is dirtier than a toothbrush and you still put that in your mouth."

"Girl, a penis doesn't have bristles."

As the commercials ended the host's voice came on once again, *"Okay, so we have a few text messages with advice for Sherry. Let's see... Mel from New Jersey wants to know where you bought the toothbrush... Donny from Long Island is reminding us that a cold sore is a form of herpes, and lastly, Jessica from Capital District says Abreva is selling for half-off on Groupon... Okay, well, there you have it Sherry... advice from the* Talk New York *family."*

An annoyed Sherry replied, *"Are you serious? You call that advice?"*

"The listeners are in charge! Have a nice afternoon," the host said bluntly. *"Okay, we have another caller on the line. Hopefully this will go a little better. His name is Franklin and he has a dilemma involving his current girlfriend."*

I leaped towards Shaniqua and yelled, "Did she say Franklin?"

"There are a lot of people named Franklin," Shaniqua said, rolling her eyes.

My heart began to flutter, I could feel my stomach twisting. Clearly my Spidey sense was tingling and my gut was telling me something. "I think it's him."

"Viola, use your head. Why would Franklin be calling *Talk New York*?"

"He knows I listen to this station. Maybe he has something special planned." A rush of excitement washed over me.

"Calm down, girl. You do this all the time—you get your hopes up for inevitable disappointment."

She wasn't wrong. I could think of plenty examples, but I still had a feeling that something remarkable was about to happen.

"What if I'm not wrong? What if all my dreams are about to come true and a marriage proposal is a few minutes away? What if it's time to share my belongings legally with the man I love?" I trembled, nervously thinking about the future.

"Viola, you don't know how to share. You have had that issue since high school."

"That's not true, I have excellent sharing skills. I always carry an extra roll of floss in my purse to share in public bathrooms."

The host interrupted our conversation. *"We have Franklin on the line. Are you there, Franklin?"*

"Yes, I'm here."

"It's him! That's my Franklin!" I shouted. My voice echoed throughout the gym, grabbing the attention of the patrons and staff.

Shaniqua turned to me and said, "Holy shit, you're right!"

Hearing the sound of his voice, I felt like vomiting, but in a good way. Was Franklin, my boyfriend of over nine years, about to propose to me on a talk show that was broadcast in over nine countries? Most importantly, was I about to become America's sweetheart to over twenty million listeners?

"Okay, Franklin, the floor is yours! Tell the listeners what your dilemma is," said the host.

After a long period of silence, Franklin finally began to speak, "Well, my dilemma involves my girlfriend, Viola."

I leaped into the air and screamed, "Oh my God! He said my name on the radio!" I turned towards the gym patrons and shouted, "Hey, everyone! That's my boyfriend!"

Shaniqua rolled her eyes and said, "You're such a dork."

The host continued speaking, *"How long have you been dating Viola?"*

"A little over nine years," Franklin replied.

"That's a long time, Franklin. Normally a relationship that long ends with a ring on a finger."

Franklin was silent for a few seconds before he replied, *"That's why I'm here."*

I turned to Shaniqua with a great big smile planted on my face and said, "You know, I wouldn't be upset if you got me two male strippers for my bachelorette party."

Shaniqua shared another infamous eye roll with me. She looked around the gym and said, "Maybe we should tell Janette to turn down the volume. Everybody is staring at you."

"No way! I want the world to hear what my man has to say." All eyes were on me and it felt fantastic. It was my day—a memory to cherish.

"Franklin, you were saying?" said the host.

"Right, I was saying... Viola and I were high school sweethearts. The thing is... I love her, but there are some doubts I'm having that are preventing me from marrying her. For example, I have always had a career path before me, whereas Viola... well... doesn't. To be more specific, I will be a full-fledged doctor soon, which means that I will be removing tumors out of patients at a prestigious hospital while Viola will be squeezing juice out of beets at The Protein Hut. Also, Viola doesn't know how to compromise."

I quickly chimed in. "That's not true. We don't even carry beets on the menu. And I can compromise—why do you think I stopped using my selfie stick in movie theaters?"

"Where are you headed with this, Franklin?" asked the host.

"Well, I don't know what to do. I just feel like Viola won't change. A part of me believes she can be a good wife, but the other part of me believes she will remain a goal-less, driveless, overweight woman for the rest of her life."

Shaniqua turned to me, fury on her face. "That motherfu—"

I interrupted her. "It's okay... I'm sure that's the worst of it."

"Well, I'm not listening to this garbage," Shaniqua yelled. "And neither should you!" She stormed into the back office and slammed the door.

The patrons in the gym were glued to the speakers, as if they were watching a reality show starring someone they wanted to see fail.

"Franklin, what exactly are you asking our listeners?" asked the host.

Franklin took a deep breath. *"I need to know whether or not I should break up with Viola."*

You know that feeling when you're walking around New York and you suddenly get hungry and you buy a double-stuffed burrito from a street vendor, only to have it fall on the pavement before you get a chance to bite into it? That's how I felt hearing Franklin's dilemma. If only the five-second rule applied to relationships.

I innocently waved at the reception desk and shouted, "Umm, Janette, can we turn this off?" She responded with a middle finger and turned the volume up.

With the damage already done, I quickly scanned the fitness area to see who I should avoid for the next few days. The regular patrons were chatting amongst themselves and laughing at my expense.

All except one person: the new personal trainer.

Why wasn't he laughing or gossiping amongst the group? He stood facing me like a statue, and as our eyes met I felt sick. I couldn't see myself, but I was positive that my face was beet red from embarrassment.

Suddenly, the host spoke up on my behalf. *"What's so bad about Viola? I'm sure she has some good qualities."*

"She doesn't," Franklin said.

"Well, what are some more of Viola's flaws?"

I couldn't believe what I was hearing. I was hoping that this was all a dream that I was having.

The chatter in the gym was getting louder. All eyes were on me and nothing was in my control.

Franklin was the type of guy who would say something without thinking about how it would impact someone else's feelings. Yes, he was *that* guy. The one who would send food back in a restaurant or file several complaints during a hotel stay.

Franklin sighed. *"Well, for starters, everything is a joke to Viola. What annoys me the most is that she doesn't even care about her appearance. She should; she is over 190 pounds!*

My heart started racing. "Okay, Viola," I said to myself, "this isn't so bad. I mean, he isn't wrong. As long as Franklin remains calm I can recover from this."

He didn't.

Franklin's voice suddenly became louder with each flaw he listed until he was at the point of yelling. *"Viola never picks up a check, she carries like a thousand items in her purse, she's as messy as the beets she juices, and I have to constantly correct her!"*

I waved at the patrons and yelled, "I just want everyone to know that despite what Franklin is saying, we do not juice beets!"

Judgmental eyes were all over me. I felt violated, insulted, and hungry for a burrito. I couldn't hear all the chatter clearly, but I could tell from their giggling and dropped jaws that they were being entertained. Several people even had their smartphones out to record my reaction.

I thought the humiliation was over. I was wrong.

Franklin continued ranting. *"Viola dresses like she's from the 90's, she dances like an intoxicated duck, and she once gave me an STD!"*

I quickly jumped to my defense and yelled across the gym, "It's not what you think. It was lice!"

With Shaniqua sealing herself in the back room, I was left to defend myself.

The host finally stopped him. *"Franklin, I'm just curious, if there were two words you would use to describe Viola, what would they be?"*

Everyone in the gym was on the edge of their seat, except for the new personal trainer, who continued to ignore the commotion.

"The two words I would use to describe Viola?" Franklin said. *"Fat bitch."*

The entire gym crowd roared with laughter as if they were watching a slapstick comedy. Believe it or not, I have been labeled worse names in high school, but never out of the mouth of someone I loved. Okay, maybe once. I think my old dog called me a whore.

"Okay, Franklin," said the host, *"we have our first caller, let's see what advice they have for you."*

At this point I figured the worst was over. Boy, was I wrong. *"We have Shaniqua on the line. Go ahead, Shaniqua."*

"Shaniqua?" I shouted, jumping up in shock.

Shaniqua's voice tore through the speakers like a knife. *"Listen to me you undernourished ass-lookin' hobgoblin! Viola don't need your sorry ass! You ain't nothin special! Boy, you can't even please her, why do you think she keeps a vibrator hidden in her big ass box of tampons?"*

"Shaniqua? As in Viola's friend?"

"Oh my God... Shaniqua," I quietly muttered to myself.

Franklin jumped back in, *"Oh no! Is Viola listening? I gotta go."* And just like that, Franklin was gone.

"Okay..." said the host, obviously delighting in the dramatic turn of events. *"Well, folks, Franklin is gone and it sounds like Viola now knows his true feelings about their relationship. I have a feeling this won't be the end of their drama. Anyways, thanks for tuning in to* Talk New York. *Up next... The Laxative Report with Joanna Lax."*

Shaniqua shrieked, *"Bitch, I am still on the line! Don't you dare hang up on m—"*

As soon as the host disconnected the call, Shaniqua marched out of the back room with a thirst for blood.

I waved my hands in front of her as if I was stopping a jet plane. "Don't say anything. I'm seeing Franklin tonight. Let's just see how this plays out." I quietly turned away from Shaniqua as she huffed and puffed in anger.

Shaniqua placed her hands on her hips. "You don't need him."

I nodded as if I agreed with her. "I need to get out of here. You coming?"

"Yeah, all right." As Shaniqua went to grab her things, I pulled out my phone to text Franklin.

Still on for dinner tonight?

While waiting for his reply, I caught a glimpse of my reflection in a nearby window. "I'm not that fat," I said to myself, twisting and turning. "I don't know what Franklin is talking about."

My cell phone buzzed.

Yes.

I couldn't help but feel a little nervous and scared. I was looking forward to going home and eating my way back to a comfort zone.

Shaniqua came out and saw me on my cell phone. "Oh, hell no! you are not still having dinner with that douchebag, are you?"

I shrugged.

"Viola, you're not the type to give second chances, remember that."

"Hey, I believe in second chances. How do you think I justify eating out of the garbage?"

"Girl, you nasty." Shaniqua strutted her way towards the front door.

I couldn't have been more happy that it was time to go home, as I'd exceeded my daily humiliation quota. I gathered my belongings and followed Shaniqua to the front door.

I cheerfully waved to the receptionist. "Bye, Janette."

"Bye, Fat Bitch," Janette replied, smiling with a condescending wave.

"Why is she so mad at me?" I whispered to Shaniqua.

"I don't know, Viola, maybe it's because you brought Taco Bell to her wedding."

"In my defense, who serves dinner after 8 pm?"

Shaniqua's cell phone began to ring.

As we walked towards my car, Shaniqua began yelling into her cell phone. "I asked you to do one simple thing! Use your head, Shamar! It's chicken! It needs to be cooked well! … You know what? I don't care if it's raw, I am still feedin' it to yo ass!" She ended the call and tossed her phone into her designer handbag.

"What was that all about?" I asked, unlocking the doors.

"Before I left work I asked that numbskull Shamar to defrost a chicken. He forgot." I didn't want to be in Shamar's shoes. Shaniqua was angrier than usual today.

As we settled into the car, I pulled out my phone to see if there were any unread messages. There weren't.

I didn't talk much as I drove Shaniqua home. I was distracted, thinking about what had happened in the last hour.

After Shaniqua calmed down and took notice of my silence, she gently touched my shoulder. "You guys are going to be okay... I would rather you dump his sorry ass, but I support whatever dumb decision you make. I got you."

"Thanks, Shan," I said with a smile, grabbing her hand. "Nine years... We have been together for over nine years. Why is he doing this now?" I was getting emotional.

"Viola, I think this is just one of those things where you are going to need to be brave."

"Oh, I can be brave. I'm like Monica Lewinsky. The only difference between me and her is that the stain on my dress is from ice cream."

Shaniqua gently squeezed my hand as we came to a rolling stop in front of her house. She looked at me and said, "Remember, you're Viola Ginamero. You don't need a man who treats you like garbage."

I nodded absentmindedly. "Or maybe I should put on some lacy lingerie, cake on the makeup, and seduce the hell out of him?"

Shaniqua gave me a dirty look. "Viola, you're as seductive as a bowl of hummus."

"Hey, I can be seductive, you should hear me speak pirate in bed."

Shaniqua couldn't help but crack a smile. It always felt good to make her smile. Even if it was a small crinkle, it still made me feel like I'd accomplished a big task.

Shaniqua's cell phone started vibrating again. "Ugh, it's Shamar. I gotta go." She left the car, yelling into her phone, "I'm outside, dumbass, you don't need to call me!"

I chuckled a little before driving home. Call me weird, but there was something charming about watching a heavy African woman cuss her way into her house.

It had been a long, eventful day and I was emotionally drained, so clearly it was time to upload another video and fill my viewers in on the events that had occurred.

After a fast-food pit stop, stomach cramps, and several bathroom breaks, I was prepared to share my life with the few subscribers I had. I sat down in front of my laptop and poured my emotions out.

"Okay, so today was an interesting day. I think I was dumped on live radio, although it's not definitive as he hasn't actually told me—he just told twenty million listeners."

I paused for a second to collect my thoughts. Tossing my hair over my shoulders, I began speaking again.

"You know what? I was planning on coming on here and sharing all the humiliating details of what happened today, but I got a better idea: let's cook!"

Shaniqua said that I had to be brave, and that's what I was going to do. I was going to hold my head up high and cook up a meal that Franklin would never forget.

"Okay, so here's the plan. I'm going to make something simple yet unforgettable: a peanut-butter-glazed turkey with chocolate stuffing. My mouth is watering just thinking about it."

I whipped open the fridge door in search of a turkey. "Hmm… looks like I don't have a turkey, so I'm going to have to use a small chicken."

Tossing the chicken on the counter, I quickly glanced at my phone for any notifications. Nothing.

"Next, I'm going to preheat the oven to 350 degrees. It's crucial that the chicken is cooked throughout, otherwise we will have an incident similar to the last Thanksgiving meal I made."

I was starting to get anxious waiting for Franklin to text or call. I suddenly felt like I needed to talk to someone about my feelings.

"Okay, maybe while we wait for the oven to preheat we can talk about what happened today. As always, feel free to leave a comment below. Oh, and please remember to click like before you leave."

I grabbed a bowl out of the cupboard and began pouring chocolate chips into it. "Basically, Franklin, my boyfriend of over nine years, called *Talk New York* today to ask advice on whether or not he should break up with me. The entire conversation was heard through the speakers of the gym, The Fitness Hut, where I work. Needless to say, it was mortifying. The last time I felt that humiliated was when I was thrown out of a Baskin Robbins because they said I was licking too suggestively."

I started to feel nauseated. Why wasn't Franklin here yet? He said he was coming, but would he show up? Was the dress I was wearing okay?

I knew I'd find out soon enough, but the wait was killing me.

The beeping oven snapped me out of it. "Okay, looks like the oven is preheated, so let's shove this bird in there."

The sound of metal screeching along the sides of the hot oven made me cringe. "Sorry about that, guys, the oven rack is still in pain from last Halloween's pumpkin incident."

I couldn't help by hover over my phone in anticipation. "Why isn't he calli—" The phone started vibrating, and I scooped it up in excitement.

A text from Franklin made my heart start racing. "He's on his way up! Okay, friends, we are going to have to put a pin in this for now. As always feel free to leave a like or comment below or both. You're watching #ViolaSwallows. Till next time."

I slammed the laptop lid shut and raced to the bathroom. Standing in front of the mirror, I flipped my hair back and forth to give it some volume, then rolled some red lipstick over my chapped lips.

I stopped and looked in the mirror for a few moments, realizing something had changed in me. For the first time in my life I felt a little self-conscious. The image of my near 200-pound figure made my heart race. I knew what I had to do: drown myself in denial.

"I'm not *that* fat," I said to myself while twisting and turning. "Besides, what guy doesn't like a girl with a big booty?"

My modeling was interrupted by the sound of a knock at the door. "Okay, Viola. It's show time," I whispered to myself.

Walking towards the front door, I felt like throwing up. Was Franklin really going to break up with me? And in this pretty dress from Costco?

I stood in front of the door and took a deep breath, gently twisting the doorknob to reveal Franklin standing in front of me.

With a great big smile, I said, "Hey, handsome!" My short, slender boyfriend was dressed casually, wearing a button-up shirt, khakis, and a new pair of glasses. "Oooh, I like the new fancy glasses."

"Thanks, Viola," Franklin said. He paused and started sniffing. "What's that smell?"

"Oh, I ran out of shampoo, so I had to use dishwashing liquid on my hair this morning."

"No, Viola, I think something is burning." Franklin walked towards the kitchen.

"The chicken!" I yelled, racing towards the oven door.

"Listen, Viola, we need to talk…" Franklin began pacing back and forth between the kitchen and living room.

"Just give me a sec, honey, a piece of the chicken was touching the broiler. Have a seat. Dinner won't be ready for a while. Plus I still need to make the chocolate stuffing and peanut butter glaze."

"Viola, we really need to talk," Franklin said in a serious tone. If I'm being honest, it was the break-up tone.

"Franklin, if it's about today's radio show call-in, don't worry about it. I mean, yes, it was embarrassing, but like a staph infection, I'll get over it."

"Viola, I'm sorry about that. Let me explain. Before I called in, I learned some big news and panicked."

"What news?" I asked, plopping myself down on the couch.

"Viola, I was offered a full-time position in a Manhattan hospital as head surgeon."

I leaped across the couch. "That's amazing! I knew you would follow through with your dream. I'm so proud of you! You should be more excited. Hey, want to go shout it from the rooftop? Literally. Oh, wait, never mind. I was banned last week for hanging my bras out to dry."

"Viola, I feel bad about what I said today. I had no idea you would be listening, honestly."

"Franklin, it's water under the bridge." I placed my hand over his.

Franklin gently pulled his hand away from under mine. "Viola, how long have we been together?"

"A little over nine years, why?"

"There's something I should have asked you a long time ago." Franklin shook nervously.

"What is it?" I don't know why, but after everything he'd said, I was still anticipating a marriage proposal.

"Where do you see yourself in five years?" Franklin asked.

"Umm… well if more people keep pissing Shaniqua off, she will eventually lose it on a customer, leaving me to become the manager."

"At The Protein Hut?" Franklin said with disgust. "Viola, do you think you even have the skills to lead?"

"Hey, I can be a leader, I have been a part of three different pyramid schemes."

"Viola, this isn't a joke. I feel like you have no plan for your future, no goals, and your weight scares me."

"Franklin, where are you going with this?"

"Look, I'm about to take the next journey of my life, and I've decided that it won't be with you. I'm sorry." Franklin walked towards the door.

The oven started beeping and I was too stunned to notice it. "Franklin, wait!" I yelled, running towards the kitchen. "Stay for dinner. We can talk about this." After pulling the chicken out, I turned around to watch the door slowly close.

I was confused. Why would Franklin invest over nine years in a relationship, only to bail out of it? I needed to talk to somebody. I scooped up my cell phone and called Shaniqua.

"Hello?" Shaniqua said. I could tell she'd been yelling just before answering.

"Shan, I think Franklin just broke up with me." I was emotional and confused, but I wasn't about to waste the meal I cooked, so I began preparing the peanut-butter glaze.

"Girl, are you serious? What did he say?"

"He said I have no future, no goals, and he implied I was fat. I'm not that fat—I'm the same cup size as Adele!"

"Viola, I am coming over right now."

"No, that's okay. I'm just gonna eat a small snack and go to bed." The small snack, of course, was a peanut-butter-glazed, oven-roasted chicken. "I might upload a video on #ViolaSwallows before bed, too."

"Girl, you *really* need to change that name."

I ended the call and began lathering the chicken with the peanut-butter mixture. I was too preoccupied with my thoughts to remember the chocolate stuffing I'd promised my viewers.

Feeling hungry and confused, I sat on the couch and began devouring the chicken, taking short breaks to swipe through photos of Franklin on my cell phone.

After a few minutes my eyelids began to feel heavy, and before I knew it, I was passed out on the couch—a common occurrence from my usual binge eating.

I woke up in a panic to the vibration of my cell phone on the hardwood floor.

Half asleep, I reached for my phone. "Hello?" I was secretly hoping Franklin was on the other end, begging to take me back.

"Viola, it's Shaniqua. Are you reading these comments? Girl, they are *cold*." I was still half asleep, my stomach was hurting, and I had no clue what was going on.

"Shan, what are you talking about? What time is it?" Dazed and confused, I dragged my body to the bathroom.

"Girl, have you been online in the last few hours?"

"Nope, I just posted one video earlier and then I passed out," I said, yawning into the phone, but I was waking up fast. Something was up. Something big was happening that would change my life forever.

"Viola, you gone viral!"

"Huh? My viral infection? How do you know ab— Oh, right... I tweeted about it last Tuesday."

"No, Viola, a video of you and the radio conversation. It's everywhere—Facebook, Twitter, Instagram, even news stations picked it up!"

"Shaniqua, it can't be *that* big. I think you're overreacting... just like the time I threw up in your purse."

"This is no joke Viola, check out MSN."

"Fine, give me a sec. I'm putting you on speaker." I opened up a web browser on my phone and loaded MSN news.

To my surprise, I was greeted with an unflattering shot of my face. The caption read: Today's Most Watched Viral Video: Chunky Woman Dumped on Live Radio.

I clicked on the link, which took me directly to YouTube, and I immediately saw that over *forty million* people had watched my humiliation.

I scrolled through line after line of insulting comments. It reminded me of that time in high school when I recorded gossiping cheerleaders in the locker room with my secret pen microphone.

"I gotta go, Viola, Shamar is barking. Maybe you're right that this will all blow over soon, but you know what this means?"

"Oh my God, I'm gonna be asked to be on *Dancing With the Stars*?

"Ugh, night Viola."

I couldn't go back to sleep, and I spent most of the night reading tweets, Facebook comments, and blog posts about me, Franklin, and my weight.

I couldn't help but wonder what the next day had in store for me. Were reporters going to await my arrival at work? Was I going to become a sex symbol for a fat camp? Most importantly, was the barista at Starbucks going to write Fat Bitch on my white hot chocolate?

The impact of the viral fame didn't hit until I found a discussion under the article titled, 'The importance of Fat Bitch and why she's trending.'

One snooty commenter believed I represented America as a whole and everything that was wrong with it. A feminist defended me and claimed that Franklin proved that men are shallow and image conscious. Another commenter discussed the power of radio talk shows and how far they would go for ratings.

As I sifted through hundreds of posts, clever memes, tweets, and blogs throughout the night, one thing was clear: everybody on social media had something to say about the situation.

Most were defending me, some were insulting me, one woman said I was too fat for love. What did that even mean?

I started off as a joke, but as the hours of the night went on something began to shift—I was gaining more and more support from people.

To show their support, hundreds of people started sharing their struggles with obesity over YouTube, Twitter and Facebook. Who knew there were so many causes? Stories were shared about everything from pregnancy to anti-depressants. One woman was living in poverty for most of her life and could only afford McDonald's meals. Another woman stress-ate her way through an abusive relationship.

It was in that moment I felt the trigger being pulled—the world knew who I was and there was no place to hide. Was Franklin right to dump me on live radio? Was he wrong for doing it? Did the radio host go to far? Am I really too fat for love?

Suddenly my stomach started gurgling. I jumped up and ran to the bathroom as I started dry heaving. The chicken was coming up, and it was coming up fast.

After a lovely vomiting session, I couldn't help but catch a glimpse of my body in the mirror. Holding my hair up, I twisted and posed.

I didn't quite feel like my peppy, optimistic self anymore. Something felt different—for the first time in my life I was looking at my true image.

"I'm fat," I whispered to myself. My eyes tried to fight off the mirror, but they couldn't run away from the truth. I grabbed my belly and said loudly, "I'm Viola, and I'm fat."

With a big grin on my face I grabbed a hold of the mirror with both hands and boldly proclaimed, "My name is Viola Ginamero, and I'm fat!" I felt a fire in me. Or maybe it was acid reflux. Either way, a spark was ignited.

So what if I was fat? I could lose the weight easily and win back Franklin. How hard could it be? This was far from the end. I whipped out my phone and prepped the most important tweet of my life:

Announcement @ #ViolaSwallows, mins away

Thankfully I wasn't working the next day, as the sun was about to rise. I'd been up all night, glued to my computer, refusing to get out of bed until I responded to my hundreds of supporters.

I grabbed my phone and began recording.

"Hi, all! Viola here, I just wanted to welcome the new viewers to my channel, #ViolaSwallows. Spoiler alert: I have finally chosen a new channel name! More on that later."

I took a deep breath to collect my thoughts.

"I read a lot of comments all night—both positive and negative—and I was deeply moved by all of the support you guys showed me. It gave me strength to do something I should've done a long time ago. For all of my supporters on YouTube, Facebook, Twitter, or any other social media platform, I have something for you: a challenge."

I walked into the bathroom and pointed the camera at my scale, which I'd received as a Christmas present from my parents.

"I'm going to show the world my current body weight. Drum roll, please… It's 198 pounds."

I bit my lips, feeling a bit naked. The internet was full of bullies and I was giving them gold, but there was no going back now.

Next, I made my way to the kitchen to show off my diet.

"Follow me to the kitchen. Those of you who subscribe to my channel will already be familiar with this place."

I began flipping cupboards open to reveal containers of cake frosting, boxes of soda, and bags of chocolate chip cookies. I then followed up with a trip to the freezer, where I stored several bulk packages of fried foods.

"As you can see, I don't eat healthy. Far from it. To put things in perspective, before Franklin my longest relationship was with a quarter pounder."

"So this is where you come in. You saw my weight, you've just seen my eating habits, and you all know way too much about my personal life. So where do we go from here? I'll tell you what. I'm turning thirty in November. I'm making a goal to lose some weight by then… with a ring on my finger from Franklin. You heard me. I am winning him back. You can count on it! This will be a tough journey and the whole world will be watching, so I won't be able to do this alone. Here is my challenge to all of you who want to lose weight: meet me at Central Park today at 8 am and take this journey with me. That's it! See you soon. Bye for now."

Then I remembered that I forgot to give the most important message of all.

"Oh, one other thing. Effective immediately, this channel is no longer titled #ViolaSwallows. I leaned into the camera with a big grin on my face. "Ladies and gentlemen, welcome to The Fat Bitch Diet."

Chapter Four

201 Lbs

November 14, 2016

After a quick shower, I was going through my wardrobe and quickly realized I didn't have proper workout attire. I was forced to improvise by slipping on a clean pair of pajamas and a bedazzled pink T-shirt.

I made my way to the kitchen and began prepping my usual meal—four eggs sunny-side up, ten pieces of bacon, five sausages, and a large chocolate milkshake in case you forgot. My high school nutrition teacher, Ms. Brinski, told me a million times that breakfast is the most important meal of the day.

I know what you're thinking, and yes, I was aware that it wasn't the most healthiest meal decision, but that's okay, because I will start eating healthier tomorrow. I promise.

I was just about to head out the door to meet my fellow supporters when my phone rang. "What's up, Shaniqua?"

"Viola, your ass is breaking the internet right now. Congratulations! I only have one question. Do you think you have the will power for this weight-loss journey? Cause I've seen you eat a full bag of rotten M&M's."

"Hey! I stopped eating halfway through that bag, and that took strength. You know how much I love peanut M&M's."

"Whatever, girl, just wanted to wish you luck. Later."

"Awww, thanks. Call ya later, Shan."

Feeling a bit nervous, I pounded down another milkshake before I took off.

After few subway stops and a quick stop at a gyro stand and a Starbucks, I finally arrived at Central Park.

It was a beautiful day, the sun was shining, and the park was full of joggers and dog walkers. I almost forgot what I came here for—I was looking for a big group of heavy people.

A large woman approached me, smiling. "Excuse me," the woman said.

"Oh, hi! You're in the right place. Welcome to the Fat Bitch Diet!" I said, jumping up excitedly.

She gave me a dirty look. "Excuse me? I was about to ask if you saw a small white poodle run by!"

"I am so sorry!" I called, watching the woman walk away.

A mysterious, manly voice with feminine tone piped up behind me. "Oh my gouda, that was totes amaze."

I turned around to see a heavy twenty-year-old Indian male, dressed from head to toe in stylish garb.

"Hi! I am Viol—"

"You're Viola!" he cried. "I am a big fan of your work. I loved the episode where your hair got caught in a blender!"

"Aww, thanks… and you are?"

"I'm Vikram, but you can call me Vik."

"Nice to meet you, Vik! You're here for the Fat Bitch Diet, right?"

"Oh my God, yes! Hey, can you join me for a quick selfie?" Vik pulled out his iPhone and snapped the photo before I could answer. "Is it okay if I tweet this?"

"Sure, go ahead. Umm, do you know if anyone else is here?" I scanned the park in search of heavyset individuals.

"Nope," Vik replied, tapping away on his phone.

I was a bit disappointed, as I was expecting a larger turn out given my newfound viral fame. It was clear that people were not taking me seriously.

"You know what, Vik. Maybe we should stick a pin in this. It doesn't look like anyone else is showing up."

"Hey, wanna join me for a churro?" Vik asked. "I think I saw a stand near the entrance of the park."

"Sure, let's go."

As we walked towards the churro stand, I thought it would be a good idea to get to know Vik. "So, where are you from?" I asked.

"Well, my parents are from India, but I was born and raised here in New York. You?"

"New Jersey, born and raised." I couldn't help but pry a bit into his life. "So... any girlfriend?"

"Umm, ya, you just missed her. I, uh, walked with her here. But she, umm, had to go," Vik said, fumbling his words.

"Oh, is she Indian, too? I think I see her over there by the trash cans."

"Viola, that's a homeless woman."

"Oh."

As we reached the churro stand I couldn't help but wonder if I made a mistake with the challenge. After all, my dieting knowledge came from binge watching episodes of *Doctor OZ*.

The vendor greeted us warmly. "Welcome to Churro Churro, what can I get for you two?" The stand was nothing more than a cart anchored under a large red umbrella, but the emanating smell of sugar and cinnamon was intoxicating.

"Can we get two churros please?" said Vik. I grabbed my wallet out of my purse. "Put that away. It's on me, Viola." Vik smiled, handing the vendor cash.

"Aww, thanks, Vik," I said, smiling warmly.

Just as I was about to take a bite, a familiar voice bellowed from behind us.

"There she is!" the woman shouted. I turned around to see a familiar 65-year-old heavy woman, dressed in Adidas running wear, walking towards me. Beside her was a large twenty-something Caucasian male wearing a plain T-shirt, shorts, and sandals.

"Hey, I know you. Barbara-Anne, right?" I said, scratching my head. Vik was too busy inhaling his churro to notice anything around him.

"Yes, dear, I am Barbara-Anne. Me and Remy are here for your challenge." She was trying to catch her breath.

"I take it you're Remy?" I said, shaking the man's clammy hand.

"Yeah, I bumped into Barbara-Anne a while ago. We got lost looking for you. I get lost a lot."

"So, Remy, tell me about yourself," I said, noticing that Vik and Barbara-Anne were chatting.

"What would you like to know?" Remy asked, looking confused.

"How 'bout something a little personal?"

"Umm, I'm not wearing any underwear. And I once got pneumonia from drowning in a tub."

"That's sounds really serious," I said.

"Oh, it is! My washer broke, so I haven't had clean laundry for weeks."

I couldn't help but chuckle, unaware if Remy was joking or not. He seemed a bit slow, but who was I to judge? "Welcome aboard, Remy. Are you excited to chase your dream?"

"Yeah! Up until now the only thing I ever chased was an ice cream truck."

I smiled warmly and said to everyone, "Well, it looks like it's just going to be the four of us today, so let's get this show on the road."

Vik was glowing with excitement. "Ooh, what are we going to start with first?"

It was a good question, one that I didn't know how to answer. Suddenly it dawned on me: I knew as much about fitness as I did about dieting. My knowledge came from Jane Fonda videos and episodes of *The Biggest Loser*. I guess that was as good a place to start as any.

I interlaced my fingers against my chest. "We are going to start with some running. You know, just a little warm-up. Oh, and guys, from here on out we have to watch what we eat," I said, biting into the churro.

Barbara-Anne raised her hand shyly. "Instead of running, can I walk briskly? I have bladder control problems."

"Sure, of course," I replied, feeling a bit uncomfortable as pressure was mounting on me. "Well, let's get started, follow me!" I shouted gleefully, jogging away from the churro stand.

I ran for about fifty seconds before I was forced to stop and catch my breath. The others weren't doing any better. Remy was dry heaving over a recycling bin, and Vik collapsed onto a patch of grass.

I limped towards Remy, looking away seconds before he vomited into the bin. "Are you okay, Remy?" I said, cringing.

Remy coughed. "I'm okay, Viola, I'm just glad this bin was here. Usually I throw up on my shoes."

I looked in Vik's direction, hoping he was okay. "Hey, Vik! Are you all right?"

Vik rose to his knees and shouted back, "There's dog shit on my chinos!"

I couldn't help but smile. We had a long way to go, but I was looking forward to it.

As the three of us regrouped on a bench, I suddenly realized that Barbara-Anne was missing. "Hey, did you guys see where Barbara-Anne went?"

Vik pulled his shirt over his nose. "No, but does anyone else smell that?"

I took a few sniffs and grimaced. "Yeah, I do."

Remy looked at us sheepishly. "Sorry, I had burritos for breakfast."

"I don't think it's you," I said, coming to his defense. "It's a pleasant smell."

"I also had fruit."

"There you guys are!" It was Barbara-Anne, gripping a half-eaten calzone.

I jumped up off my seat in excitement. "Where did you go?

"I had to use the bathroom, but on the way I got distracted by the calzone vendor."

"Oh, okay. Well, now that you're done eating we can continue."

"Actually, I still need to use the bathroom."

I was starting to feel the pain of being a leader, but I wasn't going to give up that easily.

I gently touched Barbara-Anne's shoulder, trying to sound cheerful. "No worries! Feel free to join us when you're done."

Remy jumped into the conversation and said, "She just ate a calzone. If she is anything like me she'll be in there for a while."

Vik cringed. "Eww. TMI."

With Barbara-Anne on her way to the nearest bathroom, the rest of us were ready to continue our fitness regime.

I turned towards the group. "Okay, so now that we are warmed up, we are ready to try out some aerobics."

Remy blankly stared at me. "Viola, do you know what you're doing?"

Vik quickly came to my defense, shaking his finger in Remy's face. "Excuse you? Viola knows exactly what she is doing. Don't be questioning her."

I was starting to feel a little confident. "Vik is right, you're in good hands. Shall we get started?"

I led the boys to an empty patch of grass to begin our first official aerobic workout of the day. Marching in front of them, I planted my arms on my hips. "Now, we are all here for one reason." I looked over at Remy. "Remy, tell me that reason."

"Because the mean girls kicked us off that other patch of grass?"

"Yes, that's true, but also because we are here to lose weight together. I know we will be a success together as a group. Strength in numbers, guys, strength in numbers. We have to be persistent, and I'll have you know that I have learned from the best—my parents. They are *very* persistent. They sent me to fat camp three times."

It wasn't a speech to rival the ending of *Braveheart*, but it did make me feel a jolt inside. "Let's do this!" I shouted.

Recalling the last YouTube fitness video I viewed, "*Trudy Works Her Booty,*" I started doing jumping jacks, and the others quickly followed. "Come on, guys, pick it up!" I shouted, mimicking Trudy.

After ten jumps, I felt dizzy, so it was time to switch it up.

"Okay, boys, let's start kicking! I wanna see those feet up high!"

Unaware that Vik had collapsed onto his knees from exhaustion, I accidentally kicked him in the face with my fifteen-dollar Payless running shoes.

Vik screamed in agony. "My nose! It's bleeding!"

"Oh my God! I am so sorry!" I cried, kneeling down beside him. He was too distracted to hear me, as blood was oozing through his fingers.

"Get away from me!" Vik yelled, rising to his feet.

"I think it's broken," said Remy.

Feeling horrible, I asked, "Are you sure, Remy?"

"Yeah," he replied. "I was once hit in the face with a frying pan."

Given the bad outcome of my coaching, I figured being in the park surrounded by many people was an advantage. Despite feeling queasy, I spun around in circles shouting, "Is anyone a doctor? Is anyone a doctor?"

My eyes locked onto Barbara-Anne jogging towards us. I waved at her.

Barbara-Anne looked at Vik. "What happened to his nose? Was he picking it?"

"Viola kicked him in the face!" said Remy.

Barbara-Anne looked at me in disgust. "Wow, you are a tough coach. I'm in!"

I grabbed Remy's arm and began panicking. "We need to take him to the hospital. Can I borrow your phone?"

Barbara-Anne turned to me. "You don't have a phone?"

Scratching my head, I calmly replied, "I purposely left my iPhone at home. I wasn't in the mood for Siri's cynicism this morning."

"My nose," Vik cried. "My beautiful nose!"

I grabbed Remy's phone and turned to Vik. "It's okay, help is on its way. I am getting an Uber."

"You are the worst coach ever!" barked Vik.

Remy nudged my arm. "I once threw up in an Uber."

"Oh!" I said excitedly. "Looks like there running a promo. We can get a 50% discount if we make a pit stop at the airport first!"

Vik looked at me with pure hatred.

I backed up. "Okay, okay, put those eyes away. I'll pay full price."

As the three of us waited in the crowded hospital for Vik, I couldn't help but think about the memorable visits Franklin and I made to the ER. He was a bit of a drama queen. One time he got really angry when I accidentally cut off a piece of his earlobe. In my defense, cutting hair is really hard!

"I think Remy fell asleep," Barbara-Anne said, knocking me back to reality.

"Huh? What? Oh," I replied, sitting up in my chair. I looked over at Remy and the puddle of drool he was making on his shirt collar.

Barbara-Anne stared at Remy intensely. "He has a really big head. How much pain do you think his mom endured during childbirth?"

"Barbara-Anne, can I ask you a question?"

"Sure, dear." Barbara-Anne sat back in her seat. "What's on your mind?"

"Do you think I'm in over my head?"

"I think you're doing a great job."

"But I kicked Vik in the face."

"Everybody should take a kick to the face at least once. It's refreshing."

I smiled. "Your grandkids must *love* you."

Barbara-Anne stared up the ceiling as if she was looking into Heaven. "Oh, I have no kids. My late husband and I decided to focus on ourselves and our careers."

We sat quietly for a few seconds when suddenly Remy woke up and started screaming as if he was being murdered. After grabbing the attention of everybody in the waiting room, he drifted back to sleep.

I shot a confused look at Barbara-Anne. "Night terrors?" She shrugged her shoulders and closed her eyes. I was tired of waiting and decided to shut my eyes as well.

I woke up to the sound of chattering. When my vision came into focus I noticed Vik was back and arguing with Remy. His shirt was soaked in dry blood and his nose was covered with white swabs, which probably meant he'd gotten stitches.

"Vik, are you okay?" I asked, standing up. He slowly turned in my direction and took a deep breath.

Vik leaned in threateningly. "Viola, my nose was the only attractive feature I had going for me. You are dead to me."

"I am so sorry, Vik," I said as he stormed off.

Remy started walking towards the exit, then he turned around and shouted, "I gotta go, but it's not because I'm mad. I drank too much Mountain Dew!"

I waved goodbye as Remy left. I was feeling bad when Barbara-Anne gently placed her hand on my shoulder. "You did your best, dear. He'll get over it, so try not to lose sleep over this."

"I hope you're right, cause I haven't been able to sleep properly since I swallowed my mouth guard."

Chapter five

201 Lbs

November 15, 2016

I didn't sleep well that night; I was too distracted. I felt like I'd let both the team and my followers down. Or maybe it was because I wolfed down seven fish tacos for dinner. Either way I was not looking forward to being back at work.

"Earth to Viola!" Shaniqua shouted, waving her hand in front of my face.

"Huh? Oh!" I said, looking blankly at the customer in front of me. "Sorry, Shan. I barely slept last night." I handed over a panini to the customer. "Have a nice day."

Shaniqua walked up to me. "Girl, what is the matter with you today? Did you take those pills from my purse again? Viola, how many times do I have to tell you those are not Skittles."

"I told you, I slept really poorly. The meeting in the park was a disaster." I stepped away from the cash register.

"What happened? It can't be that bad."

"Shaniqua, I kicked a guy in the face and broke his nose!"

She laughed wildly. "I would give anything to kick Shamar in the face."

Maybe Shaniqua had a point. Was I making a big deal out of nothing? I knew this wasn't going to be an easy goal to complete and fretting over the rocky start wasn't helping. I had to find a solution that would keep me moving forward. Then I realized it was in front of me the entire time.

I perked up. "You know what, Shan? I have an idea." I rolled up my sleeves and walked over to the reception desk.

"Hi, Janette, how are you?" I said cheerfully, tilting my head.

Janette was leaning over the desk, filing her freshly manicured nails. "Oh, it's you. What do you want?" Janette said in a disgusted tone.

"I wanted to ask you a question."

"Hi, Christos!" Janette shouted flirtatiously, looking over my shoulder. Her attitude completely changed, as if she had a multiple personality. I curiously turned around to see who or what triggered her good side.

Standing behind me was the new personal trainer. Being that I was one foot away from him, I was finally able to get a better look at his appearance. I was curious to see what Shaniqua and Janette saw in him.

He was a lot taller up close, probably a little over six feet. His hair was dark brown, thick, and smelled like tea leaves. He was wearing a black compressed tank top, which showed off muscle definition in his arms and shoulders. I have to admit, his beard did accentuate his chiseled face, but I was still grossed out by it.

Clearly this guy had good hygiene, fashion, and cared about his personal health, so could I now see everyone's attraction to him? Meh.

Janette reached into a drawer and pulled out a card. "Here is your parking pass, Christos. It's right next to mine. Hey, maybe we can carpool sometime."

Christos reached for the card and replied in a deep masculine voice, "Thanks."

As he walked away, I couldn't help but feel butterflies in my stomach. He walked with confidence, unlike Franklin, who was constantly hunched over like he was going to ring the bell in Notre Dame.

"Viola!" Janette shouted, pulling me back to reality. "Eyes over here. Christos is *way* out of your league. You're too innocent and fat for him."

"I am not that innocent. I was a part of Occupy Wall Street, though that was strictly for the free sandwiches."

Janette rolled her eyes. "What do you want, Viola?"

"I am interested in a group personal training session."

"You know you need a group for that, right?" Janette said condescendingly.

"Absolutely," I replied cheerfully. "Including myself, there are four of us." In truth, Barbara-Anne, Vik, and Remy had no clue what I was up to. Hopefully they were still willing to give me another chance.

Janette moved over to her computer screen and exhaled deeply as if she was annoyed. "Okay, I can book you and your freak show in to meet a personal trainer tomorrow afternoon."

"Thanks, Janette! I really appreciate it. Hey, can you do me a favor? Can you please ensure it's not Christos?"

"Fine, whatever. Roll away now," she said, waving me away.

"Thanks again. You da best!" I shouted, walking back to the Hut.

"Oh, Viola! You need a minimum of five members for a group session. Oops, did I forget to mention that?" Janette said with a devilish smile.

"Oh… Okay, I'm on it!" I replied.

Where the heck was I going to find a fifth member before tomorrow afternoon?

Halfway through my shift, Barbara-Anne stopped by the Hut. I was extremely excited to tell her the good news.

"Hi, dear," Barbara-Anne said, walking up to the till. For a sixty-five-year-old heavy woman, it was impressive to see her at the gym daily. Sure, she chatted with the patrons for most of the time she was there rather than actually working out, but she was so sweet and friendly that her presence made me feel warm inside.

"Hi, Barbara-Anne. Do you want the usual smoothie today?" I asked, figuring I'd better get a head start.

"Yes, please. Thank you, dear." She seemed a bit on the mellow side today, and I couldn't help but think that something was on her mind.

"Listen," I said, "I have something to share with you. I know yesterday was a bit of a gong show, so I decided it would be best to take the group in a different direction."

"Oh, Viola, thank goodness you came to your senses. I'm glad you agree that we should disband the group and forget about everything."

I bit my lip and shook my head. "That's not at all what I was going to say. I have signed us all on for a group personal training session. Right here at The Fitness Hut!"

"Oh, Viola. You shouldn't have done that," Barbara-Anne said, sounding disappointed.

"C'mon, what are you afraid of?"

Barbara-Anne leaned in and looked me in the eye. "Failing."

"There are worse things than failing."

"Like what?" Barbara-Anne asked.

"Well, for one thing, getting diarrhea during a Christmas recital is much worse."

Barbara-Anne smiled. "You're sweet, dear, but I don't know."

"You won't regret it, I promise. We have a fantastic female trainer who will be meeting with us tomorrow afternoon, the only issue is that we need a fifth member."

"Well, what about her?" Barbara-Anne said, pointing at Shaniqua, who was sitting at a table eating chips. "She looks like she needs to lose weight."

"Shh, she'll hear you," I said.

"What? Look at that chair leg—it's bending from her weight."

"Shh! She won't say yes, trust me," I said, handing over the smoothie.

"How do you know if you don't try?" Barbara-Anne grabbed the smoothie and walked away.

She was right. I knew what I had to do.

I quietly walked over to Shaniqua and took a seat, trying to think of the best way to persuade her to join the group.

"Hey, beautiful, how's it going?" I said, cheerfully nudging her with my shoulders.

"Why are all men idiots? Shamar hasn't replied to my texts all day. Do you think he is cheating on me?"

"What? Of course not. You guys have been together for, like, forever. You have nothing to worry about," I replied, gently touching her shoulder.

"Good, cause if Shamar is texting that greasy-haired, troll-lookin' trick Lakeesha, I am going to rip his dreads out of his head and whip her senseless with them. Did you know that bitch said I need to lose weight?"

"Pfft, you? That's ridiculous," I lied, hoping Shaniqua didn't see right through me.

Shaniqua froze and stared at me without blinking her eyes.

"Viola, you're a terrible liar. Do you agree with Lakeesha?" Shaniqua leaned in.

"No, no, I agree with you! That bitch is wrong. But I do think your gorgeous curves might be slightly above the average." That was the nicest way I could put it. Hopefully she bought it.

"So you *do* think I'm fat!" Shaniqua said. Damn, she didn't buy it.

"Listen, Shan, I am fat. I accepted it and I think you should, too. I booked us a personal train—"

"Are you out of your mind? I ain't lettin' no personal trainer tell me what to do!"

"Shan, I am desperate. We need a fifth member or we can't do it."

"This discussion is over!" Shaniqua yelled, rising from the chair. As I watched her walk away, I felt my goal slipping away.

My evening at home was quiet, as Shaniqua wasn't replying to any of my texts. She was the queen of holding grudges. I couldn't blame her, though, she had a lot of family drama in her life so eventually it became second nature to her.

I was lying on the couch in my pajamas, scrolling through the contacts in my phone, contemplating if I should text Franklin. I hadn't sent him a word since he broke up with me. He was my addiction and I needed a fix. I also had a hankering for some chocolate.

I leaped off the couch and headed to the freezer for a piece of the brownie concoction I made days ago. I placed a slice on a plate and put it in the microwave, hopefully ensuring I wouldn't get sick from the chunks of chicken. As I watched the plate spin, I couldn't help but wonder what Franklin was up to.

With Shaniqua ignoring me, there was nobody around to stop me from making a foolish mistake, so I proceeded to dial his number.

Holding my cell phone tightly against my ear, I waited nervously for him to answer. "Hi, Franklin?" I said optimistically, but I was tricked by his voicemail greeting. I contemplated leaving a message. I went for it and quickly learned why you should never call your ex when you're nervous.

"Hi, Franklin... it's Viola. Umm, I just wanted to see what you're up to. Oh, and not in a stalker way or anything like that... just wanted to see how you're doing. So, umm, call me back. I'll be here, unless I'm in the bathroom. I ate some rank fish tacos for dinner, and in that case I will call you back, unless my phone is with me, then maybe I will answer it, unless I am in the middle of number two. Okay, I should probably hang up now before I start talking about my period or something, not that I'm in the middle of my period right now—that's supposed to come next week. That reminds me... do you know where my Costco card is?"

Suddenly I was cut off. I guess I'd been talking too long.

I wasn't sure if I should leave another voicemail or hide under a rock for the next few days. As I began eating the tray of brownies, I kept replaying the message in my head, trying to create better versions that would result in favorable outcomes.

Surprise, surprise, all outcomes ended the same way—with a ring on my finger.

After eating half of the brownie tray, I passed out on the couch, only to be awoken by the sound of my stomach struggling to digest what apparently was not the best combination of ingredients.

I crawled to the bathroom, preparing for sickness, when I caught a shocking glimpse of myself in the mirror. Facial sweat clung to my greasy hair and chocolate smudges covered my white XXL Fruit of the Loom T-shirt.

I stared down at the scale. "One small step for man..." I whispered to myself, slowly stepping onto it as if it were laced with spikes. My eyes widened as I took notice of the number displayed. "One giant leap for mankind." I stared at the number for several seconds, hoping it would go down. No change.

I sighed. "So you're 201 pounds. What now, Viola?"

I had plenty of options. I could quit and spend my time binge watching *Fuller House* on Netflix.

Or there was that other option.

I grabbed my laptop and plopped myself on the couch, all set to upload a video.

"Hey, guys, Viola here. I have something to share with you all. I am now a tick over 200 pounds. Honestly, I never in my life thought I would weigh this much. It all happened so quickly. You just kind of tell yourself it will go down eventually, that you can control the weight, but you know what? You can't. At least, not without help."

Frustrated, I huffed out a deep breath, lifted up the laptop, and placed it on the coffee table. "I am not that surprised, I mean, I really don't know my body well at all. I once thought I had bedbugs, but it turned out to be eczema."

I sat back on the couch and lifted the laptop off the coffee table. "All jokes aside, I want to apologize to the three people that met with me yesterday at Central Park. Yesterday was a disaster. Vik, Barbara-Anne, Remy—I thought I could lead you to your goal of weight loss, but I was wrong. So what now? Should we quit and resume our lives? Or should we fight to find some motivation to reach our goal? I am not giving up, and neither should you, so that leaves me with one question. Tomorrow afternoon I booked a personal trainer at The Fitness Hut: Are you in?"

I finished uploading the video and set the laptop aside. I wasn't sure if my message would convince the group, but I was certain that if it didn't, there would be no hope for any of us.

Chapter Six

❷⓪❷ Lbs

November 16, 2016

The following morning, I woke up with an upset stomach and chocolate in my hair. To make matters worse, I was late for work.

Pressed for time, I was forced to shovel food into my mouth, throw on some dirty underwear from the hamper, and rinse my mouth out with orange juice.

While running out the door, I found the time to scroll through my phone messages. Sadly, Shaniqua was still ignoring me. As much as I was looking forward to seeing her at work today, I was dreading the attitude that would come with it.

It was a quarter past eleven and there was no sign of Shaniqua. And it just so happened to be one of the busiest days at The Protein Hut.

"Can I help the next person in line, please?" I called over the sound of clanging barbells.

"Hi, dear!" said Barbara-Anne, walking up to the till.

"Oh, hi. Gettin' the usual?" I asked, grabbing a handful of fruit.

"Sure. Hey, Viola, did you cut your hair? It looks short today."

"No, not going through that again. The last time I cut my hair short, people thought I was a lesbian."

"Oh, well it has a nice shine," said Barbara-Anne.

"It's just greasy. I didn't have time to wash it." I smiled politely, handing over the smoothie. "So… are you coming this afternoon to the session?"

Barbara-Anne took a sip of her smoothie and then looked at me curiously. "Were you able to get a fifth member?"

I bit my lip. "Not yet. It's not looking good. Maybe I can convince them to take the four of us."

"Try to be a little optimistic, my dear," Barbara-Anne said.

"Hey, I am very optimistic. I strongly believe Amelia Earhart is alive and working as a Walmart greeter."

Barbara-Anne gave me a warm smile and walked away. I reached for my cell phone, hoping Shaniqua had replied to my text messages.

There were several unread tweets and Facebook posts, but nothing from Shaniqua. I was starting to get worried, but there was nothing to do but hope she would walk through the door.

It was time to close up shop and prepare for the group session. My stomach was in knots as I was nervous about the intensity I was about to face. I was still worried that the group wouldn't show up.

After rinsing out the last juicer and powering down, I made my way to the bathroom to freshen up.

Staring deeply into the spotty bathroom mirror, I began the breathing exercises I'd learned from watching episodes of *Teen Mom*.

"You can do this, Viola," I whispered to myself. Talking into mirrors has calmed me down ever since my first breakdown in third grade, when a rebellious classmate stabbed my best friend, Emily Jane, a Cabbage Patch kid I'd received as a birthday gift.

"You got this, Viola," I said, a little bit louder. "Just go out there and give it your all. But not too much because you forgot to put deodorant on this morning."

"Hi, Janette!" I said cheerfully as I walked up to the front desk. "I am here for the group session."

Janette, looking annoyed, handed me a clipboard. "Fill this out. The names of your group of five is required."

"Oh, okay, of course," I said nervously, knowing I didn't have a fifth name to write down. Realizing I would have to lie, I wrote down the first name that popped into my head. I enthusiastically handed the clipboard back to Janette.

Janette scanned the list and eyed it suspiciously. "Your fifth member's name is Yolanda Squatpump?"

"Uh huh. I think she's Dutch."

"You do realize personal trainers aren't for cheap and stingy people, right?" Janette said condescendingly.

"Don't worry, I am not cheap. I stuff my bra with Bounty, the thicker, quicker picker-upper."

"Whatever," she said. "Just head over to the group training room. The personal trainer will meet your group there."

"Thanks. Bye, Janette!" I said, feeling a little relief.

Although I had worked inside The Fitness Hut for several years, for the first time I felt like I had a real purpose being there. As much as I loved the job, it was a simple day-to-day responsibility and nothing more.

As I walked into the training room, I couldn't help but feel self-conscious, realizing one wall was made of glass, which meant that anyone on the cardio equipment could look in.

My increasing anxiety was making me extremely hungry, and I was already planning a dirty drive-by at the nearest McDonald's.

I walked around the empty training-room floor for several minutes, desperately waiting for somebody to join me. At one point I was so bored I started screaming in short bursts just to test the acoustics in the room.

As I stared at the ticking clock high above, I figured I might as well do something fitness related, being that I was in a training room.

After a few minutes of stretching, I decided to do a few lunges. By the tenth lunge, my phone slipped out of my pocket and crashed onto the hardwood floor.

"Shit!" I shrieked, bending down for the phone. The loud sound of a snap alerted me to a bigger issue. "Oh my God!" I suspected my strapless bra had snapped.

Before I could run out and assess the situation, a familiar man walked into the training room—the new male trainer.

I hugged myself tightly, desperately hoping he wouldn't be able to see my bra, which was slowly edging its way to the front of my shirt. I stuck my hand behind my back to hold it in place. He walked right up to me and said, "Hi, I'm Christos, the group trainer."

Confused and embarrassed, I said, "I think there is some kind of mistake... I asked for a female trainer."

Christos shook his head. "Janette specifically assigned me to your group. Where is your group, by the way?"

"Umm, they should be here shortly, but they're expecting a female trainer. I don't want to disappoint them," I said, staring at his biceps as he brushed his fingers through his thick, dark hair.

"Viola, right?" Christos asked. Did he not hear me?

"Yeah, let me guess, you heard the radio show?" I couldn't believe I was bringing up one of the most humiliating things to ever happen to me.

"Yes," Christos said, gently touching my shoulder. "I thought it was disgusting, hurtful, and I am sorry you had to go through that."

Distracted by his soft fingers against my skin, I let go of the bra, and it slipped out of my shirt and fell to the floor.

Christos took a few steps back. "Uh, I think you dropped something."

"Nope," I said hastily, "it's not mine. Must belong to some other lady."

My eyes widened as Christos bent down and picked up the bra. "Are you sure?" he asked. "Because it says property of Viola Ginamero in permanent marker."

I bit my lip and snatched the bra out of his hand. "Why don't I just hold onto that until I find the owner." I smiled as I shoved the bra into my pocket.

"Okay, well, Viola, welcome to your first group training session! The change rooms are just outside the door and to the left. As soon as the rest of your group arrives we can begin. I will return when the full group is here."

"Okay, looking forward to it," I replied, watching him exit the room.

The second he was out of my sight I yanked the bra out of my pocket and raced across the gym floor and tossed it into a garbage can.

"Did your bra snap again?" said a familiar female voice. "Cause I got some binder clips in my car."

I turned around and shouted with glee. "Shaniqua! You came!" I ran up and squeezed her tightly as if she was a teddy bear.

"Of course I came. Look, Viola, I may get upset and act like a bitch from time to time but in the end I will never, ever let you down. Especially at times when you need me the most."

I smiled warmly. "I know. I love you, Shan!"

Shaniqua rolled her eyes. "Where is everybody?"

Before I could answer, Barbara-Anne and a barefoot Remy popped in behind Shaniqua.

Barbara-Anne looked at Shaniqua. "Oh, you're Viola's black friend!"

"*Excuse* me?" shouted Shaniqua.

I quickly intervened. "Shaniqua, this is Barbara-Anne, and the gentleman behind her is Remy. You probably recognize Barbara-Anne from The Protein Hut.

Shaniqua rolled her eyes and looked at Remy's bare feet. "Where are your shoes?

Remy scratched the back of his neck. "I had to run for this bus, and… well, I sort of threw up my shoes on the way here."

Shaniqua looked at Remy in disgust. "Boy, that is nasty."

"It gets worse," Remy continued. "I was wearing sandals."

"Oh, hell no!" Shaniqua cried, looking in my direction. "Viola, this foo is a mess, and he smells like rotting meat. Why is he even here?"

"He's one of us," I said. "Besides, he just needs a little deodorant."

"Forget deodorant, that foo needs Febreze," she said.

"Umm… I can hear what you guys are saying," said Remy.

"As can I, and oh my galoshes, that was hilarious," said Vik, coming up behind Remy. His nose was still covered in white bandages.

"Vik!" I shrieked. "You're here! Does this mean you forgive me for that?" I pointed at his nose.

Vik crossed his arms against his chest, looked me up and down, and said in a mean-girl tone, "Viola, did you even try this morning? You look like a hobbit."

"Okay, guess you're still mad… and you have every right to be. I will respectfully give you all the time you need. The important thing is you're here." I couldn't help but clap joyfully.

I looked at Shaniqua. "Shaniqua, meet Vik. Vik, meet my best friend, Shaniqua."

Shaniqua slowly walked up to Vik, her stance clearly threatening. "You better watch what you say to my girl, understood?"

Vik looked Shaniqua up and down. "Girl, please. You know, up close, you look identical to Beyoncé. Except for the nose, mouth, hair, body, talent, and face."

"*Excuse me?*" Shaniqua barked. "What did you just say?"

Thankfully Christos returned before Shaniqua could break Vik in half.

He did a quick head count. "Oh, good, everyone is here. Shall we begin?"

Christos began marching back and forth in front of the five of us like a drill sergeant. "Okay, so, looking at my clipboard we should have here today Viola, Barbara-Anne, Remy, Vik, and... Is this right? Yolanda Squatpump?"

Shaniqua turned to me with a confused look on her face. Clearly I had some explaining to do.

Christos continued. "My name is Christos and I will be your personal trainer for the duration of the program. Any questions?"

Shaniqua put her hand up. "Yeah, can you turn around so I can see your fine booty?"

"I second that!" said Vik.

"I should mention a few things about me," said Christos. "I take my job very seriously and expect a high level of commitment from all of you. I have no doubt in my mind I will not only get you guys to your goal. We will destroy it."

Barbara-Anne raised her hand. "Will this commitment conflict with my bingo night?"

"This commitment will conflict with your entire lifestyle," said Christos.

Shaniqua nudged me and whispered, "Girl, look at his biceps. How do you not find him attractive?"

"Shh! I am trying to listen. Besides, I only have eyes for Franklin. Also, Christos's beard grosses me out."

"Hey, ladies," said Christos, "I need your full attention."

Shaniqua nudged me again. "Ooh, he's assertive, too. You know, you could learn a thing or two from him."

"Shh…"

"Will you two please shut up?" Vik shouted. "I can't hear my future husband speak. Go ahead, honey."

Christos continued, slowly pacing back and forth. "As I was saying, if you want change, you're going to have to be committed to a new lifestyle. Now, don't panic. I will be guiding you every step of the way with a program that will get you closer and closer to your weight-loss goals. Each session, I will take you through one of the eight stages of weight loss and provide you with all the tools you need to get in the best shape of your life. I only need one thing from each and everyone of you. Can you guess what that is?"

Remy raised his hand. "A urine sample? If so, I have a few in my backpack."

"No, Remy."

"A stool sample?" asked Barbara-Anne.

Christos looked at Barbara-Anne with disgust. "What I need from each and every one of you is: the desire to want to get in the best shape of your life."

"Huh?" I said.

"Basically," said Christos, "each of you has to *want* to change, otherwise we won't get anywhere. It's easy to wake up one day and tell yourself you're going to try to walk more or eat a little better. And sure, you may be able to do it for a few days, weeks, or months, but at some point you will go back to your old routine. Weight loss isn't something that can be forced on somebody—they have to truly want it. You five have to want to get in the best shape of your life or we may as well disband right now."

The five of us took turns staring at each other, waiting for one of us to stand up and head for the door.

Christos posed a good question. How badly did we want to lose weight? Did I really want this? Was I doing this for myself or Franklin?

Christos began pacing back and forth again. "Great! So that leads us to the first stage of weight loss—accepting change. A lot of people are in denial about their weight. They would rather ignore it instead of actually accepting it and taking action, but most importantly, they refuse help. A lot of people are too embarrassed to ask or accept help, but realistically, change won't come until those people accept the fact that they are over weight, they eat unhealthy, they don't know the first thing about working out, and decide they are one hundred percent ready to accept help and absolutely believe that they can reach their weight-loss goals."

I raised my hand. "Umm, should we be taking notes? If so, I don't have paper. Though I do have a chocolate bar wrapper in my purse that I can use."

Vik rolled his eyes. "What's step two?" I was glad he asked, because I wanted to know, too.

Christos walked towards Remy. "Each session, I will reveal another step. That means you guys will have to wait until tomorrow to hear step two. Also, regarding tomorrow, I want you all to be dressed in proper workout attire. That means no sandals, no boots, no jeans, no jewelry. And Remy: no bare feet. So what should you guys wear? T-shirts, athletic tank tops, shorts, track pants, comfortable athletic shoes. I think you guys get the point."

Shaniqua raised her hand. "I just want to make it clear that I am just here to support my girl Viola, and that's all."

Christos looked at Shaniqua. "Actually, that brings up a good point. I am not like most trainers. I will be putting a lot of pressure on you guys with tough love and motivation. At first, you guys will struggle—"

"Oh, I know what it's like to struggle," I said, interrupting him. "I own a pair of fitted yoga pants."

Christos tried again. "At first, you guys will struggle, but then you will succeed. The key thing is you have to want the success more than anything in the world. Everything comes back to that."

Vik raised his hand. "Christos, I can't hear you back here. I think maybe you should take your shirt off and speak louder."

"I second that!" said Barbara-Anne.

I couldn't help but roll my eyes. What did they see in him? Sure, he had a chiseled face, a tall muscular body, straight white teeth, and thick hair. I admit those were all attractive qualities, but really, he was nothing special. And honestly, I really couldn't get past that big beard. Gross.

I raised my hand to ask the million-dollar question. "Christos, can you guarantee us results?"

Christos scanned the group. "Results are guaranteed if you do everything I say."

"That's what my driving instructor said before I drove over his toe," I said.

The group chuckled at my comment, but Christos didn't. Sheesh. What did I have to say to make him laugh or smile? Not that it mattered.

"I once caused a pile up," added Remy.

"Me, too!" I said. "Were you also brushing your teeth?"

"No… I was clipping my toenails," he said.

Vik, looking disgusted, took a few steps away from Remy. "Christos, honey, what's next?"

"You're not going to like it," said Christos, "but keep in mind the next step is related to stage one."

"What is it?" I asked.

"Weight. It's time to get a reading of your weight. Who wants to go first?"

"I ain't comfortable with showin' any of you my weight," barked Shaniqua. "That shit is my business!"

I raised my hand. "I will do it! The only two things that make me uncomfortable are public speaking and yeast infections."

Christos raised his eyebrows. "Great. Thanks, Viola. The scale is over there at the back of the room." I led the group to the back, and I could feel the group's anxiety wash over me.

I stared at the scale for a few seconds before hopping onto it. I closed my eyes. "Okay, my weight shouldn't be a surprise to anyone—the world already saw it." Suddenly, there was silence.

Opening one eye at a time, I looked down at the scale. "202 pounds!" I shouted. "How the hell did I gain more weight!"

Christos touched my shoulder and calmly said, "It's okay, Viola. This is what acceptance is about. If you can accept it, you will be able to reach your goal. Okay, who wants to go next?"

I couldn't help but feel a bit embarrassed. Why did I keep gaining weight?

One by one the group hopped onto the scale. I started to feel a little more comfortable learning that we were all around the same weight range.

After taking everyone's weight—except for a very stubborn Shaniqua—Christos gathered us up and continued the training session.

"There are three different basic body types," Christos said, slowly pacing back and forth. "Ectomorph, mesomorph, and endomorph."

"I think I once ate an ectomorph at Red Lobster," said Remy.

Vik rolled his eyes.

Christos continued. "Knowing which of the three you are closest to will help you plan an effective diet and create realistic, achievable goals that will lead to nothing but success."

I raised my hand. "What's the difference between the three?"

"I am glad you asked, Viola. An ectomorph has a thin build, and usually has long limbs."

Shaniqua piped up. "Oh! That sounds like my cousin Moesha. That skinny bitch can eat a bucket of fried chicken without gaining weight."

"The endomorph has a rectangular shaped body," continued Christos, "and a hard, athletic physique."

Remy pointed at Christos. "That's you!"

"No, not exactly. I will get to that later. An endomorph has a soft, round body, has difficulty losing fat, and has slow metabolism. The five of you are endomorphs."

I raised my hand again. "So… are you saying there is no hope for us?"

Christos stopped pacing. "Absolutely not! I used to be an endomorph just like you guys. With my guidance and motivation, the five of you will surpass my physique. Believe it."

"Honey," said Vik, "look at us. Do you really think we can get in better shape than you?"

"Vik has a point," I said. "How are we going to get to your level? I've tried aerobics on my own before. As you can see, it didn't stick."

"Most people rely on cardio too much for weight loss," explained Christos. "I focus on a combination of cardio and weightlifting."

"You're joking, right?" I said. "How will that be possible when I can barely lift my ass off the couch?"

"Viola," said Christos, "eventually you will be able to squat with a barbell that weighs more than your couch."

"I don't know, Christos," I said. "I am usually slow to pick up on things. I thought the Kardashians were a box of chocolates."

Vik gasped.

Christos grabbed his clipboard. "That's it for today. Get ready to bring it tomorrow."

As Christos walked out of the training room, I turned to the group. "So? What do you guys think?"

Vik was the first to answer. "Christos is sexy, but like most men I have been with, he's biting off more than he can chew. Also, this gym is more disgusting than Viola's choice of shoes. Did anyone else see that used bra in the garbage over there?"

I laughed nervously. "Let's get back on topic. So are you guys going to return tomorrow?"

As I looked around the room, I saw nothing but undecided faces. I wasn't surprised, as this was only the beginning of a long, life-changing journey.

After a pit stop at KFC, I went straight home for a cat nap. It was a bit hard getting to sleep as my cell phone kept vibrating from social-media alerts. Although it was comforting to know the world was supporting me, focusing on the goal was important, so I decided to limit my activity on social media.

Wrapped in my Snuggie, I eventually drifted off to dream land. I was quite fond of sleeping—everything from the darkness to the weird dreams compelled me to never wake up. Speaking of dreams, I am the queen of dysfunctional dreams. One night I dreamt that I was having a three way in a food court with Bigfoot and Miss Piggy. Another night I dreamt I was being chased by a burrito holding a Shake Weight. I think I ate Mexican food that night.

It wasn't until I heard a door slam that I was yanked back to reality. Two barely audible voices were seeping through my door. It was clear that the couple on the other side of the door were having an argument.

Suddenly, memories of Franklin came rushing back as I stared at the door. The last thing I remember was hearing the door shut with Franklin already gone. I didn't even get the chance to watch him walk out.

But that was okay, because I wasn't looking for closure—I was seeking a wrench to repair what was broken.

I curled up against the edge of the couch, feeling incredibly uncomfortable. My hair tickled my ears, my body was insanely warm, and hunger was creeping up on me.

I couldn't get thoughts of Franklin out of my mind. I had a thousand questions in queue. What had he been up to? What was on his mind at that very moment? Was he missing me? Did he still love me? Was he caught up on *Game of Thrones*? I admit, I was getting obsessed. I mean, it's normal, right?

I knew what I had to do to feed my obsession: Facebook stalking.

As if she could sense my impending stupidity, my phone began to ring. "Can't talk now, Shaniqua, I am about to stalk Franklin on Facebook, and this requires all my attention."

"Viola, that is not a good idea. You need to take care of yourself. Forget that foo." I could hear someone moaning in agony in the background.

"I do take care of myself, and I'm a very caring person. I took really good care of my dog during his final days, remember?"

"Didn't you sit on him?"

"That's not the point."

"Whatever. Anyways, I was calling to tell you that I need a lift to work tomorrow. Shamar needs the car for a doctor's appointment in the morning."

"I can hear him. Is he okay?" I asked, flipping open my laptop.

"He's fine. The dumbass sat on my tweezers."

"Yikes, those are sharp! That's why I get that woman on 45th to thread my eyebrows. She's the only one that's willing to thread with my used floss."

"Girl, you nasty."

"Adios, Shan."

The second my browser loaded I took a deep breath and headed over to Franklin's homepage. "Okay, Franklin, let's see what you've been up to," I said to myself.

To my shock, he'd changed his picture. What was once a cheek-to-cheek selfie of us had been replaced by a picture of him hugging another girl. A girl I recognized.

"Oh, hell no!" I said in disbelief. I immediately sprang for my phone to call Shaniqua.

Shaniqua answered. "I can't talk now, Viola. I'm watching today's recording of *General Hospital*. Carly just bitch slapped Sonny. Shit just got real."

"He's seeing Annabelle!" I shouted, jumping up from the couch.

"What are you talking about?" Shaniqua asked, confused.

"Franklin's Facebook page! There is a picture of him and Annabelle as the profile pic!"

"Wait, are you talking about that girl from your Halloween party? The skinny bitch who thought you were Franklin's alcoholic cousin from Minnesota?"

"No, and for the record, I only threw back a few shots that night."

"Oh, was it the girl that slipped on your vomit?"

"No, but that was one hell of a dry-cleaning bill."

"Was it the girl who helped you back up after you fell down that flight of stairs?"

"Okay, now I'm starting to think that maybe I did drink too much that night."

"Wait a minute, Viola, was it the girl who refused to use the bathroom because she thought your toilet would give her Ebola?"

"Bingo!"

"So Franklin's dating her?" she said, her voice going soft, "do you think he left you for her?"

My eyes widened. "Now I do!"

"Relax, Viola. You don't need a guy like that. Oh shit! Sonny just slapped Carly back!" Shaniqua shouted in shock.

"Shaniqua, come on! A new girl in the picture is going to make it harder for Franklin to come back to me."

"Viola, you're starting to sound desperate."

"Hey, I admit I have been in some desperate situations, but this is different. Franklin and I are soul mates."

"Girl, you crazy. I gotta go, Viola. See you tomorrow."

Was Shan right? Did I need to move on? Was I acting desperate? Honestly, I didn't think so. I was prepared to make big sacrifices for Franklin and that included physical changes.

Chapter Seven

❷⓪⓪ Lbs

November 17, 2016

The following afternoon I was a feeling a little anxious about the upcoming group session. Too much was at stake. On one hand, if I had success I would have Franklin. If I failed, it would have all just been a waste of time. Time that could have been better spent watching *Hoarders* on A&E.

"Viola!" Shaniqua shouted from across the gym. She was holding a large black garbage bag in one hand and a smoothie in the other. She gestured behind me.

I turned around to see a pregnant lady waiting by the till. "Oh, sorry about that. How can I help you?"

"Yes… ouch… Can I please have… ouch… a large strawberry smoothie?" the woman said, stumbling on her words. Was she having contractions?

"Ma'am, are you okay?" I asked, slowly reaching for a large cup.

"I'm fine. My maternity pants are really tight. I can barely slide my hand into them."

"I completely understand! The last time I was able to slide my hand down my pants was when I discovered masturbation."

"Ooooh!" cried the woman, grabbing her belly. I was certain it wasn't the pants that was causing the pain.

"Are you sure you're okay? You sound like you're having contractions, and believe me I have seen a lot of sitcoms to know what contractions sound like."

"Stop talking!" barked the woman. Sweat dripped off her red face as she walked over to sit at a table.

I figured nobody knew her body better than she did, so I let it go and continued making her smoothie.

"Hi, Viola!" said a familiar voice.

"Hi, Remy! How's it going?" I asked.

"Great! I got the last of my kidney stones out this morning."

"Congratulations, Remy!" I said cheerfully, still distracted by the woman.

"Yeah. Thankfully it wasn't as painful as the time I had to push out a Lego piece."

The woman was moaning, then she started screaming.

"Hey, Remy, I think that woman is going into labor."

"Really? Cause I can help. I once performed a C-section on a duck."

I walked over to the woman, grabbed her hand, and calmly said, "Ma'am, I think you're going into labor. We are going to have to call 911 or knowing my luck it will be too late and I will end up slipping on your placenta."

The woman spoke between short breaths. "I... have gone... to the hospital... three times. Three... false scares. This is... just a... fourth scare... trust me. Ooooh!"

"What if it's not? I think you're cutting it too close. It might already be too late!"

Remy jumped up enthusiastically. "I'll go get a knife!"

I ignored him and looked up to see Shaniqua walking towards us.

"Shaniqua, can you ask Janette to call 911?"

"Is this for real? Is she really about to give birth?" Shaniqua said, bending down.

"Yeah, I think so. This is about to get really messy."

Shaniqua placed her hands on her hips. "Oh, hell no! I just spent half an hour cleaning the floor!"

Paramedics burst through the front door, followed by a woman with a stretcher. "Over here!" I shouted, waving my hands in the air.

The team of paramedics wasted no time and strapped the pregnant woman to the stretcher. As they wheeled her out the door I shouted, "Wait! You forgot your smoothie!"

Remy snuck up behind me with a large serrated knife. "Can I have it?"

With the commotion over, it was time to get my head in the game and mop the various fluids off the floor. I was nervous, as we were going to learn about our greatest challenge: nutrition.

After closing up, I quickly ran into the backroom to change into my workout clothes. I was running late and the group was already in the training room. Luckily it didn't take too long to slip into a tight pink tee, navy-blue vest, and a pair of gray sweats that I frequently used as pajamas.

I rolled my uniform into a ball and tossed it on a nearby computer chair. All set, I briskly walked to the training room and I saw Vik at the door. His nose was still covered in white bandages and he was not smiling.

"Hiya, Vik!" I said cheerfully, waving both of my hands.

He crossed his arms against his chest and eyed me up and down. "Viola, what's with that blue vest? You look like a Walmart greeter."

"I know, right? The breast pocket is perfect for carrying sausages."

Vik rolled his eyes and joined the group inside. I followed close behind, noticing that everybody but Christos was present. It was clear that I hadn't missed much—Shaniqua was on her phone while the rest of the gang was chatting amongst themselves.

I was feeling exhausted from the shift I had just worked; it ended up being more stressful than I had anticipated. I couldn't help but secretly wish that Christos would walk in and announce that he was going to reschedule the session, and then I could go home and watch *Judge Judy* with a bucket of fried chicken on my lap. A girl can dream, right?

Christos entered the room hastily and dropped a large duffel bag on the floor. "Sorry I am late. A pregnant woman just gave birth in the parking lot."

I looked down at the bag. "What's in the duffel?"

"You guys will find out soon," Christos said. "Is everybody ready for the next training session?"

"Hells yeah!" I replied, fist pumping the air. The group didn't look very enthusiastic, as if they knew what was coming.

"So yesterday we learned that the first stage of weight loss is accepting change. Today we are going to learn about the second stage: effort. In other words, failing before you succeed."

I raised my hand. "Oh, I know all about that. I have stayed away from toasters ever since my Easy-Bake oven electrocuted me."

"Thank you, Viola," Christos said, pausing briefly before speaking again. "Whether it relates to fitness or the diet that accompanies it, most people trying to lose weight will fail. The reason is because in order to succeed, each individual has to learn on their own what works and doesn't work for them. It's a dusty trail that most people walk off of prematurely, which leads to failure."

"I once got lost for days on a dusty trail," said Remy. "I had to urinate in a plastic bag."

"Why didn't you just use the bushes?" asked Barbara-Anne.

"I didn't want the wolves to track my scent," said Remy.

Shaniqua turned to me. "Is this guy for real?"

I shrugged.

Vik spoke up. "So, Christos, if we are bound for failure, what's the point of even trying?"

"The idea," Christos said, "is to get right back on the horse with full motivation and an understanding of where your obstacles are so you can avoid them and aim for success."

Shaniqua rolled her eyes and locked onto the duffel. "What's in the bag?"

"Ah, we are almost there," said Christos. Clearly we were all dying to know what was in there. I was convinced the biggest obstacle of my life was related to the contents of that bag.

Vik raised his hand. "Unlike Viola's garbage-bin throwaway sweats, I spent over a hundred dollars on these Lulu Lemon's. Are we working out or not?"

"Hey," I said, "I did not get these pants from a garbage bin—I found them in a lost and found box."

Remy raised his hand. "I once found a water bottle in a dumpster."

Shaniqua looked at Remy in utter disgust.

"Absolutely, Vik," said Christos. "I will be introducing you guys to your first workout in a matter of moments. Did you all bring a water bottle?"

Remy raised his water bottle into the air cheerfully. I, on the other hand, was the only one without one. I shook my head and said, "Sorry, Christos, I didn't bring one. I'm not much of a water drinker."

Christos began pacing back and forth. "Water is key to fat loss, as it helps boost your metabolism. Be ready to drink a lot of it."

"That might be hard," I said. "The most water I ever swallowed was in a drowning incident."

Christos continued. "From here on out I will throw out random tips. Here is your first one: use a water bottle with a straw. This will allow for maximum water consumption. I also want you guys to take five gulps at a time. Get into the habit."

Shaniqua passed me her bottle. "Here, take mine. I'm good."

"Are you sure?" I asked, grabbing the blue bottle from her.

She nodded.

"Thanks," I said, lifting the bottle up to my mouth to grab five gulps.

Christos was already moving on. "So next we are going to learn abou—"

I interrupted with a choking cough. Liquid dribbled out of my mouth and onto the floor.

"Are you okay?" Christos asked, handing me a towel to wipe my face.

I continued coughing for several seconds before replying jokingly, "I was never very good at swallowing."

"As I was saying, next we are going to learn about nutrition: the third stage. It's another key to fat loss and muscle growth. I can't stress enough how important meal planning will be during your transition."

I couldn't help but feel a little nervous. I had tried dieting before. Sort of. Either way, I didn't last long.

Christos continued pacing back and forth. "So right off the bat, I will tell you that dieting is not the answer. It's a short-term solution which I avoid." Christos stopped and paused for a moment. "You guys are going to eat. A lot."

And just like that, the nerves went away. I could feel a wave of relief and excitement from the group.

"I mentioned before that I am a tough trainer, and I have no problem pushing the mental and physical capacity of you five. I am not going to be a fly on the wall, so you will have to honor the rules on your own. Remember: you have to want it."

Remy interrupted yet again. "So does that mean I can have as many Big Macs as I want? Cause I have a few squished in between my mattress at the moment."

Vik looked at Remy in disgust. "Eww. Why?"

"Duh, cause then I can stack them."

"As of right now, here is what you guys cannot eat: sweets or desserts, fast foods of any kind, sugar-sweetened beverages, junk food, whole-fat dairy, potatoes, refined grains, fruit juices, and processed meats. If you have any questions, you guys have my number. Just send me a text."

"Are you messin' with us?" said Shaniqua. "You just said that we are going to eat a lot. I ate most of those items last night in bed. If those aren't on the table, what the hell is left to eat?"

Barbara-Anne raised her hand. "Can I still drink my Ensure mixture?"

Christos asked, "What do you mix in it?"

"Vodka."

"To answer Shaniqua's question, here is what you guys will be eating: fruits, vegetables, nuts, skim milk, Greek yogurt, whole grains, lean meats, and much, much more."

I raised my hand. "So today we can go home and eat whatever we want, right? Tomorrow is when the clean eating begins, right?"

Christos puckered his lips and said bluntly, "No. Not at all."

We all paused to stare at each other's faces.

"Umm... okay," I said. "You know what? I can do this; I'm opened minded. After all, I gave ketchup Doritos a chance."

"Christos," said Vik, "I just received a case of Twinkies I ordered off of eBay. Are you telling me that I can't eat them?"

Remy raised his hand. "If Vik can't eat them, can I have them?"

Barbara-Anne waved her hands in the air to grab everybody's attention. "Wait a minute! I have a very important question."

Christos stopped. "Go ahead, Barbara-Anne."

"How do we know following this meal plan will get us results?"

Christos grabbed the bottom of his tank top and peeled it up towards his neck to unveil his tanned and toned washboard abs.

Barbara-Anne stared. "Okay, I'm sold."

Christos lowered his shirt. "Any other questions?"

Vik raised his hand. "Can you do that again?"

"Actually," he said, "it's time to show you the contents of this duffel bag."

I looked at Shaniqua and whispered, "You're quieter than usual. What's up?"

"It's Shamar," she said. "Earlier when I was on the phone he accused me of being abusive to him. Can you believe that dumbass?"

"Umm."

"What the hell, Viola! Are you siding with him?"

"No, no, it's just that… do you remember that argument you guys had in the theater a few months ago?"

Shaniqua shook her head with great attitude. "Yeah, so? It was justified! Shamar was checking out the big booty bitch in the next row. Besides, in no way was that abuse."

"You slapped him!"

"That ain't the same."

"Girls," said Christos, "please focus."

"Sorry, Christos," I said. "Go ahead." I was starting to get the feeling that he didn't like me, and that was okay, as I couldn't care less about him, either. "We are ready."

Christos bent down and unzipped the bag to reveal... nothing. Absolutely nothing.

Vik crossed his arms against his chest. "Umm... I don't know what's more disappointing, Viola's pet-store breath or the fact that there is nothing in that bag."

I turned to Vik. "Hey, I will have you know that I learned how to make my toothpaste off of Pinterest."

Christos stood back up and said, "I have been watching you guys closely, and what I have learned is that each of you is hiding food. I want you to place whatever food items you're hiding in this duffel bag."

Remy was the first to step up to the bag. He slipped off his shoe and tipped it over the bag. We watched in silence as a smashed chocolate bar fell into the bag.

"Goodbye, my friend," he said solemnly.

Christos gently patted Remy on the back. "Great job, Remy. You won't regret your new lifestyle; it will pay off. I promise. All right, who wants to go next? Viola?"

"Oh, I am not hiding anything," I said innocently, looking away, hoping he would buy it.

Vik shouted, "Oh, please, girl! Unless you have serious inflammation issues, there is no way your boobs went from a C to DD overnight."

Christos looked at me disappointingly. "Viola? Do you have something to share?"

I snorted and sauntered over to the bag, as it was clear that there was no way out. Exhaling deeply, I reached into my bra and pulled out a small bag of chips.

"Well done, Viola!" Christos said. "This is a big step towards your transformation."

"Are we done yet?" asked Shaniqua.

"Not quite. There is one more person here hiding an item," Christos said, staring suspiciously at Barbara-Anne.

Barbara-Anne looked at him in shock. "*Me*? Why are you accusing me of hiding food? You know what, Christos? It hurts to be accused of such things. How can we work together if you have no trust?" She looked genuinely sad and hurt and began to tear up.

Christos looked at her sternly. "What's in your purse, Barbara-Anne?"

"A gentleman never asks an old lady that question! Where did you learn your manners?"

"Barbara-Anne?"

After a few moments her tears suddenly vanished as if she was faking. She took a deep breath, reached into her purse, and pulled out a bag of powdered donuts.

Impressed by what I saw, I quietly whispered to her, "Oh, you're good." Barbara-Anne winked at me as she dropped the bag into the duffel.

Christos zipped up the bag and tossed it aside. "Remember, guys, you will look as good as the quality and effort you put in. If you cheat, you're only pushing yourself further from your transformation goal."

I raised my hand. "Oh, you don't need to worry about me, I have never cheated, not even in school."

"Didn't you once get caught writing answers on a tampon wrapper?" asked Shaniqua.

"Cheating is allowed in Math class; everyone knows that."

Shaniqua rolled her eyes.

Christos walked towards the door. "Okay, is everybody ready to work out?"

"I ain't going out there," yelled Shaniqua. "I don't need people watchin' me work out!"

Christos held the door open for us. "All they will see is a group of people working hard to better themselves."

I had to admit, I never really thought of it that way. I mean, up until now the public saw me as a heavy girl with barbeque sauce in her hair.

One by one, we walked through the door. It was not going to be easy working out in public, but what was the worst that could happen?

Christos led us to a row of treadmills. I felt a little tense, as the last experience I had with a treadmill was twenty years ago when they had a safety clip attachment.

"It's a treadmill," said Shaniqua, "so what?"

Christos gave a slight smirk. "You will see. Everybody hop on and wait for my instructions."

I raised my hand. "Umm… these buttons look really complicated. Keep in mind that I haven't used a treadmill since I did a face plant on one in a gym class."

"Did you break your nose?" Vik said snidely.

"No, nothing like that happened, I only peed myself a little."

Christos stood in front of the row of treadmills as if he was conducting a symphony. "All right, I want to get you guys in the habit of drinking water, so go ahead and take your five gulps."

Shaniqua was getting impatient. I figured she was still annoyed with Shamar. "Okay, now what?"

Christos began his usual pacing back and forth. "Every workout session will begin with what you guys are about to learn. Welcome to HIIT cardio."

"Oh, is that that new trend?" asked Vik. "Like a barfie?"

Shaniqua said, "What the hell is a barfie?"

"Barfie's are the next big thing on Instagram," said Vik. "It's when you take a selfie as you barf."

"HIIT," Christos continued, "or high intensity interval training cardio, is scientifically one of the most effective ways to burn fat. It efficiently replaces hours of cardio for twenty minutes of training and yields more favorable results."

Barbara-Anne raised her hand. "Exactly how long is our workout going to be?"

"Typically, an effective workout should be around forty-five minutes to an hour and a half, with the HIIT cardio included. Okay, everybody, press the start button. The treadmill will now be activated at its lowest speed."

"This feels good," I said cheerfully. "I think I can feel it doing something."

"I, too, can feel something," said Remy, "but I think it's my breakfast burrito coming up."

"Okay," said Christos, "now press the arrow button until you reach the speed of four. This will be your rest speed. Continue walking at this rest speed for five minutes as a warmup."

My initial thoughts? So far so good, but I had been anticipating that I wouldn't be able to keep up with the speed. The fastest I ever moved was when I spotted a cockroach in my Snuggie, and all that left me was a sprained ankle.

The group was holding up, which was a good sign, but I feared that Shaniqua might go into cardiac arrest. I looked over at her. "How are you doing, Shan?"

She remained silent and kept walking, beads of sweat pouring down her face.

"Five minutes are up!" Christos shouted. "Now you guys are going to sprint for twenty seconds. Bump the speed up to ten. The timer starts now!"

As the speed increased, so did my need for antiperspirant and Gravol. I could feel my long hair bouncing behind me with each stride.

Vik shouted, "How much longer?"

"Eleven seconds," said Christos. "You guys are doing great."

I wasn't buying it. I don't know what it was, maybe it was the fact that I was sprinting for the first time in my life with total discomfort or maybe it was the snugness of my new training bra. Either way, I was ready to throw in the towel.

"That's twenty seconds!" Christos shouted. "Reduce your speeds back down to four. You guys did fantastic! Keep up the good work!"

Panting like a dog, I said, "We are done? Great, that felt really good. See you tomorrow, Christos."

"No, Viola," said Christos. "You guys are going repeat that eight times."

I want to tell you that I reacted with positivity and grace, but that would be a bold-faced lie. When he said the word eight, I vomited onto the treadmill, spraying a woman on a rowing machine directly behind me.

I sat in the locker room with my head between my legs while the group continued without me. I couldn't help but feel like a failure.

Shaniqua walked in and sat down beside me. "Hey, girl, how are you feeling?"

I lifted up my pale and sweaty head. "Are you guys done?"

"For today, yeah. Christos is saving the weightlifting for tomorrow, as they called for an evacuation due to the smell."

"Oh my God, I am so embarrassed. Maybe I should just give up. I think that's what people want, anyways."

"Viola, nobody wants you to give up," said Shaniqua.

"Tell that to the woman who had to scrape my puke out of her hair."

Shaniqua chuckled. "Ready to get out of here?"

I nodded.

Feeling a new breed of exhaustion and hunger, I plopped myself on my couch. After an hour of zombie surfing on my cell phone I passed out in between the cushions.

It wasn't long before I woke up to the ringing of my cell phone. Oddly, it was a number I didn't recognize. Predicting it was a telemarketer, I answered the way I always answered sales calls.

"Thank you for calling Pizza Hut, will this be for pick-up or delivery?"

"Oh, sorry," said a masculine voice. "I must have called the wrong number."

"No problem. Have a nice day." I couldn't help but smile a little as he disconnected.

Minutes later the phone rang again.

"Wow, this telemarketer is desperate," I said to myself. This time I tried something else. "You have reached the sexually transmitted diseases hotline. For gonorrhea, please press one; for chlamydia, please press two; for genital herpes, please press thr—"

"Viola?" the man interrupted.

"Uh, who is this?" I said, feeling a little uncomfortable.

"It's Christos."

Suddenly a rush of anxiety came over me. I leaped onto my feet and cleared my throat. "Christos? Why are you calling me? Oh, wait, is this because of what I forgot in the sink? I just wanted to clean it off a little before I re-inserted it."

"No, not calling about that. Wait, what did you forget in the sink?"

"If that's not it, then why are you calling me?"

"I just wanted to check up on you and see if you were okay. You left so quickly I wasn't able to catch you after the session."

I recalled a moment in high school when a few mean girls tossed my clothes in a toilet while I was showering. Later that evening the most popular boy in school called me because he was concerned, and then he laughed and made fun of me.

With that in mind, I waited a few moments before replying to Christos, waiting for him to start laughing.

"Viola? Are you there?"

"Yeah, sorry. What was the question again?" I asked, feeling confused. What was his agenda?

"Are you okay?"

"Yes, yes I am."

"Okay, great," he said. "So I will see you tomorrow?"

"What's tomorrow?" I asked, realizing I'd just asked a dumb question.

"The next training session," Christos said.

I bit my lip. "You know what, I don't kn—"

"Oh, before I forget," he said, "I just wanted to say I really admire your drive. The group wouldn't exist if it wasn't for you. In one year's time, all of the group's success will be because of you. I hope you're proud."

"Honestly, it's been a while since I felt that way," I said, "but I did take a lot pride in my childhood goals. I taught my Firby to swear in three different languages."

Christos laughed, and I was taken aback, as it was the first time I heard his warm chuckle. Up until now I thought his sense of humor was dead. "You're not like other girls, are you, Viola?"

I smiled. "I know, right? People envy me. You should see the stares I get when I pull out my Snuggie on the subway."

"You sound like you are going to be just fine, Viola," Christos said cheerfully. "See ya tomorrow?"

"Sure, see ya tomorrow."

"Oh, wait! I just realized that you were missed when I distributed the meal-plan guide. I will e-mail it to you right away."

"Thanks, Christos."

"My pleasure. Good night, Viola."

"Good night," I replied, hanging up the phone.

I felt a sudden tingling, similar to the time when I was mistakenly tasered at Panda Hut.

I kept playing back the conversation in my head, tweaking my responses at every turn. Should I have been more serious? More funny? I was feeling confused. Why did I even care? I needed a distraction. Thankfully it wasn't long before I received the meal-plan guide in my inbox.

"All right, let's see what we got here," I said to myself. After a quick glance, it was clear that it was going to be a challenge adjusting to the guide. Morning meals consisted of oatmeal and fruit; noon was comprised of chicken breast, vegetables, and brown rice; evening included options such as fish, chicken, lean beef with whole grains. Interestingly enough, there was also a snack period scheduled mid-morning and before bed.

Sadly, there was no junk food or sweets in the guide, not even one sugary item. How was I going to satisfy my potato-chip cravings? What was I going to stuff into my mouth during *Grey's Anatomy*? Would I need to buy a muzzle off of Amazon?

The situation was reminiscent to my Aunt Lucille's addiction to eating couch cushions. Yes, you heard me right. So just like her solution to kill the craving by switching out her couch for a beanbag chair, I knew I had to get rid of all my unhealthy food.

With a large black garbage bag in hand, I began the hunt. I flipped through every cupboard and opened every drawer to fill the bag with every unhealthy item in my apartment.

There was one item left behind that I didn't have the courage to toss in the bag—the brownies I made the night before Franklin left. To me they had symbolic meaning and a purpose, and I couldn't help but feel that getting rid of the brownies would indicate that our relationship was officially over.

Afraid that I would change my mind, I quickly ran downstairs to the garbage dumpster and tossed the bag as far as I could so it was unreachable.

When I returned back to the apartment I was feeling peckish. It didn't take long before I realized my fridge and cupboard were completely bare.

As if on cue, my phone began to ring. "Hey, Shan."

"Viola, something happened today that has me concerned," Shaniqua said in a very serious tone. I immediately got butterflies as this was a new one for the books.

"What is it?" I said, taking a deep breath.

"Something's changed in me. This evening I was cruising in Manhattan when suddenly I was forced to stop for a pedestrian. Anyways, just as she walked in front of my car, the bitch kneeled down to tie her shoe!"

"Oh my God, you didn't run her over, did you?"

"No, Viola, that's what I am concerned about. I wasn't angry at all. It didn't bother me."

"Are you sure? Maybe deep down inside you wanted to at least throw your coffee at her."

"No."

"Did you hit your head on the treadmill? Maybe you have a concussion."

"Whatever. I gotta go. Later, Viola."

I couldn't help but feel worried and concerned about Shaniqua, as she was my best friend, and I knew her emotions. Typically my source of repatriating these feelings was solved by eating a bag of chips with a bucket of fried chicken.

Unfortunately, I failed to find a distraction and ultimately the cravings kicked in.

An hour passed, and the cravings were getting worse. It wasn't until I saw a Burger King commercial that I hurled myself off the couch, galloped down the stairwell, and kicked open the door to the waste stations.

I paused for a minute in front of the dumpster. "Be strong, Viola," I said out loud, looking towards the far end of the dumpster where the garbage bag I'd filled with food laid peacefully.

"Come on, Viola, you're not going to resort to eating trash now. Are you?" I asked myself.

I grabbed onto the top of the dumpster. "Fuck it."

Pulling myself up, I fell head first into the large metal bin and onto a bag of dirty diapers. I crawled over to the bag of food and ripped it open like a bag of chips, forcing the glorious scrap and mushy food into my mouth.

It wasn't until I realized I'd torn open the wrong garbage bag and was eating some other tenant's trash that I knew I'd hit rock bottom.

It reminded me of the time I walked in on Aunt Lucille slicing open her beanbag chair to shovel Styrofoam beans into her mouth.

Chapter Eight

❶❾❽ Lbs

November 18, 2016

I rolled around in bed for an additional hour after slamming the snooze button. If it wasn't for my weak bladder, I would have remained in bed all morning as I was feeling sore from the last session.

Upon my return to bed, my phone rang. "Mornin', Shan," I said in between a lengthy yawn.

"Girl, where the hell are you? You're late for work!"

"Oh, about that, I think I will play the D card today."

"Viola, diarrhea doesn't count as a sick day. Besides, you used up your last sick day to stand in line for those tickets to Frozen on Ice."

"Hey, it's important to support the arts."

"Viola!" Shaniqua shouted.

"Fine, I'm on my way," I said reluctantly.

I skipped my morning shower and threw on my uniform. With several cookies shoved in my mouth, I fled the apartment.

"I'm here, I'm here!" I yelled, barging through the door. The Protein Hut was backed up with customers.

Shaniqua stepped aside from a customer to greet me ever so politely, "What the hell took you so long?"

"Sorry, Shan, I was really sore this morn—"

"Excuse me? Don't you think I was sore, too? I was tossing around so much last night that I rolled right over Shamar and cracked his rib."

"Oh no! Well, I'm here now. What can I do?"

"Go help the indecisive bitch at the counter."

"I heard that!" the customer said angrily.

Shaniqua turned around. "I know, I said it out loud."

"Where is the manager? I want to speak to him right now!"

"Excuse me?" said Shaniqua. "Are you illiterate? Read my tag. It says m-a-n-a-g-e-r."

I could see that Shaniqua was about to lose her mind, so I intervened as quickly as I could. "Your smoothie is on the house," I said with a smile, and Shaniqua walked away in a huff.

After an exhausting morning of cleaning, blending, and smiling, I was more than ready for lunch when suddenly a voice startled me.

"Hi, Viola!" said Barbara-Anne, waving at me in excitement.

"Greetings, Barbara-Anne. What can I get for you today?"

"Nothing, my dear, I am still full of energy from this morning's meal," Barbara-Anne replied.

"Really? What did you have for breakfast?" I asked curiously.

"The usual, coffee and prescription medicine."

Shaniqua ran towards the front door in excitement. "Girl, get yo ass outside. It's open!"

"What's open?"

"In-N-Out!"

It was a bittersweet situation. I was trying to eat healthy, yet I had been dying to see what the fuss was about.

We followed Shaniqua to the parking lot and headed across the street. I could feel palpitations in my chest, the same feeling I felt when Zayn Malik left One Direction.

I grabbed ahold of Shaniqua's arm. "Wait! We committed to Christos's meal plan, remember?"

Shaniqua stopped walking and turned around aggressively. "Viola, can you honestly tell me you have been eating clean since yesterday?"

"I am proud to say I haven't cheated all day."

With one finger, Shaniqua pulled the top of my shirt towards her and peeked inside my sports bra. "Then why do you have an Oreo stuffed in your cleavage?"

Barbara-Anne smacked my shoulder with the back of her hand. "Viola! I thought you were smarter than that. Chocolate bars are for your bra; cookies go in your pocket."

I took a step back. "In my defense, I was planning on scraping off the white stuff before I ate it in the bathroom."

Shaniqua scoffed and continued walking across the street, heading towards the famous burger joint.

She grabbed the door and said, "Relax, Christos will never know."

I closed my eyes and took a deep breath as the sweet smell of oil and meat in the air made my pores salivate.

Suddenly Shaniqua shouted, "What are you guys doing here?"

I opened my eyes to see Remy and Vik in line.

Remy looked at Vik and said, "See, Vik, I told you we should have worn those masks I made!"

Vik looked at him with disgust. "Unless you're Sia, a paper bag is not a considered a mask."

"It's okay. We're here for the same reason you guys are."

"Constipation?" asked Remy.

I took a step back and addressed the situation. "We need a plan. We can't all be here; Christos is right across the street."

"As much as I hate to agree with somebody who looks like they rolled out of a coffin," said Vik, "Viola is right."

"Okay, here is the plan: Vik, you grab the burgers while Shaniqua, Remy, Barbara-Anne, and myself wait in the back alley behind the dumpster."

With a plan in place, Remy began leading us out the door when suddenly he stopped like a deer in headlights.

"Everybody get back inside!" Barbara-Anne shouted.

"What is it?" I asked, confused.

The severity of the situation became clear when I looked across the street to see Christos making his way through the crosswalk.

As if a grenade had been thrown at his feet, Remy fled back into the restaurant, knocking Shaniqua head-first into the bushes.

Shaniqua shouted, "Motherfu—"

"We gotta move," I cried. "Christos is almost across the street!"

I helped Shaniqua back up to her feet and ran into the restaurant.

Vik shouted from the front of the line. "What are you guys doing back?"

Remy explained, out of breath, "Christos… outside."

"Oh shit," said Vik. "What are we going to do?"

"We have no choice," I said. "We should be adults about this. Let's barricade the door with wood and nails."

"Viola," said Vik, "this isn't *The Walking Dead*."

Remy massaged his stomach. "I don't feel so good. I think I'm going to be sick."

"He's at the door!" shouted Barbara-Anne. "Everyone hide!"

I quickly dove under a table that was occupied by a family of four.

Just as Christos walked in, the mother at the table bent down and looked at me. "Umm, excuse me. What are you doing?" Her black curly hair dangled in my face.

I knew I had to come up with a lie, and quickly, so she wouldn't cause a scene.

"That guy," I whispered. "The one who just walked in. He has been stalking me."

"Really?" she said sarcastically. "That guy is stalking you?"

"Yes! Can you please let me know when he leaves?"

"So let me get this straight. That hot, handsome, muscular man has nothing better to do than stalk an overweight girl hiding on all fours under a table at a burger joint?"

"What can I say, I am charming."

"You kneeled down in mayonnaise. Please leave, you're embarrassing us."

"Don't be afraid of a little embarrassment," I said. "This isn't the first time I've been on all fours under a table at a fast food joint."

A woman's shriek came from the ladies bathroom. I watched as she stormed out and flagged down the nearest employee. "There is a man throwing up in the sink in there!"

I peeked my head out from under the table as I watched Christos walk slowly towards the bathroom. Then Remy stepped out with his shirt covered in vomit.

"Remy?" Christos said. "What are you doing here?"

"We were hiding from you," he said, "until I threw up on myself and that girl's shoes."

"Who's we?" Christos asked.

I bit my lip, hoping Remy wouldn't rat us out.

"Vik, Barbara-Anne, and Shaniqua."

I sighed in relief.

"Oh, and I think I saw Viola hide under the table over there," Remy added.

I lowered my head and crawled out from under the table. "Hi, Christos!" I said cheerfully. "I just came in to use the bathroom. You know how ours is always occupied."

Christos crossed his arms against his chest. We were in for a long lecture. "Where is everyone else?

An employee walked past Remy, giving him a dirty look as he opened up the door to the janitorial closet where Shaniqua, Barbara-Anne, and Vik were discovered stuffing burgers into their mouths.

Christos took a deep breath. "Okay, everybody, listen up."

The five of us gathered in front of Christos, preparing our ears for the longest lecture about healthy eating and its importance.

He quietly looked at us for a few seconds. "When we started, I only asked for one thing, and that was for your commitment. You guys failed to hold up your end of deal, so there is nothing left to say other than… I am done."

"What do you mean?" I asked.

"I am not going to waste my time helping people who don't want to be helped, so effective immediately, I am no longer your personal trainer."

My heart sunk. A few days ago I would have been more than happy to hear him say those words. So why was I suddenly feeling sick to my stomach?

"Christos, wait," I said as he walked out the door. I couldn't help but feel like I'd let him down. He was so proud of me last night. Nobody had ever shown me that kind of support, and I'd thrown it all away.

"What are we going to do now?" Barbara-Anne asked.

Christos was right. We needed to take our new lifestyle seriously, but most importantly we had to find a way to show him we were still committed. The question was, were we?

"Vik," I said, "can you take Remy into the bathroom to get him cleaned up? The rest of us will grab a table. We need to have a serious conversation."

The three of us sat down quietly at a nearby table. Barbara-Anne was the first to talk.

"Viola, I can't do this," she said. "For most of my life, I've lived on prescription medicine and fast food."

"I know how you feel," I said. "I sometimes give in to hunger, too. Last night I tried to eat my potato clock."

"Viola," Shaniqua cried, "I gave you that for your birthday!"

Vik and Remy returned to the group, chattering amongst themselves.

"You tell her," said Remy.

"No," said Vik, "you tell her. It's your fault we got caught."

"Tell me what?" I said.

Vik rolled his eyes at Remy. "We were talking, and we've decided that we are leaving the group."

"What?" I shouted, standing up. "You guys can't quit now! We were sort of making progress."

"Viola," said Shaniqua, "look around. We are the heaviest people in this joint. We made zero progress. I'm out, too."

I shook my head in disbelief. "Wait, so it's just going to be me and Barbara-Anne? We need five for a group session, remember?"

"Actually, I am out, too," Barbara-Anne said. "Sorry, dear."

As I looked around the table, I could feel myself losing emotional connections with people I considered friends. I'd had the same feeling when I was asked to leave a sweet-sixteen party after I secretly licked all the icing off the birthday cake.

"So is this the end, then?" I asked.

"I think so, dear," said Barbara-Anne.

I slowly rose to my feet and backed away from the table. "Okay, then, I guess this is goodbye. So… goodbye, all."

With my head held low, I began walking towards the door when Shaniqua asked, "Viola, aren't you going to have a burger?"

I stopped for a second and thought about it. "I'm good."

The afternoon flew by at The Protein Hut. I think it was my constant barrage of thoughts that was propelling time forward.

"Viola!" shouted Shaniqua, bringing me back to reality. "Girl, you have been mopping the same spot for the last five minutes. What's up?"

I put the mop aside and sat down at a table. "Do you think we gave it our all?"

"Viola, we tried and failed. Let's just move on."

"I just feel like we let Christos down."

"Wait a minute. Viola, since when do you care about what he thinks?"

I stood up. "I don't *care* what he thinks. I just feel a little bad, that's all."

"Wow, you just got more defensive than the time I saw you eat a falafel off the floor."

"Hey, for the record it was only the pita that was touching the floor—the meat was safely on top."

Shaniqua rolled her eyes and walked behind the register. "It's almost quitting time. Let's just get out of here."

We packed up our gym clothes, cashed out, shut down, and headed for the doors.

"All right, girl," Shaniqua said as she walked out the door, "I will talk to you later."

I waved goodbye, as I had my car keys in my mouth, followed by a second wave towards Janette as I passed the front desk.

Janette curved her lips and sneered. "I heard Christos left you guys."

"Yeah," I said, "I wonder who told him where we were?"

With a big smirk, Janette raised her hand into the air. "Guilty!" she said, laughing.

"Why?"

"Oh, puh-lease. You had no chance of losing weight." With an evil grin on her face, she picked up the phone, hit the intercom button, and spoke loudly into the receiver. *"Face it, Viola. Everyone here knows you're going to be a lonely fat bitch for the rest of your life. Just accept it."* Suddenly all eyes were on me, and I could feel myself being covered by a blanket made of pity.

Then a rush of anger engulfed me like burning flames. It was an emotion I hadn't felt since a Whole Foods employee accused me of hiding marshmallows under my shirt.

I pushed my gym bag and purse off my shoulder, and they fell to the floor with a loud thump. I walked towards the treadmill that I'd puked on and hopped on. All eyes were still on me, a heavy girl in a tight Protein Hut uniform.

I pressed the quick-start button and quietly said to myself, "All right, Viola, twenty sets of twenty seconds rest speed, twenty seconds sprint. You got this."

I took deep breaths during the first rest set and used all my anger and energy to pace myself through the sprint.

By the fifth set, I could feel nausea knocking at my door, but like a Jehovah's Witness, I was not going to let it in.

After the tenth set, the strangest thing started to happen—people came from all over the gym to cheer me on. Maybe I was gathering attention because of what I was wearing, or maybe they felt bad after hearing Janette humiliate me.

"You're doing fantastic!" shouted a woman on a nearby elliptical.

I smiled back, afraid to open my mouth. Sweat was pouring down my face and neck, and I didn't have to check to know that my shirt was getting soaked.

"You're doing great, Viola!" Barbara-Anne said, sneaking up behind me.

"Don't stand back there," I said, feeling like my lungs were about to collapse.

"Why? Is it dangerous?" Barbara-Anne asked, looking concerned.

"No, I farted."

By the fifteenth set I could feel fatigue setting in, and my audience could tell.

"Just a few more sets to go," said a fit, gray-haired man taking a break from his weights.

I smiled back.

"Your legs are trembling, Viola," Barbara-Anne said.

"The last time I felt my knees tremble like this was when I spilled a cup of hot coffee on them."

I approached the final set, stumbling through the twentieth sprint, my entire body went numb.

Barbara-Anne was raising her hands into the air and shouting, "You did it!"

I brushed the hair off my sweaty face and slowly lifted up my head to see both a spinning room and a handful of people surrounding me, clapping and cheering loudly. It reminded me of the time I was once escorted off the stage at a karaoke bar.

With one foot off the treadmill, I looked in Janette's direction and mouthed the two words she deserved the most: "Thank you."

She, of course, replied with her middle finger and stormed off.

Barbara-Anne helped me off the machine. "Viola, can you feel the fat burning?"

"I don't know, up until now I've only ever felt the burn from a urinary tract infection."

All of a sudden, I started feeling light-headed and weightless, which forced me to an abrupt stop.

"Are you okay?" asked Barbara-Anne.

"Uh huh," I said. "I just have to pee really badly." Then I collapsed onto the floor as the brightly lit gym faded to black.

Before I even opened my eyes, I could hear mumbling between a male and a female.

"I think she's waking up," the female voice said as my eyelids slowly opened, taking in the bright light. "Viola? It's Shaniqua."

"What happened?" I asked, realizing I was waking up in the treatment room.

"Girl, you passed out."

"Is that all? I can live with that. That doesn't sound so bad."

Shaniqua leaned in and quietly whispered, "You also pissed yourself. Barbara-Anne called me to bring you a change of clothes."

"Oh my God! Did anyone notice?" I asked, covering my face in a blanket in embarrassment.

I heard the door open and a familiar male voice said, "Oh good, you're up."

I pulled the blanket off my face to reveal Christos standing by the door holding a garbage bag. I quickly lifted it back up again in the hopes that he would magically disappear.

"I'm feeling okay now; you can go," I said, hiding under the blanket. How did Christos find me? Had he been watching me on the treadmill?

"Okay," said Christos, "I will just leave your bag of clothes over here."

I dropped the blanket off my face and nervously asked, "Why are my clothes in a garbage bag?"

"Girl, your clothes stunk so bad we had no choice but to wrap them in a garbage bag."

"Are you sure you're okay?" Christos asked. "You still look pretty pale. Maybe you caught a bug?"

"I never get sick. The only thing I have ever caught was my hair on fire."

Revealing his perfectly straight white teeth, Christos smiled. "Viola, I am glad you haven't lost your sense of humor."

I smiled back, feeling more embarrassed than that time I fell into a coin pond on my first date with Franklin. "No, but I have lost my top a few times." Did I just say that? Why did I say that?

Christos laughed as he opened the door. "Oh, by the way, you kicked ass on that treadmill."

I gave him a wink as he closed the door behind him.

"What the hell was that?" Shaniqua shouted.

"What?" I asked, sitting up on the cot.

"Girl, you ain't foolin' me. You like Christos," Shaniqua said, smiling.

"*What*? Are you crazy!" I was shocked and mortified. "Why on earth would you think that? I am with Franklin, remember?"

"Viola, I know you better than anyone. You have a tell."

"I do not, and besides, Christos is way out of my league. He couldn't care less about me."

"Girl, you need to open your eyes and move on. Franklin ain't coming back."

I remained silent, staring at the door. Sure, there was a possibility that Franklin was gone forever, but nothing was going to stop me from at least trying to win him back.

"All right, let's get out of here," I said, peeling the blanket off my body. "I think I can still catch the last half hour of *The Bachelorette*. Oh, and thanks for putting a blanket on me."

"It wasn't me," said Shaniqua. "Christos noticed you shivering and spread the blanket over you. He even warmed it up in the microwave."

"Oh," I said, trying to hide my surprise.

Shaniqua opened up the door, turned around, and asked, "Still think he couldn't care less about you?"

Sadly, the evening was a bust, and I missed *The Bachelorette*, so I did a Walmart run to grab chicken breast for dinner. After my successful second run at the treadmill, I felt the confidence I needed to give healthy eating a shot.

I eagerly entered the store, marching towards the frozen-foods aisle when suddenly I was stopped by the manager. He was a sweet fifty-year-old Hispanic man who was always eager to help me.

"Welcome back, Viola! You came at just the right time. We're having a sale on feminine-hygiene products, face products, and laxatives."

"Thanks, Alex, but I am here for something else," I replied, grabbing an empty cart.

"Oh! Silly me, I forgot it's a weekday. You must be headed for the bulk aisle, I will go get you some boxes."

"Oh, that won't be necessary, Alex, I am actually here for some chicken breasts."

Alex looked confused and concerned. "Oh, do you have a new dietary restriction? Cause I've never seen you step foot in the fresh meat section."

"That's not true. I've stopped by in that aisle for free samples."

Alex scratched his head. "Okay, well, what else do you need?"

"Umm… brown rice and some vegetables."

Alex gently placed his hand on my shoulder and whispered, "Are you dying, Viola? It's okay, you can tell me, I won't tell anybody. Is it your heart?"

I shook my head, smiling uncomfortably. "I'm trying a new thing."

"Oh, okay, well, if you need anything just ask your good friend Alex."

"Thanks, Alex," I replied, quickly walking away.

Just as I reached the poultry section, I felt a pat on the back.

"Oh, hi, Crissy," I said, turning around. She was my junk food hookup. Whenever anything I liked was on sale I always received a heads-up from the most talkative employee, Crissy Wilkinson.

"How are you, girl? Listen, I heard what happened with your boyfriend. What a jerk. Oh, before I forget, stop by the deli. Naomi filled a bottle full of bacon fat just for you. Can you believe this weather? I wish I wasn't so thin and beautiful. I am really tired of getting hit on at the clubs. Hey! You should come out with me and my girlfriends sometime. I would love to see how you big girls twerk!"

"That won't be happening," I said. "The last time I tried twerking I fell down a flight of stairs."

Crissy burst out laughing, grabbing the attention of other shoppers. I slowly inched away from her with my cart and raced over to the rice bags. I sped over to the cooler area to grab random bags of veggies and headed straight for the cash registers, figuring I was home free... for about three seconds.

"Hi, Viola!" said Shaista, a middle-aged Pakistani woman who had been trying to find a girl for her thirty-five-year-old son. I only know this because it's all she talked about whenever she scanned my items.

"Hi, Shaista. Any luck with Kurram?" That was the name of her bachelor son.

"Oh, Viola, he is so picky. We picked out three girls for him, and he rejected every single one."

"Really, why?"

"All ridiculous reasons. He complained that the first girl had unattractive fingernails. How ridiculous is that? Nobody's nails are perfect, just look at yours."

"Hey, I file my nails to perfection with my teeth. So what was the issue with the second girl?"

"Her breath, can you believe that? He said her breath smelled like a rotting pakora gave birth to a decaying samosa."

"And the third?" I asked as Shaista scanned through my last item.

"He didn't like the way she dressed. He said that she looked like she stole her clothes off a hit-and-run victim."

"Yikes," I replied, handing over cash.

"Just keep him in your prayers. I fear he will be living at home forever. Have a nice day Viola!" Shaista said, waving and smiling.

"Bye, Shaista," I said, pushing my cart and heading out the door. Mission accomplished.

Preparing the meal was a cinch. I kept it simple as Christos's guide advised, and all that I placed on my plate were the breasts, some brown rice, and a cup of vegetables. I believe the rule of thumb was groups of three for meals.

For my bedtime snack, I toasted a piece of multi-grain bread with peanut butter spread on it. It was a big departure from my typical midnight pantry raid of chips and chocolate desserts, but oddly enough, I felt good.

Chapter Nine

❶❾❺ Lbs

November 19, 2016

I woke up feeling less nauseated and sluggish than I usually did. After my morning bathroom routine, I decided to do something adventurous: check my weight.

I closed my eyes and nervously stepped onto the scale.

"Please, please, please, please, please," I whispered to myself, crossing my fingers.

I slowly opened my eyes. The message on the scale was loud and clear.

I'd lost seven pounds!

Leaping off the scale in excitement, I began whipping my hair back and forth in the bathroom mirror. You may not see this as a big deal, but for me this was huge! I had lost many things in life—a boyfriend, respect, a tooth in a bowl of soup, but one thing I had never lost was weight.

Feeling like I was on cloud nine, I whipped out my phone to share with the world my excitement—and unknowingly, my vibrator in the background.

"Hi, all! Viola here. Listen, I have some big news, and no, it's not that I got rid of my fishy burps or my vaginal itch. It's day three and I *lost seven pounds*! Can you believe that? Seven pounds! Anyways, I just wanted to keep you all updated. Oh, and if my group is out there listening—don't give up. Let's kick ass together. Meet me on the treadmills in thirty minutes. Okay, Viola out!"

For breakfast, I microwaved a bowl of oatmeal. I'm not going to lie, it tasted like the personality of a mean girl—artificially sweet and awful.

Nonetheless, I downed every drop with the motivating reminder that I'd lost seven pounds.

I arrived at the gym almost forty-five minutes before my shift actually began and headed straight for the changing rooms. As I slipped into my tie-dyed T-shirt and plus-size sweatpants I got off of Craigslist, I couldn't help but wonder if any of the group members would show up.

The gym was filled with a handful of members, including their mainstay member, Barbara-Anne.

"Good morning, Viola! We are ready to go," Barbara-Anne said, following me to the treadmills.

"Who is we?" I asked, seconds before I found out for myself. "Vikram!" I shouted gleefully as I saw him walking out of the changing room. Did his presence mean that he'd finally forgiven me for breaking his precious nose with my foot?

Vik smiled warmly, leaned in, gently pinched a piece of my hair, and said ever so softly, "Viola, your hair looks like it committed suicide."

Well, that answered that question.

"Yeah, but you can't deny how groovy my shirt is."

"Honey, please, what's with all the color? You look like you threw up all over yourself."

Suddenly Barbara-Anne blurted out, "Oh! I forgot that thing in my car. Vik would you be so kind as to come help me find it?"

"What thing?" said Vik.

"Just come," Barbara-Anne said, yanking him towards the door.

I was confused until I looked behind me and saw Christos filling up his water bottle at a nearby fountain. Was Barbara-Anne trying to set us up? Is that why she'd fled with Vik so quickly?

"Good morning, Viola," said Christos, tightly screwing the lid on his bottle.

"Same to you, sir. How are you today?" I said like a rich debutant. I was feeling extra witty.

"Charmed, milady. May I?" Christos said, reaching for my empty water bottle.

"You may," I replied, handing him my Hooters water bottle. Christos looked at it for a few seconds before he began filling it up.

"Interesting cup, Viola."

"I know, right? I won it in a contest," I said, acting important and smug.

"At Hooters? What kind of contest was it?" Christos asked, spilling a bit of water on the floor between his muscular calves.

"A wet T-shirt contest," I replied, raising my eyebrows.

"Are you serious?" Christos said, wide-eyed.

"No, but I have been in one before," I said with a great amount of pride.

"Really?" Christos said, handing me the bottle.

"Well, it was more of a battle with a water cooler jug but the outcome was the same."

Christos laughed, once again revealing his pristine white teeth, which contrasted with his dark brown beard.

"You're funny, Viola. You kind of remind me of someone I once knew."

"Really, and who would that be?" I asked.

Christos backed away slowly and winked. "Me."

I stood frozen and puzzled. Was Christos hiding something from his past? I was about to start brainstorming when Barbara-Anne startled me.

"Are we all set?" she asked.

"Let's do it," I said, leading them over to the treadmills.

With five minutes to spare, I slipped out of my sweaty clothes and waddled over to Shaniqua at The Protein Hut with every ounce of energy I had.

Shaniqua plugged her nose. "Damn, girl, you stank. Are you using hairspray as deodorant again? I told you that shit don't work."

"How bad is it?" I asked. "Never mind, I'll just spray myself down with perfume."

"So, how was it?" Shaniqua asked, wiping down the stained countertop.

"I didn't pass out, Barbara-Anne didn't have a heart attack, and Vik didn't get injured, so that's progress, right?"

Shaniqua rolled her eyes.

"Oh! I forgot to ask. How was the burger?"

She inhaled deeply and sighed. "Let's just say when you left the table yesterday we all made a pact to follow Christos's meal guide."

"Shan!" I shouted cheerfully. I couldn't help but wrap my arms around her large bosom and jump up and down like I was a nine-year-old on Christmas Day.

"Girl, you gotta calm down." Shaniqua slipped out of my grip and took a step back.

"This is huge! If we can stay consistent and motivated, we will be the sexiest women catwalking down the aisles of Walmart, and best of all, I won't have to stuff my bra with water balloons for attention anymore! So what did you pack for lunch? Wait! Don't tell me yet. Wanna see what I brought?"

"You got a customer, Viola," Shaniqua said, walking towards the small office.

I turned around to greet a tall red-headed woman who looked like she'd just walked off of a Maxim photoshoot.

"Wow! You're so pretty. I bet you have a lot of Instagram followers."

She smiled uncomfortably, then looked away and replied in a stuck-up tone. "Kale smoothie, please."

The Fat Bitch Diet

"Sure, coming right up," I said, suddenly realizing we didn't have any kale. Leaning away from the cashier, I looked towards Shaniqua and yelled, "Hey, Shan, I think we need to restock!"

Shaniqua leaped off her chair. "Oh shit, I totally forgot. I was late thanks to my meal prep."

I looked at the woman and said, "Sorry, it will be just a moment."

She rolled her eyes behind her long, perfectly lifted eyelashes. "Whatever, just hurry." By the tone of her voice and gestures, I couldn't help but feel like she was judging us.

"So, Shan, wanna know what I brought?"

Shaniqua handed me a bunch of kale. "You seem to really want to tell me, so just tell me."

"Go have a look in my purse. You might have to dig deep, though."

"No way! The last time I put my hand in your purse it came out sticky."

"That wasn't my fault. When Franklin first inserted it, it was hard as a rock. Who knew it was going to start discharging everywhere uncontrollably?"

The red-haired woman took a step back and gasped. "Eww! What is wrong with you?"

I leaned over the counter. "Relax, it was a jelly donut."

Just as Shaniqua replenished the vegetables, the woman rudely walked away in a huff.

I turned around, biting my chapped lips. "I don't think she wants her kale smoothie anymore."

"Fine, whatever," Shaniqua said without a hint of anger.

"Are you okay? Normally you would have threatened to shove that woman's hair into the garbage disposal."

"I'm fine, Viola. Just let it go."

I'd known Shaniqua long enough to know that she was hiding something. The last few days she was quieter, distant, and calmer than usual. These were all indications that something was on her mind, but what?

Before I could investigate further, my cell phone vibrated. It was a cryptic text message from Christos:

> *5th stage, same place, same time.*

I turned to Shaniqua with a confused look on my face. "I just got a text from Christos."

"I just got the same message. Didn't he say he was out?"

Feeling a bit of relief, I said, "Guess not."

The afternoon flew by thanks to a steady stream of customers and a brief dramatic incident where a Zumba instructor locked herself in the bathroom after learning that she'd gained a percentage of fat.

I missed most of the action as I was busy eating my mid-afternoon snack, where I discovered what almonds tasted like without a chocolate covering.

"Viola, are you ready to go?" Shaniqua asked, walking towards the training room with her bedazzled gym bag.

"Yeah, I just want to class myself up a bit. I found a half-used lipstick on the subway that I have been dying to try out."

"Viola, you don't know how to be sophisticated."

"I can be sophisticated. I once ate a Big Mac with a knife and fork."

"Girl, please, that's only because they forgot to give you the top bun."

When we arrived at the training room, everyone but Christos was present.

As I entered, Remy greeted me with a big smile. "Hi, Viola!"

"Hey, Remy. Where is Christos?" I asked, looking left and right.

"Viola," said Vik, "what's with the lipstick?"

"You like?" I said, gleefully puckering my lips like a Cover Girl model.

"You're like a Quiznos sub. You try way too hard."

Christos entered, carrying a large box. "Good, you're all here," he said, placing it down. "Don't worry, this box won't be used to take anything from you. It's actually about to give you all something."

"Honey, what's going on?" asked Vik. "I thought the group disbanded, and you left."

Christos crossed his arms against his chest. "You guys hit stage four yesterday: failure. As I said when we first started, it was inevitable, and now that's in the past and I know the five of you are fully committed. A wise person once said you have to make mistakes to learn lessons."

"I think I once read that on a box of condoms," I said.

"So does everyone remember the first four stages?" Christos asked with enthusiasm.

"Dear," said Barbara-Anne, "I barely remember to put on underwear."

"Okay, so the first stage was accepting change. The second was effort. The third, nutrition. And the fourth, failure. This brings us to stage five: supplements."

There was a long period of silence, so naturally I decided to speak. "Oh, I know all about supplements, I've been taking Flintstone Chewable Vitamins daily."

"That's great, Viola, but there is a lot more to it than that."

"I have also been taking a lot of Lax-A-Day," I said with pride.

"Okay, maybe I should highlight that I am only focusing on sports nutritional supplements."

"I ain't taking that!" said Shaniqua. "My cousin Fonesha once took fat-loss pill. The poor girl was constipated for three weeks straight."

"The truth is that there are good supplements, borderline supplements, and avoidable supplements," said Christos. "The key is to do your research and be responsible. For us, my focus is going to be solely on good supplements, which consists of protein, creatine, caffeine, fish oil, and amino acids."

Vik raised his hand. "Unlike Viola, the rest of us can't put multiple things into our mouth at once."

"Hey, that skill comes in handy for speed dating," I said.

"Christos," said Barbara-Anne, "how much will this cost us?"

Christos bent down and opened the box. "Everything in here is free. It's part of the program."

We approached the box, which was full of various-sized plastic containers.

Shaniqua bent down and picked up a large container of protein powder. "For real? This is all free?"

"That's right," said Christos. "As long as you guys are in the program. Like I said at the very beginning, you will be given all the tools you need to succeed. Wanting the change is on your shoulders."

Shaking a small bottle of multivitamins, I asked the million-dollar question. "So do these come with an instruction manual?"

"Absolutely," said Christos. "The timing and serving for each supplement will be e-mailed to all of you after today's session."

Shaniqua suddenly started sniffing around Remy's legs. "What's that smell?"

"I brought a bag of onions with me today," he said.

Christos closed the box. "All right, is everybody ready for the first bodybuilding exercise of the program?"

We regrouped at the adjustable benches, and Christos explained the session plan.

"Welcome to day one: chest and arms. Most of everything we will be using is in this area of the gym. Now, that being said, everybody grab an adjustable bench."

This area of the gym was usually filled with bodybuilders and body odor. Luckily today was not one of those days.

Vik cringed. "Gross, my bench has sweat all over it."

"A tip," said Christos. "Always wipe down equipment that you used. It's standard gym etiquette."

Barbara-Anne reached into her bra and pulled out a handful of tissue. "Here, Vik, use this."

Christos pointed across the room. "Most gyms carry wipes. I believe they are over there by the wall."

Vik gave Barbara-Anne a dirty look while wiping off the bench.

"Don't judge," said Barbara-Anne. "The twins get sweaty."

I chimed in with excellent advice. "Barbara-Anne, just do what I do—wipe them down with flatbread."

Vik looked at me strangely. "Why do I get the feeling you were one of those fanny-pack girls?"

"Hey, fanny packs were fantastic for holding condiments."

After we settled into our cushiony benches, Christos gave us the first set of instructions. "All right, folks, here is the plan: five exercises, each containing three sets of ten reps."

Barbara-Anne raised her hand. "What are sets and reps again?"

"A rep," said Christos, "or repetition, is one whole motion of an exercise and a set is a group of those repetitions."

"Oh, I get it," said Remy. "It's like if I had to change my briefs ten times in a row. That would be one set of ten reps."

"But what if each of those briefs are different?" I asked.

"Oh, you mean like if one pair is clean and the next is full of skid marks?" said Shaniqua.

"You guys have it all wrong," said Vik. "Type and condition of his underwear doesn't matter. He does the same motion every time, right, Christos?"

"Right," Christos said. "Moving on. The exercises we will be doing today are the following: dumbbell chest press, incline dumbbell chest press, cable biceps curl, cable triceps pull-down, cable cross shoulder raise, dumbbell overhead triceps press, dumbbell biceps curl, and dumbbell shoulder press."

As the list was delivered, it became clear that I wasn't familiar with any of the exercises. In fact, up until then the closest I'd been to weight training was lifting up my couch to locate a Fudgee-O.

Shaniqua lowered her head. "Are we gonna be here all night?"

Christos shook his head. "Typically a workout session should be between forty-five minutes to an hour and a half."

Barbara-Anne eagerly stood up from her bench. "Can we go get weights now?"

Clearing his throat, Christos grabbed our attention to make an important announcement. "One last thing before we start. The key to your success will be working together as one unit. I want you guys sharing meal tips, exercise techniques, encouragement, obstacles, etc. Going forward, you five are no longer independent individuals working towards one goal. You five are now what I like to call… a fitness guild."

Cheerfully jumping up and down like a child, I shouted, "Oh my God, that's so nerdy! I love it!"

"Christos," said Barbara-Anne, "I have a nutrition-related question."

"Go ahead, Barbara-Anne."

"I have a recurring dream where I am sexually assaulted by a baked potato. Do you think that means I am eating too many carbs?"

Christos paused for a second and then said, "Umm… no, I don't think that's related. Any other questions?"

The guild remained quiet, giving each other short stares. "I think we're good," I replied.

"Great, let's grab some weights."

After an hour of intense weightlifting and a short dizziness spell outside where I threw up on some freshly planted petunias, I was in dire need of relaxation and entertainment. Fortunately I didn't have to wait too long, as I found a YouTube channel dedicated to commuters chasing after their bus.

Just as my eyelids began to close, my phone started buzzing. Incoming e-mail from Christos, enclosed with a PDF of the exercises and supplement guide. The guide was fairly straightforward but required that doses be taken at specific times.

I curiously gazed over at the kitchen counter where I'd placed my share of the supplements that the guild received. Confused as to whether I should wait to start the supplements today or tomorrow, I suddenly remembered what Christos had told the guild about nutrition. Clean eating started now, not tomorrow, not on a scheduled future day. It started now.

During my third read-through of the e-mail, I received a call from Shaniqua. I had a feeling as to what she was calling about.

"So… I take it you read the e-mail?" I said, walking over to the counter.

The Fat Bitch Diet

"Has Christos lost his mind? Protein three times a day with skim milk? Shamar ain't gonna drink that shit. And if he thinks I am going to buy two different types of milk, he may as well milk the cow himself."

I leaned down onto the counter, fumbling through the bottles. "You know what? As you know, I am not very good at measurements and calculations."

"Not very good? Girl, a meth addict can measure better than you."

"Hey, give me some credit, remember that French onion soup I once made? It got tons of comparisons."

"Yeah, to Buckley's."

"Anyways, Shan, my point is, why don't you come over and we can try this stuff out together."

"Aight."

Of the many bottles I rummaged through, the most intriguing one to me were the amino acids, mainly cause of it's caffeine ingredient. "Hey handsome… I like what you got to offer," I said seductively to the bottle. "Mmmm… I want you inside me."

"Is this your new man?" Shaniqua said, startling me as she walked out of the bathroom.

"Umm… no," I said, hugging the bottle. "We are friends with benefits."

Shaniqua joined me over at the counter. "All right, let's get this show on the road."

I slipped my phone out of my pocket. "So... according to Christos's schedule, it's time for our post-workout protein shake and amino acids. But I don't see instructions on how to mix the protein."

"Relax, we pour some protein in a glass, add some milk, and stir. Not everything has to be hard, Viola."

I sat quietly as Shaniqua stirred up her first protein shake and poured it into her mouth. "How does it taste?"

Shaniqua turned around and spit into the sink. "Viola, this tastes clumpier than your banana bread."

"Those weren't clumps. I accidentally blended an eggshell into the batter."

Shaniqua emptied out the glass into the sink. "This can't be right. Let me see that e-mail."

I pointed the screen at Shaniqua. "See anything?"

"Yeah, it says to use a shaker bottle. What the hell is that?"

"Oh! That's what I call my vibrator. Well, that and Margaret."

Shaniqua rolled her eyes. "Viola, you're not helping."

Tossing my hair over my shoulder, I shuffled through the scattered bottles. "Is this it?" I said, holding up a clear bottle containing what looked like a bouncy ball."

"Let's assume it is, what now?" Shaniqua said, placing the ball in my court.

Spinning the bottle of protein on the counter, I searched for the directions. "Found it! One scoop in six ounces of milk." After a few seconds of searching for a clean spoon, I realized that a scoop was provided in the bottle. "Hey, should we maybe wash the bottle? It looks kinda dirty."

"Viola, I've seen you share a burrito with a hooker."

"Hey, she asked for a bite," I said, pouring milk into the bottle.

After dumping the scoop in and screwing the lid on tight, I shook the bottle vigorously. The motion reminded me of my patronizing Magic 8-Ball from high school, which consistently said I had no chance of getting asked to the prom.

Starting with a deep breath, I took a short sip, quickly followed by a lengthy chug. I finished the entire mixture.

"Damn, girl, you inhaled that shit! How was it?"

I tossed the bottle in the sink and wiped off my lips. "Tasty. Can I have another?"

Shaniqua grabbed my phone. "Nah, it says to take it in the morning, post-workout, and before bed."

"All right, what's next?" I said, feeling hyper.

Shaniqua looked at her cell phone. "What's next is driving my ass back home to unlock the door for Shamar. The foo forgot his house keys again!"

"When is he getting home?" I asked, gently rinsing out the shaker bottle.

Shaniqua crossed her arms against her chest. "An hour ago."

"He's been waiting outside the whole time you've been here?"

"Yup."

"Isn't is raining?"

"Yeah, so? That dumbass needs to learn a lesson. In fact, momma might make a pit stop at Payless beforehand."

While watching her prepare for her exit, I couldn't help but wonder if Franklin would have still been in my life had I had the same level of assertiveness as Shaniqua.

"All right, looks like I am on my own with the aminos."

"Oh, Viola, be careful with the aminos. There's caffeine in there, and we all know your weakness to that," Shaniqua said before closing the door behind her.

She wasn't wrong. My first encounter with caffeine was in grade school at recess, when I ate a pound of coffee beans, mistaking them for chocolate. All was good until I threw up all over my notebook when I was asked to stand up and read from my journal.

As I aged, the effect of caffeine on my body intensified. What began as nausea in grade school morphed into a state of hyper activity by my college years. I recall a moment at a party when after three Red Bulls I spun around like Julie Andrews in *The Sound of Music*, only she gracefully twirled towards the peak of a mountain, whereas I not-so-gracefully tumbled into the DJ booth.

"All right, aminos," I said to the thick purple bottle. "Let's see how to shake you up."

The directions were fairly simple—twelve ounces of water with two to five scoops, two being mild and five being intense. With a big smirk on my face, I carefully measured five scoops into the shaker bottle and chugged it down in one go.

Chapter Ten

❶❾❷ Lbs

November 20, 2016

After eating a Christos-approved breakfast, I received a text reminder to arrive early for a HIIT cardio session with the guild. It was a habit that we were trying to get into—HIIT cardio in the morning, weightlifting in the afternoon.

When I arrived at the treadmills, Shaniqua was the first to greet me with pleasant compliments. "Viola, you look awful, did you sleepwalk and pass out in a dumpster again?"

"I wish. No, I was up all night hopping to my Dance Mix '96 CD." I started the treadmill.

"Aminos?" Shaniqua asked just before she started her final sprint.

"Five scoops," I replied, rolling my eyes. "How was your night?"

"Fantastic, the aminos gave me the extra energy to shout at Shamar without feeling fatigue. I even broke a few dishes for dramatic effect."

"What did he do?" I asked.

"Wet towel on the bed," Shaniqua replied, huffing and puffing. She looked exhausted. "All right, my twenty minutes are up. Enjoy the rest of yours."

As Shaniqua left, I was able to see Vik on the other side. "Hi, Vik!" I said, panting like a dog. Beads of sweat were collecting onto his bandaged nose, and he looked like he could use a smile. I flipped my sweaty, greasy hair over my face and stuck my tongue out. "Can you believe I woke up like this?"

Vik looked in my direction. "Viola, your face looks like it was beaten by a tire iron."

"That can't be true, a sexual predator once told me that I could be a model."

Vik rolled his eyes and walked off the treadmill the second his time was up.

As Barbara-Anne and Remy were too far away to converse with, I quietly focused on my final sets. I couldn't help but feel a little pride—my first attempt at HIIT cardio had turned me into a walking disaster. Now I was just a sweaty mess.

After a fulfilling day of blending fruits, plating paninis, and plunging toilets, it was time for the guild's daily workout session with Christos.

Christos entered the training room and announced, "Before we begin, I just wanted to say that last night I received a call from Barbara-Anne from the emergency room in regards to some minor side effects from the multivitamin that you're all taking."

"Oh!" said Remy. "That explains the itchy welts on my body from last night. I had no choice but to rub mayonnaise all over my legs."

Christos took a few steps back from Remy. "Umm, no, those sound like bedbugs. I am referring to neon-colored urine, which is completely normal for anyone on a multivitamin."

Remy raised his hand. "Also, let it be known that it doesn't glow in the dark. I already checked."

"Wait a minute," said Vik, "is that why bathroom floor is wet?"

"I'm not stupid," said Remy. "I used a water bottle."

Vik took a step back, cringing.

Shaniqua seemed to be in her own world. I could tell there was something on her mind. "Everything okay?" I whispered as Christos began laying out the exercise plan for the day.

She sighed and looked at me. "Shamar and I had another argument this morning. The same one we had a few months ago about him wanting to enroll in graphic-design classes. I don't get it. I was sincere, honest, and respectful when I told him he shouldn't pursue it."

"Didn't you say it was a stupid idea?"

"Viola, I never told him it was a stupid idea, I told him he was stupid for suggesting it."

"Remind me again, who won that argument?"

"We both agreed that it wasn't a good idea and made peace with it. It was all good."

"Shan, didn't you make him sleep on the couch for a week?"

"I am not that cruel. He slept in the tub."

Suddenly Christos interrupted our conversation. "Are you guys listening?"

"Absolutely," I said proudly. "I am amazing at multi-tasking. I once parallel parked a car while eating a bag of Cheetos."

Christos cleared his throat. "As I was saying, the next stage of weight loss is music. It may sound crazy, but listening to energetic music during a workout is almost as important as a balanced diet."

Music had always been a part of me, sandwiched right between my love for Franklin and chipotle-themed potlucks.

From my first introduction to radio to my leaning tower of cassettes and collection of skip-free Discmans, the majority of my life was driven by music.

"Where are you going with this?" asked Vik.

"I want you guys to listen to music throughout your workouts," said Christos. "Focus on creating a playlist that gets your adrenaline going. The goal here is to use music as a source of energy to push yourself through each exercise."

"I forgot my headphones at home," said Vik.

"As did I," I said, "but I think I saw a pair of tangled earbuds in the garbage earlier. Should I dig those out?"

"I once swallowed an earbud," mumbled Remy.

Christos looked at Remy in confusion. "For our group sessions, we will be using the wireless speaker over there in the corner, so if you have any song requests, let's hear them."

"What do you listen to when you work out?" I asked.

Christos bit the bottom of his lip as he assembled his thoughts. "I like a good self-empowering, bass-heavy, rhythmic tune."

The Fat Bitch Diet

I nudged Shaniqua. "What do you think a guy like Christos listens to?"

"I don't know," Shaniqua said, "probably some classical shit."

"I wouldn't be surprised. Franklin had bland taste, too. Where are the guys who are into old-school hip-hop?"

Vik jumped into the conversation. "I only listen to the one artist who also happens to be the greatest singer, songwriter, and rapper… Kesha."

"My late husband and I loved the Rolling Stones," Barbara-Anne added. "We used to make love to 'Paint It Black.'"

"Me too!" I shouted happily. "Well, not the making love part, but I was trampled on Black Friday to that song."

"So are there any other questions before we start?" asked Christos. "Or does anyone have anything else they would like to share?"

Remy raised his hand as if he had a very important statement to make.

"Yes, Remy, go ahead."

"I was once trampled by a pregnant cow."

"Okay…" Christos said awkwardly. "So today I want to see you guys taking five gulps of water between every set. A few of you slacked off the other day. Don't forget that water is crucial for fat loss."

"If I drink anymore water, I am going to need to switch to Depends," I said.

"Trust me, your body will get used to it after a few weeks." Christos took a few steps back and scanned the guild. "You guys are doing fantastic, by the way. I noticed the morning HIIT cardio sessions. Keep up the good work."

"Whatever," said Shaniqua. "Can we get a move on? I need to get out of here and put an end to Shamar's drama."

I playfully smacked her arm. "Shaniqua, he was praising us, don't take that away from me. The last time I was praised was when a barista thought I lost weight."

"Viola, that's because she originally thought you were pregnant."

"It's still a compliment."

"Shaniqua is right," said Christos. "We should get started. Today we will be focusing on our legs. I hope you all ate well today because a legs workout requires the most amount of energy."

Vik rolled his eyes. "Yes, Christos. Morning meal, mid-morning snack, lunch, and mid-afternoon snack. Later on, dinner and post-dinner snack."

Christos raised his eyebrows. "What about supplements?"

I raised my hand. "Umm... vitamins, fish oil, protein, and my new love... amino acids."

Christos smiled. "Ready to sweat?"

Climbing up the stairs to my apartment, I wasn't sure what I would reach first, the doorknob or heart failure. Luckily I was able to prepare and down a protein shake and amino acids before fatigue set in.

My plan to cat nap was interrupted by a loud knock at the door. It was Shaniqua, gripping a large carry-on suitcase tightly with both hands as if she was about to detonate a bomb.

The Fat Bitch Diet

My Spidey sense was tingling. The last time Shaniqua unexpectedly stood at my door was when she needed a place to lay low after she set her neighbor's car on fire.

"Hey, Shan. You look really angry. Did somebody mistake you for that girl from Precious again?"

"Viola, I need a place to stay for a while. Can you do me a solid?" Before I could answer, she walked past me, dragging the heavy carry-on.

"Umm… sure," I replied, locking the door behind her. All of a sudden the carry-on tipped over, slamming onto my glass coffee table. "Careful, that table's from Italy!"

"Viola, I caught him in bed with that two-bit trick, Lakeesha!" Shaniqua shouted, pacing back and forth. She was shaking with anger.

"Shamar?" I asked, acting dumb.

"Who else? Oh, and get this, his excuse was that he thinks I don't treat him right. He said I verbally abused him and pushed him away. Can you believe that garbage? I have been nothing but nice to that piece-of-shit good-for-nothing asshole!"

"Okay, calm down. Want some aminos?" I asked seductively.

Shaniqua took a deep breath. "It's over. I thought he was the one." She puckered her lips and looked at me. "I need to clear my head. Can I borrow your golf club?"

"Please tell me it's for mini-golf."

"Viola, you know me better than that. I was thinking of something a little more therapeutic, like smashing the windows of Lakeesha's car."

"I'm sure you guys will work it out; you always do. Remember the time you chased him with a knife? After the doctor stitched his finger back up you guys were right as rain."

"I should have aimed for his body. Now where is that club?"

I grabbed her by the shoulders and looked her straight in the eyes. "Hey, whatever happens, I am here for you. You're welcome to stay here for as long as you need."

Shaniqua leaned back into the couch and stared blankly at the ceiling. "You know what would be perfect?

"World peace, with tolerance for all races, religions, and equality for all sexes?"

Shaniqua turned her head and mumbled, "A bucket of fried chicken."

"You know what, that would be good, too," I replied, leaning back into the couch. "You're the strongest person I know, Shan. You're going to be just fine."

I can't say that I was surprised that Shamar hooked up with Lakeesha, but I enjoyed being a little naïve. I always thought that Shaniqua would end up with Shamar, and I still do. After all, I was still in the race for Franklin's heart, so anything was possible.

Around 3:00 AM I woke up to the sound of a thump. I knew logically that it could be only one of two things: a demonic presence trying to force me out of my apartment or Shaniqua was sneaking fast food into the apartment.

"Shaniqua?" I said, pulling back my hair away from my eyes. "Is everything okay?"

There was no answer, so I slid off my bed and stumbled towards the living room. To my surprise, she wasn't on the couch, but I couldn't help but notice that the bathroom light was on.

I knocked on the door gently. "Shan? Everything okay in there?" There was no answer. "Okay, I'm coming in. I hope you're not on the toilet, cause I tend to be a little nauseated after waking up from loud noises, and that's the last thing I need to see."

Thankfully, she wasn't on the toilet, but my heart dropped as I heard the sound of her tears behind the shower curtain.

"Don't open the curtain!" Shaniqua cried, sniffling loudly.

Shaniqua never let anyone see her cry, even that time she was accidentally hit in the face with a baseball, she masked her face with the glove and ran after her assailant.

I sat down beside the tub, knowing that I couldn't leave her alone. She was like the sister my parents never wanted to give me.

A few minutes of silence passed before Shaniqua spoke again. "I don't know how to be nice."

"Huh?" I said, staring hypnotically at the dripping tap.

"All my life I've had to protect myself. You saw how cruel people were to us."

"I know, Shan… If it wasn't for you I would have dropped out."

"I wasn't always this way. I never told you this, but before I met you I let people bully me. It was easier to be passive and just live with it."

"I didn't know. I always assumed you were the type of child who pushed others down in the playground. What changed?"

"One day, I was stupid enough to accept a peace offering from this one bitch named Priscilla. It was a bowl of chocolate pudding. I didn't realize it until after I took a few bites that they'd mixed dog shit into it."

"What did you do?"

"Something changed in me that day. I guess I'd had enough. I walked over to the popular clique table where Pricilla sat laughing hysterically with the others, scooped a handful of the dog-shit pudding into my hand, and shoved it right into her mouth, smearing it all over her pretty face."

"Oh my God! Then what happened?"

"I was expelled. Had to go to another school, and that's when I met you."

"You know what, Shan? You don't have to change a single thing about you. You are who you are and that's the person I love."

There was no response, and I could barely keep my eyes open.

With help from the toilet tank, I safely lifted my sore body off the cold tile and was ready to make my exit. "Nite, Shan," I said, closing the bathroom door behind me.

Chapter Eleven

189 Lbs

November 21, 2016

I woke up to the loud clattering of pots and pans, clearly having forgotten that Shaniqua was an early riser.

Forty minutes later, after scrubbing dead skin off my body with a dermabrasion cloth I found abandoned in the laundry room, I was all set to make my entrance.

"Good morning, lovely!" I shouted, cheerfully prancing into the kitchen. I was stunned to see multiple breakfast meals prepared and laid out on the kitchen island. Everything from crepes to pancakes to eggs to fruits to oatmeal to simple smoothies.

I couldn't help but be drawn into the aroma of the crepes, which were decorated elegantly with sliced fruits and sprinkled with cinnamon.

"Good morning!" Shaniqua said, entering the door carrying a basket of clothes. "I hope you don't mind; your hamper was disgusting. It smelled like fish and rotten eggs."

I was too distracted by the food to realize that hell had frozen over. I couldn't remember the last time Shan lifted a finger for me.

"What's with all the unhealthy food? You were doing so well," I said, stealthily sniffing the pancakes.

"Relax. Everything there is Christos approved."

"What do you mean?"

"I couldn't sleep last night, so I googled bodybuilding breakfast recipes. Did you know there are like a thousand recipes up in there?"

"Clearly you found most of them, that explains why I heard cupboards slamming all night."

"Well, what are you waiting for? Try one of the dishes and let me know what you think," Shaniqua said, folding the clothes on the couch.

"Are you sure these are Christos approved? Because when it comes to peer pressure I cave easily, I was once pressured into taking ecstasy at a club."

Shaniqua gasped. "Viola, that's really dangerous!"

"It's okay, it turned out to be Viagra."

I forked a piece of a crepe into my mouth, followed by a second and a third.

"So you like?" Shaniqua asked.

"Oh my God, Shaniqua, this tastes amazing! What's in it?"

"Mostly vanilla protein and other simple ingredients. It was actually pretty easy making all these dishes, and they're low in fat, calories, and barely have any sugar in them."

I scooped another piece into my mouth and said, "Well, ma'am, you certainly know your way around a healthy gourmet breakfast. I think you found your niche."

"Viola, be realistic. Just because I can follow a few online recipes doesn't mean I can open up a restaurant or some shit like that. People like me are stuck in dead-end jobs for life."

I stepped over to the smoothie. "After this sip, we gotta get going. I don't wanna be stuck with the broken treadmill again."

"Hey, Viola, what are your thoughts on me paying half of the rent?" Shaniqua said, wrapping up the plates for later.

"Are you saying you want to be my permanent roomie?"

"Well, Christos did say that the guild should stick close together. And besides, you're my best friend, and we're both on new journeys."

"Hmmm, I like the sound of that. I have never split rent before. I have split the crotch seams in my jeans, but never rent. Let's do it!"

Just when I thought I had my fitness regimen and nerves under control, Christos came swinging in with a curve ball.

"You did *what*?" Vik shouted, going into instant panic mode.

Christos closed the door to the training room. "You guys have nothing to worry about. It's a simple seven-mile marathon on the 7th of December."

"But I can barely complete the HIIT cardio without heart palpitations," said Barbara-Anne.

"Relax everybody," I said. "Christos is joking. He wouldn't sign us up for a marathon. Isn't that against the law or something? I once heard on *Talk New York* that a woman in Texas was sued by her friend for signing her up for an AIDS walk."

"One word sums up why I signed you guys up," said Christos. "Motivation. Motivation is one of the keys to your success and also the seventh stage of weight loss. Without a purpose or drive, your goal will be more challenging to obtain."

"Christos, look at us," said Shaniqua. "Do you really think we can run a marathon?"

Christos scanned the room and smiled. "I do." His gaze froze on me for a few seconds. "I believe in you—all of you. That being said, I will see you all at the finish line."

"Aww, honey that was really touching," said Vik.

"I agree," I said. "Up until now the most flattered I have ever been was when I was roofied at a bar, but it turned out to be a Skittle."

After Barbara-Anne alerted me to a hole in my only pair of workout pants, I raced over to the nearest mall. To my surprise, I wasn't the only guild member there.

While sifting through the clearance racks at the locally owned Clothes by the Pound, I spotted Vik.

"Hi, Vik!" I said and waved cheerfully from the opposite end of the store.

After spotting me, he covered his face and crouched behind a short Indian woman.

"Vikram!" she shouted as he bumped into her, accidentally shoving her into a clothing rack.

The Fat Bitch Diet

Of course, the good friend I am, I ran over to help. Plus I was curious as to who that woman was.

"Are you okay?" I asked, helping the short woman up. Her traditional clothing was a little distracting to me, as I had always admired Indian culture. To put things in perspective, after watching *Slumdog Millionaire,* I tried to emulate a saree using my bed sheet and pillowcases.

"What are you doing here?" Vik asked, untangling a hanger from the woman's necklace.

"Do you know this woman, Vikram?"

"Hi, I am Viola, a friend—" The woman cut me off before I could finish my sentence.

"Vikram, is this your girlfriend? She is white! You know how your father and I feel about that. We want a fair Hindu girl for you. This girl probably can't even fry a samosa."

I laughed lightly. "There seems to be a misunderstanding. I am not his girlfriend."

"You can't fool me! You're his girlfriend, and do you want to know how I know? Vikram has never once had a female friend. He has only brought guys over, day and night, but no girls. You're his girlfriend, and that only means one thing."

"Okay, you're not wrong about the samosa thing," I said, "but you are wrong about one thing, Vikram is a hom—"

Suddenly, Vikram jumped in front of me, grabbing my hand tightly.

"Okay, you got me! She is my girlfriend!" It was followed by a look that I deciphered fairly quickly. He was wasn't out to his parents. "Viola, this is my mother, Sarasvati."

I lightly touched her shoulder. "It's a pleasure to meet you, Sarasvati."

"In our culture it's rude to call elders by their name," she said. "Call me Aunty."

"Umm... okay, Aunty. Oooh, I kinda like that." Vik rolled his eyes.

"Viola, you remind me of my sister, Agni".

"Aww, Aunty, that is so sweet of you to say!" I nudged Vik and said, "Your mom is so kind. Where have you been hiding her?"

"Viola, Aunt Agni is nearly three hundred pounds," said Vik.

"Okay," said Aunty. "Let's get to business. We need to set a date for the wedding. Viola, come over tonight with your parents so we can all sit down and plan out your life together."

My eyes almost fell out of my head. I grabbed Vik's arm and dragged him to the other end of the aisle.

"Vik, you need to come clean with your mom. Did you forget I'm planning on marrying Franklin? I can't be in a polygamist relationship—I don't have that kind of stamina in bed!"

Vik grabbed my shoulders. "Relax, Viola, we can pull off a fake marriage. Just look at Jay-Z and Beyoncé."

"I do love Beyoncé... But seriously, you have to come out to your parents. Living in a closet is not fun, I would know—mine smells like mold and stale nachos."

"Are you *insane*? I can't come out to my parents, they will discard me like a hard piece of naan."

"Vik, do you really believe that? You're their son. Wouldn't they would want you to live a happy life?"

"Girl, please, South Asian families only care about two things: reputation and religion."

"Vik, do you see that little Asian girl at the entrance picking her nose?"

"Yes… Eww… Somebody needs to show her how to use a napkin. What's your point, Viola?"

I shrugged. "Nothing, I just wanted to lighten the mood for what I'm about to say next." I gently touched his shoulder. "I can't marry you, and you can't live a lie for the rest of your life. Your parents will eventually find out. You know that, right? Remember, whether they accept you or not, you won't be alone. You got the guild at your back."

Vik looked far into the distance at his mother, who was arguing loudly with a cashier. "You're right. I have to tell them. I will do it tonight."

As I watched Vik mosey on back to his mom, I couldn't help but wonder if I said the right thing. Let's face it, I was no better than the nose-picking girl, so who was I to give him advice?

On a typical night, I would be flung over the couch like a throw, updating my knowledge on the latest news gossip. Sadly, those nights had ended, as Shaniqua talked my ear off over the television volume. But it was all good, as she was cooking meals for the both of us. Besides, there was no harm hearing about how her cousin Ronaldo's mistress texted the secret of their affair to his wife after he gave her a knockoff Prada purse. Hell hath no fury, hmm?

As Shaniqua went on about Ronaldo, I stealthily slid my phone out of my pocket, curious to see what Franklin was up to.

I didn't make it very far in my quest.

"Girl, you better not be checkin' up on Franklin!" Shaniqua shouted, startling me. My phone slipped out of my hand and hit the floor.

I bent down to pick it up. "Shan, you don't understand."

"I do understand. You get like this when you need to get laid."

"Ugh, I can't deny that. The last time my legs were spread open was when I slipped on a patch of ice."

A loud knock on the door grabbed our attention.

Shaniqua looked at me with disgust. "Girl, is that Franklin? Were you texting him in the bathroom earlier? Did you lie about clogging the toilet?"

I began walking to the door. "Good news and bad news—I wasn't texting Franklin, and yes, the toilet is still clogged."

Shaniqua rolled her eyes and followed me to the door. "Well, then who is it? It's almost midnight."

Thankfully I had Shaniqua there, as living without Franklin was raising my nerves. Anytime I heard a loud voice in the hallway or a thump in the ceiling I was convinced somebody was coming to attack me. One night, to calm my nerves, I placed a mop with a top hat against my bedroom window. It worked until a gust of wind blew the stick on top of me while I was sleeping. Let's just say I had to throw out my bedsheets after that.

I gracefully placed my cheek against the door. "Who is it?"

"It's Vik." He didn't sound like himself; something was wrong. I unlocked the door to reveal a teary-eyed Vik standing next to a large Louis Vuitton carry-on.

At that moment, I knew exactly what had happened.

"Come in, Vik. You can stay as long as you want." Vik quietly dragged his belongings in and sat down on the couch, completely lost in thought.

Shaniqua looked at me in confusion. "Viola, what's going on?"

After explaining the situation to Shaniqua in private, we sat down beside Vik, who hadn't said a single word since he'd arrived.

An hour of silence was too much for Shaniqua to bear. She turned to Vik and said, "If it helps, my cousin Rafael was disowned for being gay, too, but he bounced back and is now the manager of a low-end department store in Brooklyn."

Vik startled bawling, covering his face with his hands.

I looked at Shaniqua. "Okay, that didn't work."

Vik needed cheering up. It wasn't realistic to solve all of his problems in one night, but a smile was a good place to start.

I raced to my bedroom and searched high and low for the most outdated, hideous, and mismatched articles of clothing I owned. It wasn't very hard as I paired yellow socks, red sandals, baggy beige corduroy pants with a bright green belt, and a denim shirt with a navy-blue fanny pack.

It didn't end there. I whipped out all the makeup I owned and plastered enough makeup on my face to make me look like a clown's assistant.

It was time for the icing on the cake. I blasted En Vogue's classic runway song 'Free Your Mind' on my cell phone and tossed it into the hallway.

It was time for my catwalk.

With a supermodel ego, and more makeup applied to my face than the entire cast of *Toddlers and Tiaras*, I strutted my stuff down to the living room.

I looked at a speechless Vik and said, "Give me all you got."

He remained quiet, but he did stop crying.

"Oh my God," said Shaniqua. "Vik, are you gonna let her get away with this? She is wearing socks with sandals, for crying out loud! My cousin Carlton got shot for that. And they stole his sandals after."

Lifting up my fanny pack, I said, "You know, I forgot how attractive I look with this around my waist. I think I might wear it during our workouts."

Vik made a noise under his breath. "Ugh…"

I smiled. "What was that? Sorry, I couldn't hear you over the sound of my corduroys. On a side note, I really think this denim shirt brings out my eyeshadow. What do you think?"

"Viola, it looks…" I couldn't hear the rest of his sentence as he mumbled it quietly.

"What was that, Vik? I can't hear you," I said tauntingly.

He slowly rose to his feet and crossed his arms against his chest. "Did you apply the makeup to your face with your feet?"

I was jumping with joy. "What else do you got?"

"That shirt should be sent to death row, and those pants should be the executioner."

"Bitch, please," I said condescendingly. "Is that all you got?"

The Fat Bitch Diet

Vik took a step towards me and looked at my sandals and socks. "Viola, your feet look like the offspring of an incestuous couple."

I wrapped my arms rightly around him. "Welcome back!"

"Viola if I was a billing clerk, I would invoice you for ugly."

"Okay, let it all out."

"Don't even get me started on that catwalk. You looked like a disabled duck."

Vik sat back down on the couch and began sulking. "I haven't cried this much since Kim married Kanye. She could have done so much better."

I sat down beside him and grabbed his hand. "I meant what I said earlier. You have the entire guild at your side, and you're welcome to stay here for as long as you want."

"Viola, I appreciate you letting me stay here, but can you please go wash your face? It's making me nauseated."

I would have been insulted, except for the fact that the makeup was from a nearby liquidator and I was pretty sure it was toxic. Sure enough, when I got to the bathroom, it had turned my eyebrows green.

Chapter Twelve

❶❽❼ Lbs

November 22, 2016

The following evening, Vik and Shan had mysterious plans after our workout, which left me alone in the apartment.

The stress of having two roommates was creating a craving in me for something sweet. What Shaniqua and Vik didn't know was that I'd stuffed my frozen Franklin brownies into an empty ice tray and cleverly hid it under a second ice tray. It was perfect, as Shaniqua hated ice in her drinks, and Vik was too concerned about chipping a nail when it came to removing a cube.

Like a dog, I rested my chin on the dining table, staring obsessively at a single piece of brownie. Licking my lips, I examined its crusty edges and the elegant way light bounced off of the wavy frosted top.

I needed help.

Whipping out my cell phone, I contemplated texting Franklin, but since Christos's name showed up first on my contacts, I texted him instead.

> *SOS... brownie craving!*

I started feeling nervous. Waiting for his response was making it worse. Thankfully I didn't have to wait long.

I am coming to get you.

As I sat there in my stained pajamas and ripped T-shirt with my greasy hair, it couldn't have been any clearer that I didn't want him or anyone to see my appearance.

Oh don't worry about me, I will be fine.

Thinking he would accept my response, I sat my phone back down and walked away, only to hear it vibrate the entire table seconds later.

Omw.

Realizing I had lost the battle, I tossed the brownie back into the freezer and raced to my bedroom. I didn't know what to do, so I called the only person I knew who could help.

"Hey, Shaniqua, are you free? I need to tell you something."

"Viola, is this about the bloody tampon you left in the bathroom sink this morning? Girl, that is nasty."

"Christos is on his way over here. What do I do?" I asked, running back and forth between the bedroom and bathroom.

"Wait, what? Why?"

"It started with a sugar craving, and the next thing I know he is on his way over here. I have no decent clothes, my hair smells like fish, and to top it off I forgot to record *The Bachelorette*!"

"Girl, you gotta calm down. Grab something to wear from my suitcase and just be yourself. You got this."

I sighed deeply. "You're right, I can do this. Worse comes to worst, I can hide in the bathroom and tell him I have kidney stones."

Just as I finished drying my hair, a loud knock echoed throughout the empty apartment. I felt a little out of my comfort zone as I was wearing Shaniqua's black and white cocktail dress. It was the only thing I could find that wasn't loose on me.

"Coming!" I shouted, dodging opened carry-ons and suitcases on the way to the door.

The door lock was jammed, but I eventually got it open, and a bit too quickly, as it slammed into the wall.

"Hi," said Christos. I was surprised by his casual look—a white T-shirt, blue jeans, and black open-toe sandals. I guess I was too used to his tank top and shorts appearance. I admit I felt a little disappointed that his shirt was covering his plump muscles. Don't get me wrong, I wasn't attracted or anything, I just didn't mind not seeing them. Does that make sense? It sounded more clear in my head.

"Hiya, Christos!" I said cheerfully, checking the wall for door dents.

"I should probably tell you—"

"Oh, don't worry I didn't eat the brownie," I said.

"Great, but I was going to say that there is a confused woman urinating on the steps of your building."

"Oh, that's Benita, she's harmless. Anyways, you didn't have to come all this way here, the craving is gone. So, see ya tomorrow?"

"Come with me, Viola."

"Where are we going?" I couldn't help but wonder what his motive was. Did he secretly have a bucket of pig's blood in his car?

After fifteen minutes of uncomfortable small talk in Christos's car, we found ourselves in Walmart.

"Christos, what are we doing here?" He bent down to grab a box of low-fat graham crackers.

"You have to be prepared for sugar cravings. The last thing you want is to throw off your diet."

"Don't worry, the only thing I have ever thrown off was my pH balance."

Christos laughed and handed me the graham crackers. "Get in the habit of checking nutrition labels. A lot of them can surprise you."

"Alrighty, are we good?" I said, staring down at the box.

"Just about. We have one more stop to make in the frozen section."

My eyes were glued to the nutrition label as we rounded the corner, when I regretfully bumped into a woman, spilling the contents from the stack in her cart.

I hastily got down on all fours to pick up the woman's pasta cans. "I'm so sorry!"

Christos bent down to help me back up as I placed the contents back on her cart, and that's when I realized I knew the woman. It was the last person in the world I wanted to see: Franklin's new girlfriend, Annabelle.

I'd just made a fool out of myself in front of the woman who stole Franklin from me. She should have been the one on all fours begging for my forgiveness.

"Viola? I haven't seen you since that crazy party. I am so happy to see you!" Annabelle said, tossing her long brunette curls over her shoulder and down her thin waist.

"I am so happy to see you, too!" I replied, feeling embarrassed and small.

"You probably know by now that I'm dating Franklin. I just wanted to let you know that we didn't plan for this; it just sort of happened."

I wanted to tell her, 'Acne just sort of happens, you thieving two-faced tramp,' but instead I said, "No need to be sorry. It's all good."

"Oh," she said smugly, "I never said I was sorry."

I smiled nervously, hoping the humiliation was over.

Suddenly, a familiar voice startled me from behind. "Oh, Viola, I am glad you're here!"

I turned around quickly, accidentally poking Christos with the edge of the graham cracker box. "Hi, Alex, what can I do for you?"

"Are you still having that bladder leakage issue?" he asked.

I was too stunned to reply coherently. "Huh?"

"I discussed your issue with some of the staff here and they recommended a brand called Quantum."

"I think my grandmother uses those," said Annabelle.

I don't know what was worse, being humiliated in front of Annabelle or being humiliated in front of Christos.

"Excuse me," said Christos, "I have erectile dysfunction. Do you have any recommendations for that?"

I looked at Christos, and couldn't help but smile admirably. I couldn't remember a time when Franklin jumped on his own sword for me.

Smiling politely, I turned back to Alex. "Thanks, Alex, I will keep that in mind. Have a good night, bud." I looked back at Annabelle. "It was nice catching up with you. Give my best to Franklin."

It was finally over. Or so I thought.

"Tell him yourself," said Annabelle. "He's around here somewhere."

My eyes widened and my heart began racing. I hadn't felt this way since my mom caught me French kissing the family dog.

I lightly grabbed Christos's arm and gave him the look. "Umm… we gotta go, but it was nice seeing you."

We were too late. Franklin quickly appeared next to Annabelle holding a jug of milk.

"Viola?" Franklin said, looking like a deer caught in headlights.

"Hi, Franklin," I said, "you look good."

"Viola, did you lose weight? You look good."

"15 pounds!" I replied cheerfully.

Annabelle smiled mockingly. "Well, hopefully you don't quit, I read that the first fifty pounds are the hardest to lose."

It didn't take Franklin long to notice I was grabbing Christos's arm.

I released my grip from Christos as Franklin leaned forward to shake his hand. "I'm Franklin, Viola's ex-boyfriend."

It was getting harder to maintain a positive upbeat attitude, and Christos could see it on my face.

"Hi, Franklin, I am Christos, Viola's current boyfriend."

Franklin's face turned pale. "Viola, I didn't know you were seeing anyone." He turned his focus to Christos, obviously feeling a bit threatened by his masculine athletic appearance. "So what do you do for a living, Christos?"

I was stunned and didn't even know what to say. What was happening?

"I'm a personal trainer."

"Hot!" said Annabelle.

Franklin looked at me. "When did you guys start dating? Actually, never mind, it doesn't matter. I am with Annabelle now." I could tell by the tone of his voice that he was annoyed.

I grabbed Christos's arm and said, "Well, we should get going, we were headed to the frozen foods section. Don't want to keep those frozen strawberries waiting."

Franklin interlaced his fingers with Annabelle and waved. "Take care, Viola."

I let out a huge sigh of relief once we were out of their line of sight.

Christos stopped in front of the freezer doors. "I'm sorry about that, Viola. I shouldn't have told him I was your boyfriend."

I playfully slapped his shoulder. "Oh, don't worry about it. But why did you do it?"

"I was disgusted by what he did to you on the radio. You didn't deserve that."

"Thanks," I said. Maybe Christos was right. I could do better.

"Okay, so back to the final item," Christos said, reaching into the freezer to grab a tub of low-fat Cool Whip.

I jumped up gleefully. "Oh, yum! If only my inventions took off as well as the creation of Cool Whip."

Christos dropped the tub into the cart. "What do you mean?"

"I dabbled with a few inventions. My first idea was a duvet that sprayed a mist of water in the air as you slept. I called it the Wet Dreams Blanket."

Christos laughed. "That's amazing. I would buy one."

"Oh, that's nothing, my other invention was a portable patterned toilet cover for the on-the-go fashionista. I called it Sittin' Pretty."

Christos smiled. "Those inventions are brilliant. You can't give up on them."

"So now that we got our items, what's the plan?"

"I hope you have a good freezer, cause we are going to need to use it next."

"You're coming over to my place?"

"Bingo!" Christos began unloading.

"That might not work," I said, panicking. "My place is a disaster thanks to my new roommates. Clothes are everywhere, seriously. This morning I found a pair of panties in the vegetable crisper."

It didn't take long for me to learn that Christos was one persistent guy. Like a tennis match, he successfully back-handed all my excuses back into my court.

"Well, here we are, home sweet home," I said, tossing the items onto the cluttered kitchen counter. "In my defense, I expected more from a gay man and an African fashionista."

"Are you talking about Vik and Shaniqua? From the fitness guild?" Christos said, scanning the apartment with his hands in his pocket.

"Shocking, right?" I said. "So, what are we doing next?" I was eager to get the show on the road as I was really uncomfortable having Christos this involved in my personal life.

Christos walked over to the counter, grabbed two graham crackers, and spread a one-inch-thick layer of Cool Whip between them, resembling an ice cream sandwich.

Christos lifted the sandwich into the air with both hands. "I give you the healthy alternative to the famous ice cream sandwich—the Cool Whip sandwich."

I teasingly slapped his wrist. "Oh my God, you are such a dork."

Christos smiled, lowering his hands. "The plan is to make around ten or so of these, slide them into the freezer, and eat one every time you get a sugar craving."

"How long do I need to leave it in the freezer?" I asked as I assisted with the sandwich building.

"Two hours if you are really desperate, but leaving them overnight would be better."

After our task was complete, awkward silence hounded us. Luckily it didn't take long for me to break it.

"So… how long have you had the beard?" I couldn't help myself from asking, as I was so disgusted by it.

Christos's face glazed over. I could tell the question had hit a nerve. He quickly wiped it from his face and smiled. "For a while now. So how do you like working at The Protein Hut?"

"It's all right. Some days I feel it's a great fit, other days I feel like my skills could be better utilized doing something else. But it's hard getting onto a different track in life, you know what I mean?"

"I get that, Viola. My dream is to be a gym owner, but that will never become a reality as I have no equity to make that dream come true."

"No trust fund left by mommy and daddy?" I teased.

"My parents died in a car accident when I was sixteen," said Christos.

My eyes widened with embarrassment as I gently squeezed his shoulder. "I'm so sorry, Christos. I shouldn't have said that."

Christos smiled and placed his fingers over mine. "That's okay, Viola, you didn't know."

My phone started vibrating. I would have ignored it, but it wouldn't stop vibrating as somebody was sending me multiple single-line text messages.

I rinsed my hands off and reached for my phone. "Maybe I should get that. Shaniqua may have driven over a pedestrian or something."

Christos laughed. "Let's hope not. Would it be okay if I used your bathroom?"

"Of course. It's just over there at the end of the hall."

As Christos made his way down the hall, I unlocked my phone to reveal that the sender wasn't Shaniqua—it was Franklin.

My body quivered with excitement as I read his text messages.

> *It was nice seeing you tonight, Viola.*
>
> *You looked good.*
>
> *Hope you have a good night.*

I couldn't help but smile. My initial plan was working. It was only a matter of time before Franklin came back to me with a glamorous engagement ring. Only one thing remained: What the heck should I reply back?

It didn't take me long to call Shaniqua for advice.

"Shaniqua, guess who just texted me!" I shouted, jumping up and down.

"Viola, I already told you, Apple doesn't just give out free iPhones."

"Franklin wants me back!"

"That foo finally texted you back?" I could barely hear her over the sound of loud clanging and crashing in the background. "Where are you? What are those loud noises?"

"I can't find my silver bracelet anywhere. I think I left it at Shamar's place. Let's just leave it at that. So Franklin said he wants you back?"

"Well, not exactly. He said I looked good. I know that doesn't mean much, but keep in mind that he hasn't said that since the first time he unhooked my bra."

"Viola, why you reaching? Let him go. On a side note, before I get home, can you please move your vibrator? The edge of the tub is no place for it."

"Oh shit!" I shouted, realizing that Christos had probably found it.

"What is it?"

"I gotta go! Talk to you later, Shan."

I paced back and forth, trying to think of clever excuses. I could say it belonged to Shan, but then remembered I'd labeled it with 'Property of Viola Ginamero.'

Maybe I should just own up to it? It wouldn't be the first time my bathroom made a man uncomfortable.

Before I could find a solution, Christos stepped out of the bathroom. I bit my lip and turned away. The last thing I wanted to see was his facial expression.

"Umm, Viola… I think you forgot something in there." His slow expression of words gave away his discovery, and I figured that the best way to soften the blow was to lay it all on the table.

I turned around and uncomfortably said, "I'm so sorry you had to see that. I completely forgot I left that in there!"

"It's no big deal, I placed it on top of the sink."

"You *touched* it?"

"I hope that's okay. It looked like somebody was chewing on it."

"Oh, that's totally normal… Google it."

"Viola, won't that cause damage?"

"No, it's silicone, silly. You can't damage it that easily, but it does kind of smell after overuse."

"Wait, what are you talking about?"

"The vibrator, of course. What are you talking about?"

"The silver bracelet that was sitting under the toilet tank."

I could only stare at him, dumbfounded.

Chapter Thirteen

❶❽❺ Lbs

November 23, 2016

I avoided Christos at work like the plague, the entirety of the day was spent thinking of excuses for skipping out of today's workout session.

"Are you still thinking about it?" Shaniqua said, trying to contain her laughter.

"You're not going to start laughing again are you?" I asked, placing my head down on the counter.

"It's not a big deal; can't you take a joke?"

"Hey, I can take a joke, my Oprah magazine is addressed to V. Gina."

Shaniqua rolled her eyes. "So… did Franklin text you again?"

Rubbing my neck, I said, "Not since yesterday."

"Don't you think it's ironic that he texted you shortly after he saw you and Christos together?"

Before I could answer, Remy popped up out of nowhere. "Who texted you?"

I smiled politely. "Hi, Remy!" Quickly looking back at Shaniqua, I continued my defense. "Trust me, I know irony, I have been hit by three different food trucks."

"I was told I have really high iron," said Remy. "I think it's because I swallowed a bag of pennies when I was a child."

Shaniqua gave Remy a puzzling look for a few seconds before returning to me. "Viola, I guarantee that if you post a picture of you and Christos on Facebook, Franklin will be all over it."

I thought about for a second. Was Shan right? "All right, game on. I will prove to you that Franklin's motive isn't jealousy."

Shaniqua turned to Remy. "Do you have anything to add?"

"I once ate a Rubik's cube," said Remy.

The work day flew by, as there were only a handful of customers, and it couldn't have been any clearer that, as contract obligations were fulfilled, gym patrons were dropping out like flies.

As usual, I was the last guild member to enter the training room, but we were still waiting on Christos.

Tripping on my unhemmed pants, I gracefully composed myself and joined in the chatter amongst the guild.

Barbara-Anne looked at me. "Are you okay, my dear?"

Keeping my eyes locked on the door, I said, "Yeah, I just need to go shopping for some new active wear."

Vik playfully smacked my arm. "Two letters: H and M."

I shook my head profusely. "No way, I am boycotting that place."

"Is this because they thought you were transgendered?" asked Shaniqua.

"No, I took that as a compliment. I don't get many."

Barbara-Anne gently touched my shoulder. "I am sure when you apply some makeup, men flirt with you."

"Well, a construction worker did whistle at me once, but it turned out he was warning me about falling debris."

Suddenly Christos barged through the door. "I'm so sorry for being late." The second I made eye contact with him, a storm of butterflies brewed in my gut.

"It's all good, honey," said Vik. "What are we doing today?"

Christos planted himself in front of us. "Today we learn about the eighth stage of weight loss, but before we get to that I just wanted to give some feedback to the guild."

"Uh oh," said Barbara-Anne.

Christos smiled. "Relax, you guys are doing great, but there are a few things to work on. For example: water intake and eating five meals a day."

"How often do you suggest we eat?" I asked.

"You should be eating every two hours."

"You can't put something in your mouth every two hours," said Vik. "This isn't Tinder."

"Also," Christos continued, "don't forget to gulp five times from your water bottle between each set. As you sweat you will get dehydrated—water will make up for this."

I raised my hand and proudly said, "I got this, I am really good at holding my bladder."

"I'm not," Remy said. "I once peed myself in Ikea."

After a brief moment of awkward silence, Christos continued talking. "All right, so let's get to the final stage. How many of you have worked out next to somebody who, unintentionally, made you feel a little insecure about yourself?"

That was a no-brainer; the five of us raised our hands. There was nothing more distracting than the heavy feeling you get when working out next to a woman who you wished you looked like.

"Maybe you envy the amount of weight the person next to you is lifting," Christos added, "or maybe altogether you don't like the way you look while working out."

"Where are you going with this?" asked Shaniqua.

"In life, one of the biggest obstacles that we all share is how we view ourselves in the eyes of somebody else. We care a great deal about what others think. In order to overcome this obstacle, one must adopt stage eight: the D.G.A.F. attitude."

I was confused. "I haven't heard of that acronym before. Is that slang? Because I am not very good at understanding slang. I once slapped a guy for asking me to go Dutch on a restaurant bill."

"The D.G.A.F. attitude stands for Don't Give a Fuck attitude."

Barbara-Anne smiled innocently. "Oh, I could use that at bingo."

Shaniqua grinned. "Oh, hells ya! I like where this is going!"

Christos's tone suddenly became louder, as if he was at a political rally. "The second you step foot in this gym, believe that you own it, believe that you are the most hard-working person in the facility, believe that you are going to surpass all those people you are envious of and destroy your goals. You can do all this because you have the D.G.A.F. attitude."

"I can get behind this," said Vik.

Christos pointed at the other members outside the window. "Going forward, that person working out next to you won't make you feel insecure anymore because you're going to surpass them. They just had a head start."

Remy raised his hand. "Are you saying it would be okay to throw my shoe at people?"

He tapped the side of his head. "The D.G.A.F. attitude is all mental, not physical. Never forget gym etiquette."

"I am still confused," I said.

"Don't give a fuck about what others think," said Shaniqua. "See, do. Just focus on your own self."

"Exactly," said Christos. "Insecurities in the gym are poisonous. Don't get infected and don't give a fuck."

I admit, I was getting a little turned on by Christos's fierce attitude. It was quickly starting to rub onto me, so what if he knew about my vibrator? Who cared? I wasn't going to let that get in my way of success. To think I was going to skip today's session because of it.

"Okay, I got this," I said confidently.

Shaniqua rolled her eyes. "Are you sure? The only time I've ever seen you rebel was when I used the last roll of toilet paper."

"Hey, I can be rebellious. I sneak food into theaters all the time. Remember the time I stuffed a churro in my bra?"

Christos grabbed his clipboard. "I think Viola is going to be fine. Now everybody grab your headphones, your water bottle, your D.G.A.F. attitude, and let's get to work."

After an hour of lifting barbells, dumbbells, and my loose pants, the workout session came to an end. Instead of running off to the changing rooms I took a different approach and decided to take Christos's advice and apply the D.G.A.F. attitude.

Stealthily and carefully picking my post-workout wedgie, I walked over to Christos and said, "So any plans for Thanksgiving?"

Christos smiled politely. "I do. Every year I go up to New Jersey for dinner with my sisters. What about you? Any plans, Viola?

"I am going to Jersey, too!" I shouted cheerfully. "My parents live there. This year I am going to surprise them with a drop in."

Barbara-Anne rushed over. "Aww, did I hear that you have plans for Thanksgiving? What a shame, I wanted to invite the fitness guild over to my place for dinner."

"That's too bad," I said. "But yeah, Christos and I are both headed to New Jersey."

Barbara-Anne gently elbowed Christos's arm. "Why don't you give Viola a ride? It would be better on the environment." Clearly Barbara-Anne leaned more towards matchmaker than environmentalist.

"That's a great idea," I said. "And it just so happens that I have two passes to Coney Island from when a roller coaster screw hit me in the head."

Christos laughed. "Count me in!"

Then I just realized I'd just committed to a road trip with the wrong man. What was I thinking? The prize was Franklin, not Christos.

"Oh, you know what?" I said. "I just remembered, I have to take my own car and go at it alone. My, uh, dad wanted to do some work on it."

"Oh, well, that's a shame," said Christos, "but I understand."

Barbara-Anne jumped in. "Well, can't Christos go with you, then, Viola?"

I smiled uncomfortably. "The thing is, I get distracted too easily by passengers. It's a safety issue, really." It was a lie I didn't think they were going to buy.

Christos smiled politely. "No worries. I hope you have a wonderful time."

As he walked away, I turned to Barbara-Anne and gave her a look of playful disgust.

Barbara-Anne grabbed my hand. "Viola, you remind me of myself when I was your age, and I too was blind to see that my late husband was in love with me. Thankfully, I came to my senses before it was too late."

She made her exit, leaving me alone in the training room with my thoughts. While Barbara-Anne was wise, she couldn't have been more wrong. Why on earth would Christos be in love with me? He could have any girl in the world.

I found myself on my hands and knees, my body rocking back and forth, back and forth. My lady parts were sticky and wet, and no, it's not what you think. I spilled a chocolate protein shake all over my pants and rug, and most of the evening was spent patting and scrubbing it out. Note to self: Always make sure the shaker bottle is snapped shut.

After making a new protein shake, I was ready to upload the pic I'd secretly snapped of Christos to Facebook. I even thought of a perfect caption: The new guy? It had a bit of mystery and left room for open possibilities.

I posted the picture, pausing briefly afterwards to realize that a year ago I would have never done something like this.

As I stared at my phone obsessively, Shaniqua and Vik walked in with several grocery bags.

"Girl," Shaniqua barked, "unglue yourself from your phone and help us."

"Ooh, are we having fish tonight?" I asked, cheerfully emptying out the bags.

Vik took one look at my pants and said, "Oh my God, Viola, what the hell happened?"

I rolled my eyes. "A time-consuming protein shake disaster."

"Go change," said Shaniqua. "It looks like you shit your pants."

Jumping up and down, full of excitement, I said, "I love fish nights. Can I help cook?"

Shaniqua placed her hands on her hips. "You're joking, right?" She turned around and began unwrapping the fish. "I love you, Viola, but you can't cook."

I gasped. "Hey, I can cook. Remember that unforgettable dinner party I hosted?"

"Didn't you give everyone food poisoning?" Shaniqua said.

"Yes, but to be fair I used a meat thermometer that I bought at a garage sale."

My cell phone began vibrating. It was the expected text message from Franklin.

"Is that Franklin?" Shaniqua asked. "That didn't take long."

"What? How did you know?"

"Girl, I saw that pic of Christos you posted. I bet Franklin is mad with jealousy."

"Wait, what's this now?" asked Vik. "Somebody show me this pic."

While Shaniqua caught Vik up, I went to change my pants and read the text.

> *Hey Viola, can I ask you something?*

I had a feeling I knew where this was going.

> *Sure, what's up?*

After a few minutes of waiting nervously, Franklin replied.

> *Are you and the new guy serious?'*

I must have re-read his text message thirty times before I thought of a response.

> *Why do you ask?*

Franklin replied.

> *I think I still have feelings for you.*

Now was my chance to pounce on Franklin. I needed to send a text that would get him fired up and take action. I took a deep breath and replied.

> *You think? Better figure it out before it's too late. I gotta go. Packing for a road trip.*

Franklin quickly replied.

> *With him?*

I clearly had him pinned in the corner. It was time for the knockout.

> *Nite Franklin.*

Nobody said the D.G.A.F. attitude couldn't be applied to everyday life.

It wasn't until Vik knocked on my door that I stopped obsessing over the text messages. "Dinner's ready, Viola."

"Be right there."

I left the bedroom with two things: a fresh pair of panties, and a smile on my face.

Vik was quick to catch it. "Viola, reset your face. You look like the Joker."

Shaniqua gracefully set down two plates of baked salmon, with a side of quinoa and vegetables. "Does this have anything to do with that text?"

I couldn't contain my excitement anymore. "Franklin wants me back! But I am playing hard to get, and it's kind of fun. Who knew?"

Shaniqua sat down beside me. "Careful, Viola, you're playing with fire. You're using Christos to get to Franklin."

Confused, I said, "What do you mean? Christos is totally cool with it. He proved that at Walmart." I scooped a piece of fish into my mouth and tried to change the subject. "Shan, this is delicious! What's your secret?"

Shaniqua took a sip of water. "Oh no, you're not changing the subject. Viola, Christos really likes you."

I rolled my eyes. "You're giving me too much credit. I wish I had it as easy as Vik—he can grab any guy off the street thanks to apps."

"Hey, cruising the streets of New York is a lot harder now," protested Vik. "I can't tell if a guy is on Grindr or playing Pokémon Go."

"That can't be true," I said. "What about the guy you met up with last week?"

"Viola, that guy had nothing to offer but judgment and gonorrhea."

Shaniqua set down her fork and looked me in the eyes. "I wasn't going to tell you this, but at our first training session, Christos asked me if you were single, and that was *before* you lost all the weight." She picked her fork back up and scooped quinoa into her mouth. "Unlike Franklin, Christos likes you for who you are."

"Come on, Viola," teased Vik. "Jump on the Christos bandwagon."

"I don't jump on bandwagons," I said. "For example, most women want to be tied up by Christian Grey, whereas I would rather be tied up by Ronald McDonald."

Shaniqua rolled her eyes. "I'm grabbing my protein shake and going to bed."

It was a great feeling to know how much Vik and Shan cared about me, but it was clear that they didn't understand.

I admit Christos was attractive, charismatic, goal-driven, all great qualities. But I knew nothing about him, whereas I'd spent a decade with Franklin. There was nothing about him I didn't know, and in many ways that made me feel safe and comfortable.

Chapter Fourteen

184 Lbs

November 24, 2016

I woke up to an empty apartment, which I took advantage of to pack. The plan was simple—after my morning breakfast, protein shake, and run, I would be on the road to New Jersey for my Thanksgiving Day surprise to my parents.

The morning was problem free until I tried to start my car. "Come on, come on, come on," I said to myself, listening to the sound of a dying automobile. "Don't do this, come on, come on."

I gave up after five minutes and was forced to call my savior.

"Hey, Shan, what are you up to?" I said cheerfully, hoping she wouldn't guess my car was dead. She'd warned me tirelessly to get an annual check-up.

"Vik, Remy, and myself are at Barbara-Anne's house helping with the dinner. Where you at?"

"Umm… small issue. I seem to have lost my license. Do you think you can drive me up to Jersey?"

"Your car died, didn't it? Girl, I warned you about this. Why are you so stubborn?"

"I am not that stubborn."

"Viola, remember your bird-chirping ringtone?"

"I eventually changed it."

"Yeah, after a blind man mistook it for a road-crossing signal and walked into oncoming traffic."

"It wasn't as serious as it sounds."

"Viola, he got hit by a car!"

"Shan, are you gonna help me or not?"

"Not," Shan replied, ending the call.

I had one other obvious option, but I wasn't going to play it out until I was absolutely sure I couldn't think of any other way to get to New Jersey.

I couldn't afford an Uber, and the last time I took a bus to Jersey I threw up on the lap of the woman sleeping beside me, so that wasn't an option.

After being absolutely certain there were no other viable options, I made the call.

"Hi... Christos? It's Viola."

"What's up, Viola? Hey, how's the weather in Jersey?"

Biting my lip, I said, "Actually, I am sitting in my car outside my apartment. It won't start... is your invitation still available?"

"Say no more. Just gonna pack some snacks for us and I will be on my way." He sounded really excited.

"Thanks, Christos, I really appreciate it. See you soon."

Having some time to kill, I went back into the apartment to empty my nervous bladder and make sure my hair and face were presentable.

Time must have flown by, because before I knew it, Christos was knocking on the door.

"Coming!" I shouted from the bathroom while gently applying foundation. I quickly rinsed my fingers, accidentally sprayed perfume in my face, and galloped towards the door.

I whisked the door open with a big smile on my face.

"Hey, Viola," Christos said, smiling. He was clearly dressed for the weather with his slim-fit shorts, sandals, and a black tank top which displayed his shiny triceps. He paused. "Do you have a stigmatism?"

"No, why do you ask?" I said, grabbing my carry-on.

"Your left eye won't stop blinking. Are you okay?"

"Oh, that? Don't worry, I accidentally sprayed myself in the eyes with Dior." I slipped my shoes on and tossed my purse over my shoulder. "I am all set."

After Christos placed my bag in the trunk of his car, we were well on our way to Jersey. As we made small talk, my nerves slowly settled.

"So, Ms. Ginamero, what kind of tunes do you want to hear?" Christos asked, fiddling with his radio.

"I will let you decide. Franklin hated my taste in music."

Christos accelerated onto the freeway. "Try me."

I shuffled my legs towards him in the passenger seat and said, "Old-school hip-hop."

Christos furrowed his brow in confusion and looked at me. "Why would that be in bad taste? My workout playlist is loaded with old-school hip-hop."

"Shut up!" I said, gently smacking his shoulder. "We figured you out for a guy who was into classical music."

"I like classical music, too. And rock, folk, jazz, you name it. It's good to keep an open mind."

"My parents weren't really open minded, so I wasn't exposed to much as a teen aside from our next-door neighbor's penis at the community pool."

Christos laughed. "Try growing up in a traditional Greek family with nothing but women. As a guy I know way too much about feminine hygiene and menstruation cycles."

"Are you fairly tight with your family?" I asked, stealthily adjusting my wedgie.

"You could say that. After my parents died it was just me and my three sisters."

"I can't imagine living without parents. It was my mom's persistent nagging that got me through high school and dental appointments."

Christos smiled warmly. "We managed. I had to grow up quickly to become the man of the house, but in the process I kind of lost my old personality. It's strange, but around you I feel like that piece of me still exists."

With a puzzled look on my face, I asked, "Really? I'm not afraid of getting old. I'm looking forward to constipation."

Christos laughed, giving me the opportunity to scan his gloriously straight white teeth. He must have been a braces kid, no doubt about it.

I took advantage of the moment to pry once again into the reason for the full beard, which was still the bane of my existence as it disgusted me to no end. "So, Christos, now that we are friends, I gotta know… what's with the beard?"

Within a few seconds, Christos's smile morphed into a serious stare into the distance. He took a deep breath and looked at me ever so innocently. "It's a reminder of a chapter in my life I am not ready to forget." Christos looked away, and I once again felt guilty for asking, but I couldn't help it.

As the car became infected with awkwardness, I decided to break the tension immediately with a very thought-provoking and elegant discussion, "So… the protein shakes are making me really gassy."

Christos laughed. "Viola, you're an open book, aren't you?"

I smiled devilishly as I laid my head against the passenger window and closed my eyes.

A gentle push on my shoulder woke me up from a weird dream. "Viola? Are you okay? You were screaming a bit in your sleep."

Rubbing my eyes, I said, "I dreamt that I was being crushed in the center of an Oreo."

Christos laughed.

I playfully punched his shoulder. "Hey, it's not funny! I could have died. I once read that a woman in Venezuela was attacked by a turkey in a dream. She woke up to beak marks all over her skin."

Christos laughed harder. "You're too cute, Viola. Is this your parents' house?"

I turned around and looked out the window, and a rush of memories washed over me. "Oh, looks like they finally replaced it."

"Replaced what?"

"See that window over there?" I pointed at the side of the brown stucco house.

"Yeah, what about it?"

"My parents never trusted me with a key to the house, so I used that window to crawl in and out of until one day I got stuck. It was so embarrassing. My neighbor had to call 911; three firetrucks came to the scene. I am really glad to see that they replaced that window."

Christos smiled. "Well, I hope you have a wonderful Thanksgiving."

"You, too!" I said cheerfully, unbuckling my belt. I stepped out of his car and rubbed my shoulders.

"Are you cold, Viola? I think I've got a jacket for you in the backseat." Christos turned around and reached into the backseat. "Oh, I must have forgot it at home. I'm one of those people who loses their jackets wherever they go."

"That's okay," I said. "I am one of those girls who loses their top wherever they go." I ran towards the house. "Bye, Christos!"

Like a gentleman, Christos waited in the car until I entered the house safely. I recalled a time when Franklin drove off while I was using a gas station restroom.

I walked up the brown wooden stairs and rang the bell multiple times, just like I did when I lived there. For sure, they would know it was their beloved daughter.

The Fat Bitch Diet

There was no answer.

"Hello? Mom?" I said, trying to listen for voices or footsteps inside the house. There wasn't a peep.

I looked back at Christos and shrugged my shoulders.

He rolled down the window and shouted, "Try calling them. Maybe they stepped out!"

"You're a genius!" I yelled back, whipping out my cell phone.

After a few rings, my mom answered, "Hello? Who is this?" Her shrill sixty-five-year-old voice forced me to turn down the volume.

"Hi, Mom! Where are you guys? I have a big announcement!"

"We already know—Franklin left you. Honestly, I can't say that I'm surprised. We always thought he was way out of your league."

I rolled my eyes and replied enthusiastically, "I was going to announce that I'm here in Jersey for a surprise Thanksgiving pop-in! I'm here to spend it with you two!"

"Viola, your stepfather and I are in Mexico."

"Oh," I said as my smile slowly vanished from my face. "I didn't know that."

"It doesn't matter. Even if you called in advance, we would have still gone. We can't base our lives around you."

"Yeah... Yeah, you're right." I took a deep breath and cheerfully said, "Well, I hope you two have a good time. And Happy Thanksgiv—"

"Viola, I gotta go," she said, cutting me off.

"Everything okay?" Christos shouted. He clearly noticed the emotional change in my face as I got off the phone.

I moseyed over to the driver-side window and leaned in. "You know, if I was showing more cleavage right now I would feel like a prostitute, but a classy one, like Julia Roberts in *Pretty Woman*."

Christos smiled. "So are your parents on their way?"

I stood back up and replied in utter disappointment, "They're in Mexico."

"Oh, sorry. I know the surprise meant a lot to you." The truth was, it did, but I was starting to realize that I was more close with the fitness guild than my actual parents.

"Pfft, it's all good. I'll catch a bus back. You go on ahead."

Christos hopped out of the car and opened the passenger door. "Hop in, Viola."

"Where are we going?"

"You're spending Thanksgiving with us, and I won't take no for an answer."

"That's not true, if I told you I had pink eye, you would take no for an answer."

Christos laughed. "Come on, hop in."

I thought about the pros and cons of getting back in his car. Pro: when Franklin found out I'm spending Thanksgiving with Christos's family, his jealousy meter would go through the roof. Con: the last thing I wanted was to lead Christos on.

Biting my lip, I said, "Sure... what the hell. Just give me a sec to text your address to my mom, just in case she comes back early." Yes, I knew I was reaching, but can you blame me? I just wanted to feel loved.

As we rolled up to Christos's childhood home and parked in the driveway, one word came to mind.

"Bonkers."

Christos looked at me in confusion. "What was that?"

"Oh, it's nothing. Brick houses always remind me of my neighbor's cat, Bonkers. I was seven when he passed away, and I am still traumatized."

"Aww, poor little guy, hopefully he didn't suffer."

I looked down at my knees. "Umm… he may have suffered a little."

"How so?" Christos asked, unbuckling his seatbelt.

"My Dad accidentally ran him over with our lawnmower."

Suddenly a loud knock on my window startled me. "Christos!" a petite teenage girl with long black hair shouted. "Lina! Zeta! Come, Christos is here!"

Christos leaped out of the car. "Hi, Tonia! How is my baby sister? You've grown so tall. What are you, six feet now?"

"No, silly," said Tonia. "I'm almost five feet." Tonia looked at me. "Is this your girlfriend?"

Christos laughed. "Tonia, this is my friend Viola."

Tonia reached out for a handshake. "Nice to meet you, Viola. I'm Tonia, Christo's youngest and most spoiled sister."

Christos smiled. "It's true, we spoil her rotten."

"It's all good," I said. "I spoil myself all the time—just the other day instead of regular, I bought quilted toilet paper."

Tonia laughed.

A dominant female voice joined us. "Did I miss a good joke?" I turned around to see two beautiful Greek women walking out of the large brick house to join us by the car. It didn't take long for me to guess their ages. The one with no expression was clearly around thirty years old, whereas the other woman, showcasing a beautiful and elegant smile, looked like she was in her early twenties. The taller woman's dark, untidy shoulder-length hair complemented her drab clothes and flat footwear. The other woman was the complete opposite, packing on a designer outfit, shimmering jewelry, heels, celebrity-quality makeup, and long bouncy curls that I could not take my eyes off of.

"Tonia, I assume you're out here because you've done all your homework," scolded the older woman.

The middle sister quickly interjected. "Lina, why are you always so bossy? Can't you see Tonia came out to greet her brother?"

Christos smiled awkwardly. "Viola, these are my sisters Lina and Zeta." Before I had a chance to greet them, Zeta jumped onto Christos for a peck on the cheek and a tight hug.

"Aww," I said, clutching my fist against my chest.

"I missed you so much!" Zeta cried. "Why haven't you come around? Is there a new girl in your life? Is this her?" Zeta pointed at me. "I like her; she looks promiscuous."

"No, she doesn't," Lina said.

"I can be promiscuous," I said. "I've had some wild sex dreams about the Pillsbury doughboy."

Zeta laughed and wrapped her tanned arms around me. "Come inside. I bet you're dying to hear all about Christos's childhood."

As I walked through the front door with Zeta, I felt an overwhelming amount of warmth throughout the house. Photographs of the family from the last thirty years decorated the walls of the living room.

I picked up a picture frame off a side table. "Are these your parents?" It was a wedding photo of a tall, handsome man wearing a dark suit and a glowing woman dressed in a puffy white dress.

Zeta nodded. "It was taken on their wedding day." She paused briefly as a wave of emotion washed over her.

While I gently placed the frame down, Christos and Lina joined us in the living room.

Lina looked in my direction and emotionlessly said, "Dinner is in an hour. Zeta will show you to the guest room."

"She's not sharing Christos' room?" asked Zeta.

"I don't see a ring on her finger," Lina said, walking out of the room.

Christos tapped Zeta on the shoulder. "We aren't dating. We're just friends."

Zeta looked at me in disappointment. "But you guys are so cute together."

Christos thankfully teared through the awkwardness. "Zeta, could I bug you for a glass of water?"

"Sure, be right back."

Zeta leaving the room gave Christos and myself a chance to chat.

"I'm so sorry for my sisters, Viola."

"What do you mean? They are lovely."

"I have always gotten along with Zeta, but Lina and I are very different people. She is more conservative in nature, which made living here difficult." Christos motioned an invitation to sit down on the couch with him.

"Is Lina older then you?" I asked, squeezing onto a nearby sofa cushion.

Christos took a deep breath. "Actually, she is my twin."

"*What?*"

Christos leaned over and looked into my eyes. "When my parents died, Lina and I jointly looked after the house, but as the years went by she became more and more miserable and she was taking me down with her… until I met somebody who kept me in balance."

Suddenly Zeta barged into the room, chewing on an apple. "Come with me, Viola. I'll show you to your room."

———◦○◦♦◦○◦———

I followed Zeta up a short flight of stairs that led to a hallway of rooms. Similar to the lower floor, the walls were covered with family photos.

"The guest room is at the end of the hall," Zeta said, leading me into a room with painted pink walls, a white dresser, and a queen-sized bed.

"I love the color. Was this your room? It's so bright and inviting."

"Actually, this was Lina's room. Before she became a complete bitch," Zeta said.

A loud knocking on the bedroom door startled us. "You're needed downstairs, Zeta," Lina said with a blank stare.

"I'll be right back, Viola," Zeta said, quickly running out of the room, feeling embarrassed. Had Lina heard her?

"Maybe I'll help them out, too," I said, walking towards Lina.

"No, stay," Lina said, closing the door.

I swallowed nervously. "I think I'll grab some water downstairs. I forgot to put a water bottle in my purse today."

"Do you typically carry water in your purse?"

"Absolutely," I said. "I don't have a problem carrying a water bottle wherever I go. I have also been carrying an unused diaphragm in my purse for the last nine years."

Lina crossed her arms against her chest. Her blank, emotionless stare was beginning to frighten me. "Viola, I see the way Christos looks at you."

"Who? At me? I'm sure it's nothing. The garbage man gives me the same look whenever I wear my pajamas out to the curb."

Lina took a few steps back and to my relief opened the door slightly. "He's not as strong as he lets on. He's been hurt once before, and I won't let him go through that again."

"I can't imagine what it was like to lose your parents."

"No, not them. I am talking about Helena. She shattered his heart."

I took a second to sift through my thoughts to see if that name rang a bell. "Who?"

"He didn't tell you? Well, ask Christos. It's not my place to tell."

As I watched Lina exit the room, I couldn't help but wonder if she was just messing with me. After all, she seemed like the passive-aggressive type.

I was starting to feel like the world was holding a cigarette up to my lips, pressuring me to do something I didn't desire. The guild was pushing me towards Christos, fate was pushing me towards Christos, and now Lina was inadvertently pushing me towards him by hinting that I should stay away. Forbidden fruit was a bit of a turn-on for a girl like me, and honestly I never really had a taste of it, unless you count that one time I accidentally ate a fungus-covered peach.

In an attempt to clear my head, I decided to wander the hallway and poke my head inside rooms. All of the rooms looked fairly dull except for one, which looked like it belonged to a teenage boy who was obsessed with science fiction movies. Movie posters, spanning the last few decades, were plastered on the ceiling. Everything from *Alien* to *Blade Runner*. The walls were splattered with newspaper clippings and random memorabilia, and to tie it all together, a giant life-sized Chewbacca guarded the room from the corner.

"I see you found my room," Christos said, popping up behind me.

I turned around gleefully. "Oh my God, you were such a geek, I love it! I was Princess Leia for Halloween last year! I looked amazing, except I couldn't get her infamous hair bun right, so I rolled two mini cinnamon buns into my hair."

"Did that hold?"

"Oh yeah! I mean, I was chased by several wasps at one point in the night, but it all worked out in the end."

Christos laughed. "Well, hate to disappoint you but I am not the same guy I was when I was eighteen."

Tired from standing, I sat down on his queen-sized bed, "Same here. I stopped rolling food into my hair. Well, that's not entirely true; I still curl my hair with bananas."

Christos smiled warmly and sat down next to me, and our thighs touched, sending my heart into a fluttering mess. "I'm glad you're here, Viola."

"Me, too," I replied nervously. The truth was that the more I learned about him, the more I was starting to feel an attraction. Don't get me wrong, I hadn't gotten over Franklin. It was just nice to be in a place where I felt like there was another option.

We sat quietly for a few seconds when suddenly Christos's lips moved towards mine.

Lina's serious tone interrupted the moment. "Dinner is being served downstairs." She gave me a really dirty look before exiting the room, and I was reminded of the time an elderly woman caught me licking Cheese Whiz off my bra in Central Park.

Christos leaped to his feet. "Shall we?" He put out his hand.

"Lead the way," I said.

Zeta sat me down at the dining table next to Christos as Lina and Tonia brought out several Greek dishes.

Tonia smiled. "I hope you have room for dessert, I made my special brownies for Christos."

"You also dropped the batter on the kitchen floor," Lina added. "Aren't you going to tell them that?"

Tonia's smile quickly faded.

"That's all right, Tonia," I said. "I once ate cheesecake off a dustpan." Lina rolled her eyes, dropping off a plate of spanakopita's.

After several more dishes were placed on the table, the five of us were finally seated and ready to eat.

Zeta looked over at me. "Do you prefer red or white, Viola?" She rose from the table to grab a bottle of wine.

"Oh, I'm good. No wine for me."

"Red it is," Zeta said, pouring a full glass of wine and handing it to me.

Christos smiled warmly. "Zeta never takes no for an answer. She is the type of person who always says yes to everything."

"Yeah," said Lina. "It's a miracle she hasn't gotten pregnant yet."

"Lina, you're just jealous!" Zeta bit back. "When was the last time a man touched you?"

Lina rolled her eyes and scooped food into her mouth. "You have a point. Maybe I should follow in your footsteps and spread my legs and bend over for every man I meet on a dating app."

In a furious rage, Zeta leaped from her seat and threw her glass of wine into Lina's face. Red wine slid down her cheek and onto her blouse.

"Hey, come on, guys," said Christos. "Let's not bring dirty laundry to the dining table. You're making Viola feel uncomfortable."

I nervously took a sip of wine. "Oh, I don't mind, I feel like I'm in *Downton Abbey*."

Lina dabbed her face with a napkin. "Don't act so perfect, Christos. How come you haven't told Viola about Helena and how she left you at the altar?"

I choked on my wine and began coughing intensely.

"Lina, you are such a bitch!" said Zeta.

Christos gently patted my back. "Are you okay?" I nodded quietly, rising from my seat to excuse myself.

Lina gave me a dirty look and walked away from the table.

Leaning towards Christos, I asked, "Is she going to be okay?"

Zeta overheard me and replied, "She will be fine. She's a drama queen."

I looked around the table and noticed an empty seat. "Hey, where did Tonia go?"

Zeta shrugged.

I patted my lips with a napkin. "I'll go check up on her." As I left the table all I could think of were the two shocking revelations I just learned: One, Christos was left at the altar and two, I just remembered I'd forgotten to pack extra underwear."

Knocking gently on Tonia's door, I slowly walked in, mesmerizing myself with her dazzling walls covered in glitter, lots and lots of glitter. I was so focused on that I barely noticed the duffel bag she was filling up.

"Running away?" I said, plopping myself on her bed.

"I can't stand their fighting anymore!" she shouted. "Why can't they just get along?" I watched as she tossed socks, shoes, and a bag of oranges into the bag.

"Wait, why are you taking oranges?"

"Every day the two of them argue about something petty. Groceries, bills. Last night they had a three-hour fight about toilet paper."

"Oh, really? Was it 2-ply or 3-ply? I'm not a big fan of 3-ply. I understand that it catches more but it's just not worth the effort."

Tonia stopped, took a deep breath, and looked at me. "I've been tempted to run away for some time now."

I placed my hand on Tonia's shoulder. "We all have temptations. I personally have always wanted to throw a cactus at someone."

Tonia burst into laughter.

Christos entered the room, smiling. "What's so funny?"

I grabbed Tonia's hand. "I am dying to try your brownies. Shall we?"

Tonia nodded.

I winked at Christos as Tonia led me out of the room. Christos mouthed the words 'thank you.'

After Christos and I shared one of Tonia's famous brownies, I decided to take a short cat nap. Unfortunately, a loud knock at the door prematurely woke me from a lusty dream.

I sprung out of bed to open the door, and to my surprise it was Christos, wearing a tight black T-shirt, shorts, and running shoes. "Oh, sorry, Viola. Did I wake you?"

"Actually, I'm glad you interrupted, I was in the middle of a really messy three-way with George Clooney and a cheeseburger… What's up?"

"I was just wondering if you wanted to go for a late-evening jog."

Of course, my answer was yes; I didn't have to think twice. But I would be lying if I said I didn't have a motive. I had to find out more about Helena and what exactly happened between her and Christos.

Regretting my laziness to do a load of laundry last week, I was forced to slip into a dirty pair of jogging pants. I grabbed my phone off the bed and slipped it into my pocket before meeting Christos on the porch. I was restraining myself from texting the guild, as I didn't want to interrupt their Thanksgiving dinner, but boy was I ever tempted as there were like a thousand text messages from Shaniqua. I figured she just wanted to wish me happy birthday.

Yes, it was my 30th birthday. So why wasn't I celebrating and surrounded by friends? The truth was that I wasn't very big on birthdays; I have always kept it on the down low. I guess I got used to spending them quiet and alone, as Franklin was usually working.

"Hey, Viola, beautiful night for a run, huh?" Christos said, bending over to stretch.

"I love it. This is the perfect weather to go bra-less."

Christos laughed. "Ready?"

"Let's do it," I said, jogging closely beside Christos.

After five minutes of small talk I was ready to ask Christos the million-dollar question. "So... you were engaged?"

Christos came to a halt and started walking. "Yeah, I was. I don't usually talk about it, but you already know the ending, so I will tell you whatever you want to know."

"Who was Helena?" It was just me, Christos, and a bunch of questions. Thankfully there were no distractions as it was too dark outside.

"Helena was the last and only girl I fell madly in love with. My sisters hated her as she was a little controlling."

"Did that bother you?"

"No, not at all, actually. I had my hands full with helping at the house, and work, that I didn't mind having somebody tell me what to do. It was kind of a nice break."

My jaw dropped and I gasped mockingly. "Is Christos a little submissive?"

Christos laughed. "For the record, Ms. Ginamero, I'm versatile."

I burst out laughing. "Oh my, I'm clearly becoming a bad influence on you."

Christos smiled warmly and flirtatiously bumped his shoulder into mine. "Okay, what's your next question?"

"So you guys eventually got engaged, you were madly in love with her, I'm sure she felt the same way, the wedding day comes, and then what happened?"

"She never showed up. I stood alone at the altar for forty minutes before her sister announced that Helena wasn't coming. I begged her sister to tell me why, but she wouldn't reveal what Helena texted her.

To this day I have no clue as to why she never showed. The whole thing feels incomplete, you know what I mean?"

I knew exactly how he felt. I'd felt the same way about how Franklin left things with me. I was done prying into Christos' past. "Let's head back. I just remembered that I left a protein bar in my gym bag and I need to rescue it before it tastes like a foot."

Christos laughed. "All right, race you back!"

After a quick shower and tossing back a mint-chocolate protein shake, I was more than ready for bed. Unexpectedly, just as I slipped into my good pajamas—the ones with the hole in the crotch—a gentle knock came from the door.

I foolishly walked up to answer the door, assuming Zeta was behind it. "Zeta? If that's you, do you have any deodorant I could borrow?" I swung it open to discover Christos behind it, one arm was mysteriously behind his back.

Christos smiled. "I have an unopened extra stick of deodorant if you're interested."

"Well I suppose I should take you up on the offer. I don't want to use bathroom freshener—that tends to irritate my skin."

Christos laughed. "I know it's late, but I have something for you." He swung his hand out in front of him, revealing a single chocolate cupcake lit with a candle. "Happy Birthday, Viola."

I jumped back in shock. "How did you know? Come in, come in. Did Shaniqua tell you?"

"No, I just made a note of it from your registration form." Christos gently placed the cupcake in my hands. "It's a protein cupcake, but I promise it tastes as good as the real thing."

I smiled warmly. "Aww, thank you." I don't know what was causing it, but I could feel my heart racing and my libido kicking into high gear. Was I falling for Christos? Or was it the sweet scent of the cupcake under my nose? Either way, I was feeling an attraction I hadn't before. To restrain myself from jumping his sexy bones, I took a step back.

He slowly inched closer to me. "Want a bite?" I asked nervously. We could both feel what was happening—the sexual energy was intoxicating. Without talking about what was happening, we could both feel a magnetic pull towards each other.

He leaned in and replied with the sweetest, most elegant, and sexiest six words that would make a girl like me melt. "No, thanks. Protein makes me gassy."

I grabbed the back of his head and pressed his lips fiercely into mine, sliding my tongue along his, tasting chocolate protein.

Christos stopped to ask, "Are you sure you want to do this?"

I didn't know what was coming over me, but I wanted him more than anything. I pushed him against the door and slid his shirt off, dropping to my knees to kiss his tight and firm abs with my moist lips.

He lifted me into the air as I wrapped my legs tightly around his waist, continuing to kiss his warm neck. From his gentle moans, I could tell he was loving it.

I slipped off my shirt and flung it across the room as we collapsed onto the bed.

Wait, why am I telling you all this? I'll just skip ahead.

If I could describe the last fourteen minutes in one word it would be: fireworks. That is all, just fireworks.

What I didn't expect was that the most shocking moment of the night was about to come as we were lying down. Moments before I fell asleep, Christos wrapped his arms around me and pulled me tightly against his naked, sweaty body and whispered into my ear, "I think... I think I'm falling in love with you, Viola."

Entering panic mode, I closed my eyes forcefully, pretending to be asleep. Thankfully, I was facing away from him, which allowed me to fake-snore for realistic effect.

Luckily, it didn't take too long before I actually fell asleep, with Christos gently pressing his hand against my bare breast. I admit, it was nice. I felt safe, warm, and loved.

Of course, I didn't feel the same way as Christos, but was loving him a possibility? Who knew? I used to hate eating hummus, now I bury my head in it like it's a trough.

Chapter Fifteen

184 Lbs

November 25, 2016

On any typical morning the first thing I opened my eyes to was my potato clock, so you can imagine that I was stunned to wake up the next morning to Christos's eyes gazing into mine. Quickly covering up my face, I yelled, "Don't look at me! I look like crap!" I aggressively pulled the bedsheet over my face.

"Viola, you're beautiful," said Christos.

"You clearly didn't see the trail of drool going down my neck, and don't get me started on my morning breath. I've been told it's a cross between sewage and blue cheese."

He gently pulled the sheet off my face, leaned in and softly kissed my lips. "Like I said… you're beautiful."

After a few minutes of staring at each other, Christos sprung out of bed. "How 'bout some protein pancakes?"

I smiled. "That sounds lovely. I'll be right down." He bent down to kiss my forehead and ran out of the room full of energy and excitement.

I rolled onto my side and swiped my phone off the end table. "All right, time to catch up on some text messages," I said to myself. Among just over thirty text messages, there were several missed calls from Shaniqua. Suddenly I felt very nervous. It was that feeling you get when your intuition kicks in that something is really wrong and a lot of anxiety and stress is about to come your way.

Most of the messages were in regards to her wondering where I was as I hadn't told her I was staying with Christos's family. I was fairly calm until I started listening to my voicemail, where Shan was yelling so much I couldn't understand the message. All I could decipher was that it was something about Franklin, and then of course my phone died.

There was a knock at the door, followed by Zeta poking her head in. "Good morning, Viola. Umm, somebody is waiting for you downstairs."

"Really? That's odd. Nobody knows I'm here. I'll be right down Zeta." I tossed my phone aside and quickly got dressed, thinking that Christos had a romantic surprise waiting for me downstairs.

As I made my way towards the stairs I could smell the sweet aroma of pancakes in the air. I grabbed onto the railing, closed my eyes, and took a deep breath when all of a sudden I was interrupted by a familiar voice.

"*Franklin?*" I said, tripping on the last step of the staircase. He was dressed in a suit and tie, holding a red box. Lina was standing next to him with her arms crossed against her chest, walking away the second I entered the room. "Franklin, what are you doing here? How did you know I was here?"

Franklin was breathing heavily, as if he just ran around the block. "First I called Shaniqua, and she said you were at your parents' house. I checked there and nobody was home, so I called your mom, and she gave me this address. Viola, I have to talk to you."

"This couldn't wait until I got back home? Or at least till I used the bathroom?"

Franklin shook his head. "Viola, it took me a long time to realize how special you are to me. I clearly took you for granted and I am here to make up for it."

Confused and hungry, I said, "Are you... are you saying you want to date me again?"

"No." Franklin dropped to one knee and opened up the lid to the red box, which revealed what looked like an engagement ring. "I want you to be my wife."

Stunned by Franklin's proposal, the last twenty-four hours suddenly vanished from my thoughts.

"Yes! Yes, I will be your wife!" I said, jumping into his arms.

Franklin removed the ring from the box and placed it on my finger. A lot of things felt muddled, but one thing was clear: I, Viola Ginamero, was getting married to the man I was destined to be with.

"Viola, how quickly can you get packed? If we leave now we can make it back to the city by lunch."

I was too distracted by the glare from the diamond to respond coherently. "Umm, okay, dinner. Yeah, let's do it."

"I'll wait in the car," Franklin said, walking out the door.

I closed the door as Franklin left. "Oh my God, I'm getting married... I'm getting married," I said to myself, turning around to see Christos holding two plates of pancakes.

In complete silence, we stared at each other from opposite ends of the room. I will never forget the look on his face—a cross between sorrow and humiliation.

I wanted to run up to him and tell him that his friendship meant a lot to me, that last night was incredible, that I was thankful to him for showing me how a lady should be treated and that his true love was out there, but I didn't do any of that. After a few seconds of silence, I slowly took a few steps back and walked up the stairs while maintaining full eye contact with Christos.

With my baggage in hand, I made my way downstairs, where Lina was waiting for me at the door.

Leaning in for a hug, I said, "Thank you so much for your hospitality. I would love to visit sometime again." She leaned away as if I had a pungent body odor.

She took a deep breath, then leaned in, glaring. "You are not welcome in this house ever again. You're not welcome into our *lives* ever again, and most importantly I am going to make damn sure that you're not welcome into Christos's heart ever again." She swung the door open. "Now get out of my house."

Walking out the door, I quickly turned around. "Tell the girls I said goodby—" The door slammed on my face before I could finish my sentence.

I could understand Lina's anger; I can't say she didn't warn me. She told me that Christos was more fragile than he let on and that she was going to protect him from the damage Helena caused. I only hoped that Christos understood why I did what I did. I mean, how could he not?

The drive back to the city illuminated two things: Franklin hadn't changed one bit and I had a shiny rock on my finger.

"You're quiet," Franklin said, glancing quickly in my direction. My head was resting against the passenger window. I was drowning in thoughts and not in the mood to talk.

"I'm just tired. I missed both my morning protein shake and breakfast. Meals are super important in the fitness world."

"You're still doing that? You look great now, just quit."

"Umm, yes I'm still doing it. It's a lifestyle, Franklin, not a bad television series that I fall behind on and eventually lose interest in."

"All I'm saying is that you're getting married. You're going to be busy with planning."

I turned and gave Franklin a look of disgust. "You're not going to help?"

Franklin laughed. "Viola, come on, I'm a doctor now. I don't have time for planning a wedding. Just take my credit card and be reasonable."

A bit annoyed, I turned my head and laid my head on the window again until I eventually fell asleep.

When we reached my place, I woke up with a sore neck and a bit of nausea.

"We're here, Viola. You don't need help with your bags, do you? I'm kind of in a hurry, and it's almost noon."

I rubbed my eyes, trying to comprehend where we were. "You're not coming in?"

"I have a lot of work to do. Maybe I'll come see you later." I grabbed my bag from the backseat.

"All right. Bye, Franklin," I said, leaning in for a kiss.

Franklin backed away. "No thanks, you still have morning breath."

"Okay, well… have a good day, Franklin," I replied, exiting the car.

Just my luck, the elevator was broken, and I was forced to drag my bag up the stairwell. However, there was a bright side at the end of the tunnel: I was excited to see the guild.

When I reached my door, it was quiet. I sighed in disappointment and opened the door.

"Surprise!" yelled the guild before I even got a chance to open the door fully. Shaniqua, Vik, Barbara-Anne, and Remy rushed at me with a birthday hat.

Shaniqua wrapped her arms around me. "I have two things to tell you. The first this is, bitch, how come you don't answer your phone? The second, happy birthday, girl!"

I was completely taken in. "Oh my God, you guys surprised the hell outta me. I think I peed a little."

"I gotta admit," said Vik. "I missed your silly wit."

"Oh, I'm not joking. Franklin refused to make any pit stops on the way here. My bladder is about to explode."

Suddenly Shaniqua aggressively grabbed my hand, noticing the ring on my finger. "What's that? Did you get this off Craigslist?"

"Come on, Shan, you of all people should know that I only use Craigslist for birth control. Franklin proposed!" I jumped up and down like a child.

Barbara-Anne hugged me. "Congratulations, my dear! Now you won't have to die alone."

"Wait a minute," Vik said. "When did you guys get back together?"

"Duh, you're not listening, Vik," said Remy. "She met him on Craigslist when she went to pick up the birth control. Go on, Viola, some of us are paying attention."

I raised my hand into the air to watch the diamond sparkle. "Well, he showed up this morning with a ring out of the blue and just asked."

Shaniqua looked at me in confusion. "What did your parents say?"

"Oh, they don't know yet. They're in Mexico."

Vik walked towards the kitchen to pour a glass of water. "So you were at your parents' house all alone?"

"No, I was with Christos."

Vik started choking on his water. "You and Christos spent Thanksgiving together at your parents place?"

"No, I spent it with his family. You guys are totally missing the point. I'm engaged! Break out the flutes! Momma wants some sparking wine."

"I don't think we have any," said Vik.

"Oh, yes, we do. It's hidden under the sink marked as poison."

"So let me get this straight," Shaniqua said. She took a deep breath and exhaled, giving me a dirty look. "Franklin proposed to you after he found out you were staying at Christos's place for Thanksgiving?"

"Yeah, so what, Shan? I'm confused."

"Girl, I have three words for you."

I smiled cheerfully. "I love you?"

"You're a fool!" Shaniqua barked.

"Technically that's four words," said Vik. "The you and are make up the you're." Shaniqua turned around and gave Vik a glare. "Hey, I'm on your side. He is playing you, Viola."

Barbara-Anne grabbed my arm. "Don't listen to them, he loves you and wants to be with you. Why else would he propose?"

"On the farm I once witnessed a goat proposing to a chicken," said Remy.

Silence and confusion filled the room.

I broke the silence. "Barbara-Anne is right. He proposed because he wants to be with me, let's end the argument there and start partying!" I threw my hands in the air and danced as if we were in a club.

Vik scrunched up his face at me. "Viola, what the hell are you doing?"

"I'm dancing! Join me!" I waved my arms in the air, twirling on my tippy toes.

"Viola, your dancing is as graceful as a free-range chicken."

"Awww, thank you, Vik."

It was clear that Shaniqua was not impressed by my acceptance of Franklin's proposal, but just like my black lipstick phase, she had no choice but to suck it up and respect my decision.

The day was filled with fun, laughter, and lots of chatter. I couldn't remember the last time I'd enjoyed being surrounded by a group of individuals who cared so deeply for me. But all the distraction still wasn't enough to keep me from thinking about how things were left with Christos. I figured that we would talk about it at the next group workout session. I was wrong.

Typically, birthday celebrations are filled with shots. Mine, however, was filled with something much more different. Shaniqua yelled from the kitchen, "All right, guys, come and get it."

We gathered in the kitchen with shaker cups as Shaniqua poured a finely blended amino and Vodka mixture into each cup.

Vik raised his cup. "What should we toast to?"

Barbara-Anne raised hers as well. "Let's toast to Viola and Franklin on their engagement, but before we do that I just wanted to say that I won't be around as long as you guys, so I want you all to know that I love you and I think of the four of you as the children I didn't have."

I leaned into Barbara-Anne. "Aww, you're going to make me cry. You're going to outlast all of us, just watch and see."

"How many shots has Barbara-Anne had?" Shaniqua asked.

Vik raised his cup. "We love you, too, Barbara-Anne. To Viola and Franklin on their engagement."

Shaniqua added, "Hey, where's Christos?" I looked away, biting my wet lips. "He was supposed to be here."

I wasn't very good at keeping secrets from Shaniqua, and the fact that she didn't know the whole truth was killing me.

Several hours later, while the guild was watching viral videos on YouTube, I was able to sneak Shaniqua into my bedroom for a very confidential conversation.

"Viola, what are we doing in here? You're not going to show me your body hair again, are you? I told you already, just wax it or shave it."

"I slept with Christos," I blurted out, covering my mouth with my hands.

"*What*? When?" Shaniqua's eyes looked as if they were about to roll out of their sockets.

Biting my lips, I said, "Umm... last night."

"Girl, why didn't you tell me earlier? Does Franklin know?"

I shook my head in silence. "He showed up the next morning without any warning."

"Girl, I left you several messages!"

"Shan, keep it down, the guild will hear you."

"It's too late." I turned around to see the door cracked open with Vik poking his head in. "Don't worry, it's just me." I motioned quickly with my hand for Vik to come in.

Vik plopped himself down on the bed. "How did Christos take the news of engagement?"

"I don't know... he witnessed the proposal and we just parted ways."

Vik shook his head. "You're a heartbreaker, Viola."

"Hey, I am known for breaking wind, not hearts."

"Girl, you need to go talk to Christos!" Shaniqua yelled.

"Shh! The rest of the guild will hear you."

Vik leaped off the bed and walked towards the door. "Actually, I lied; I wasn't the only one eavesdropping." He swung open the door as Remy and Barbara-Anne entered the room.

Barbara-Anne pointed at me. "You need to tell Franklin about you and Christos right now."

"I agree with Barbara-Anne," said Shaniqua. "End the engagement and go be with Christos."

"No, don't do that!" said Barbara-Anne. "Just go tell him what happened. You can't start a marriage on a lie."

I dramatically flopped onto the bed. "I don't know what to do. This is painful."

Remy sat down beside me to offer support. "I know how you feel, Viola. I once dreamt that I gave a birth to the Easter bunny, and there was chocolate everywhere."

"I have an idea," said Vik. "Why don't we hit the pause button and move this party somewhere else, where you don't have to think about either man."

Leaping up off the bed, I smiled gleefully. "Let's do it!"

After an hour of debating on where to go, we settled on a gay nightclub on the west side of town. The five of us were extremely excited and were ready to let loose after all the hard work we had put in.

The five of us hopped out of our Uber, and I cheerfully clapped as we walked to the back of the line. "I'm so excited! I've never been to a gay club before!"

I admit I was a little drunk, but not drunk-girl drunk; more like in-control-buzz drunk. I stopped in my tracks to initiate a group hug. "Can I just say how much I love you guys, and I am so glad that I was fat and that you all came into my life." Okay, maybe I was drunk-girl drunk.

Shaniqua broke out of the hug. "Viola, you need to watch your drinking in there. Remember the last club incident?"

"So I got a little sick? Everyone does."

"You vomited on the dance floor, and a girl slipped and was carried off on a stretcher."

"That's why I carry a bottle," said Remy.

"It's okay," said Barbara-Anne. "I will keep an eye out on you guys. And how about you all spend the night at my place? I live close by."

Tearing up a little, I wrapped my arms around Barbara-Anne. "I love you so much! You're my favorite guild member, but don't tell the guild that, they will get jealous." I followed up with a burp into her ear. "Oops, sorry."

"We can hear you, Viola," said Vik.

Placing a finger on Barbara-Anne's lips, I whispered, "Shh… they can hear you."

After I strutted through security, and the guild picked me up off the floor after I fell down a short flight of stairs, we were greeted with loud bass, darkness, and a lot of people dancing to a mashup of top-forty pop songs.

The blaring music was drowning my hearing, and I could barely hear what Vik was saying. I nodded anyway. Now that I think back, I think he was saying something about my shoe. Realizing I had to get the guild up to my level of drunkenness, I ran up to the nearest bar.

"Five shots of tequila!" I couldn't help but dance as I watched the shirtless bartender pour the liquor.

Shaniqua tapped my shoulder. "Girl, I'm cutting you off after this." I stuck my tongue out like a child as I distributed the five shots to the guild.

I quickly noticed that we had one unclaimed shot glass. "Hey, where's Barbara-Anne?"

Vik pointed at the dance floor, where Barbara-Anne was dancing like a frat girl, sandwiched between two men. "That woman is my hero."

"To Barbara-Anne!" I shouted, pouring both mine and her shot into my mouth. The four of us cringed as we placed the empty glasses back on the bar. "Who's ready to dance?"

As the night went on, the five of us remained glued to the dance floor. A highlight was watching Shaniqua twerk in the middle of a dance off with Remy. Who knew Remy had the moves? That was the first of three surprises of the night. The third surprise was the most pivotal moment in my life. I will get to that later.

Suddenly the music fell silent and an announcer came on the mic. "If anyone is looking for a red high heel, it's at the bar."

I looked at Vik and frowned. "Ugh, clearly some cheap drunk girl does not know how to hold her liquor. Like, come on, girl, have some class."

"Viola," said Vik, "look at your feet."

"Oh no! I lost mine, too! I bet that cheap drunk girl took it." Crawling up onto a nearby table, I began hollering and waving at the crowd. "Can I please have everyone's attention! My shoe is also missing! If you see it, please return it to my foot!"

I slipped off the table and tumbled head-first onto the floor. A tall drag queen came to my rescue. "Honey, are you okay?"

I crawled towards her, and she kneeled down to help me up.

"Yes," I said, "but I think I'm gonna be sick." Then I vomited all over her dress. Needless to say, the entire dance floor cleared faster than when I backed up the toilet at IHOP.

The rest of the night was spent gripping onto a toilet seat in Barbara-Anne's bathroom, while the guild took turns holding my hair back as I did my thing into the bowl. Despite the gross circumstances, they really proved how much they cared for me, that was surprise number two.

After an hour, I was able to walk out of the bathroom without the assistance of a wall. I couldn't help but feel guilty; it was my first time in Barbara-Anne's beautiful home, and I was spending it bouncing off the walls. Luckily most of the alcohol was out of my system by the time I joined the guild in the dining room.

Barbara-Anne pulled out a chair. "Have a seat, Viola. How are you feeling?"

"A little foggy, but I think I'm okay."

Shaniqua walked in with six plates, placing them down on the table.

Vik was playing on his phone. "Is it already ready? I thought it needed more time."

Confused, I asked, "What's going on?"

Then Remy walked in with a brightly lit birthday cake as the guild started singing 'Happy Birthday' to me. Looking at the beautiful ice-cream cake, I was full of sentimental emotion. And nausea.

Barbara-Anne clapped her hands enthusiastically. "Home-made low-fat, sugar-free, ice-cream cake."

"We made it while you were in Jersey," said Remy.

I nearly teared up. "Oh, you guys are the best! I'm so sorry I ruined your night."

"Stop right there!" said Vik. "First of all, that shirt you're wearing looks so cheap that it belongs on the McDonald's dollar menu, and second of all, we all had an amazing time tonight."

Remy placed a small piece of cake on my plate. "It's true, Viola, and the men were so friendly. Some of them kept inviting me over to their place to play. I assume they meant video games."

Smiling at Remy, I noticed for the second time that a sixth plate was placed down. "Who is that plate for?"

The guild looked at Barbara-Anne as if they wanted her to explain. She gently placed her hand over mine. "It's for my late husband, dear. On special occasions like Thanksgiving or birthdays, I put a plate out for him. It makes me feel like he is with us." She laughed nervously. "Viola, you probably think I'm crazy."

"I think that's beautiful," I said. "Do you think he would mind low-fat, sugar-free ice-cream cake?"

Barbara-Anne laughed. "I could have put a shoe in front of him and he would have eaten it."

"I once choked on a flip flop," added Remy.

Sitting back in my chair, I quietly listened to the amusing back-and-forth chatter of the guild. I couldn't help but smile. For the first time in my life, I felt like I was surrounded by family.

It was just after midnight, and I needed some fresh air after feeling a second wind of nausea. I made my way to the porch swing while Vik gave the guild makeovers in preparation for a lip-sync video upload.

Swinging gently, I stared up into the starry sky, wondering what Christos was doing and if he was still hurt.

Barbara-Anne walked onto the porch. "Mind if I join you, dear? Vik's idea of a makeover is making me look like a prostitute."

I laughed. "Of course!" Shimmying down to make room, I couldn't help but blurt out, "I think I made a big mistake."

"What mistake is that?"

"I can't stop thinking about him."

"Franklin?"

Feeling a need for comfort, I lowered my head onto her lap like a child. She gently stroked my hair, "I can't stop thinking about Christos... I think I love him." The third surprise of the night.

"Viola, I had cold feet on the day of my wedding. I, too, was in love with two men, thankfully my mother was there to help me out. Do you want to know what she said?"

I nodded quietly.

"Close your eyes, I want you to imagine that you're in a nursery, holding a beautiful baby girl in your arms way past her bedtime. You tell her all about her father, how the two of you met and fell in love. After a while when she finally falls asleep, you gently lay her down in the crib. As you watch her, the door opens with the father entering to give you a warm hug from the back, and you both watch your little girl sleep. Viola, whoever you imagined as the father is one you desire to be with. Do you know who that is?"

Slowly opening my eyes, I turned onto my back. "Thank you, Barbara-Anne... I do." I rolled back onto my side as she continued to stroke my hair. I wanted to bask in her motherly love for the rest of the night; that night made it clear that she was the mother I wish I had. "Your mother sounded very wise."

"Oh, she was, and she was very crafty as well, she taught me how to crochet beautiful afghans."

"I've always wanted to learn how to crochet. I feel like it would be a productive way to kill time on the toilet."

Barbara-Anne laughed. "Well, come over tomorrow evening, after our guild training, and I can teach you."

"It's a deal!" I said cheerfully.

Resting comfortably on her motherly lap and listening to the gentle hum of cars driving by, I slowly fell asleep.

I woke up at some point in the middle of the night, quickly realizing that Barbara-Anne had fallen asleep on the bench with me. Feeling concerned about her comfort, I carefully escorted her back into the house and upstairs to her bedroom.

After gently covering her up with a blanket, I quietly tiptoed out of the room, whispering, "Good night, Barbara-Anne."

I found the rest of the guild members passed out in the living room, sleeping like babies. Feeling a bit cold, I placed blankets over the three of them. Wide awake and unable to sleep, I decided to take an Uber home to get a few hours of shut eye and to wash the smell of vomit out of my hair.

The following morning, I rose out of bed with a great big smile on my face. If there was ever a time that singing birds were to land on my shoulder, it would be now. Looking back, why was I afraid of turning thirty? I looked and felt fantastic. Everything was going so right, what could possibly go wrong?

After a quick shower, breakfast, and a poorly mixed protein shake, I was out the door and ready to meet the guild at the gym for our morning HIIT cardio. Secretly, I was also hoping I could catch Christos at the gym, as he wasn't replying to any of my text messages.

I arrived at The Fitness Hut safely. I only say that because during the drive I was belting out Beyoncé's latest single so enthusiastically that I drove through a red light. Note to self: work on distracted driving… and hitting those high notes.

Noticing that the guild was nowhere in sight, I dropped off my bags at The Protein Hut and made my way to the locker room. I couldn't help but hum and make annoying sounds with my mouth. I was full of so much energy and I hadn't even had my aminos yet!

Forgetting to put deodorant on at home, I lathered and rubbed some soap under my armpits, followed by a quick filing of my nails with the rusty zipper in my jeans.

I made my way to the training room where, to my surprise, I saw Shaniqua, Remy, and Vik somberly sitting in a corner. The second they saw me their faces went blank, and proceeded to make awkward glances at each other as if they were hiding a secret.

Smiling warmly, I cheerfully shouted, "Good morning, guys! Where's Barbara-Anne?"

After a few seconds of silence, Shaniqua finally broke the news to me.

"Barbara-Anne passed away this morning."

Chapter Sixteen

183 Lbs

November 26, 2016

There were two times in my entire life when I completely shut down and kept to myself quietly for the entire day. The first was when my parents sat me down and told me they were getting divorced. The second was the day Barbara-Anne passed away.

"We found her unconscious in her bed this morning."

I crossed my arms against my rapidly beating chest and sat down beside Remy.

"Did anyone tell Christos?" asked Remy.

"I called," said Vik, "there was no answer."

Remy rose to his feet, looking at Vik. "What happened?"

Vik shrugged. "I don't know; the paramedics spoke with Shaniqua." Remy and Vik looked at Shaniqua in hope of a comforting answer.

"It was probably her heart," Shaniqua said.

Remy scratched his head. "Couldn't they save her?"

Shaniqua shook her head. "It was too late. And they found a DNR document on file."

Confused, Remy asked, "DNR?"

"Do not resuscitate," said Shaniqua.

The training room fell silent for several minutes; all that could be heard was the sound of treadmills and clanging barbells on the other side of the door.

Vik broke the silence. "What was that paper for?"

Shaniqua, dazed and confused, said, "What paper?" I could tell she was trying to keep it together.

"When the mortuary picked up her body, they give you piece of paper," said Vik. I couldn't bear to listen to anymore, so I switched my focus to staring at the patrons working out outside the room.

"It was a checklist of what to do when a loved one dies," she said.

"Shouldn't we give it to a friend or family member of hers?" said Remy.

"She didn't have anyone in her life," said Vik.

"That's not true," said Shaniqua. "She had us."

Vik followed Shaniqua to her bag, and she pulled out the list. "Where should we start?"

Shaniqua scanned the checklist for several seconds. "The first thing on the list is to get a legal pronouncement of death."

Vik leaned over her shoulder to read the list. "Didn't the paramedic already do that?"

"I think so. The next thing is to arrange for the body to get picked up if no autopsy is required… We did that already, too."

Vik read off the next item. "We need to inform her doctor… How do we do that?"

"She had some bottles of medication by her bed," said Remy. "Her doctor's name is probably on them."

"Good idea," said Vik. "We have to head back to her house anyways to clean out the fridge and freezer. What else is on the list?"

"There is a lot," said Shaniqua. "But we got this. We need to inform her past employer, arrange for her funeral and burial or cremation, cancel her mail, obtain the death certificate, etc."

Vik bent down to grab his bag. "Well, let's get started. Meet you at her house?"

Shaniqua nodded and then looked in my direction. "Coming, Viola?"

Thirty minutes later, I met the guild at Barbara-Anne's house, and it felt like the longest drive of my life. Confused and distracted, I had trouble following the GPS and people behind me kept honking as I couldn't stay in my lane.

When I came to a stop in front of her house, I was extremely relieved to step away from the car, but the second my eye caught the porch bench, any sense of relief was gone.

I couldn't stop thinking about how my head had rested on her lap just eight hours ago.

"Oh, good, you're here, Viola," Vik said, holding on to a large box of frozen food. "We need your help finding some documents."

After staring at the bench for a few more seconds, I proceeded quietly into the house and stood in the corner.

Shaniqua entered the living room with a large empty box. "Hey, Viola, can you look for Barbara-Anne's birth certificate and marriage certificate? It might be upstairs."

Remy popped up behind me, holding on to a tote. "What should Vik and I do with all this food?"

"I just got off the phone with the food bank," said Shaniqua. "They will take it, but it has to be dropped off right now."

"All right, we're on it."

As Vik and Remy left the house, I began my ascent up the wooden staircase. My heart skipped a beat with every step I took towards the bedroom.

I looked in, imagining Barbara-Anne's lifeless body under the scattered blanket. My thoughts grew wilder, thinking about how the mortuary carried her body out of the room or what kind of pain Barbara-Anne felt the moment her heart gave in.

Suddenly I felt nauseous and desperately needed air. I raced down the stairs and bolted towards the front door.

After a couple deep breaths and closing my eyes for a minute, I walked to my car and drove away.

Exhausted and desperate for the day to be over, I turned off my phone the second I entered my apartment.

It was tough to fall asleep—the afternoon sun kept me awake while my thoughts forced me to toss and turn. When I did finally fall asleep, a loud door slam woke me up.

"Get your ass out of bed!" Shaniqua shouted, bursting into my bedroom. "We needed your help, and you bailed!"

Vik stepped in from behind. "It's okay."

"No, it's not okay!" Shaniqua ripped the blanket off of me. "Viola, she's dead! You have to accept that and move on!" She stopped to take a deep breath. "Get your shit together and meet us back at the house in thirty minutes."

I quietly hugged my knees as Shaniqua stomped out of the room. I could hear faint yelling as she made her way to the door.

Feeling guilty, I forced myself into the bathroom, undressed, and stepped under the warm showerhead.

As I closed my eyes and soaked my hair under the warm water, a wave of emotions rushed over me. It started with a quivering mouth and led to teary eyes. Before I knew it, I was crying uncontrollably into the palm of my hands.

Chapter Seventeen

❶❽❶ Lbs

November 27, 2016

We arrived back from Barbara-Anne's house after giving the house a good cleaning and collecting all the documents on the checklist.

Slipping on some worn clothing, the guild and I regrouped in the kitchen for breakfast.

"Good morning, Viola!" said Remy.

I smiled half-heartedly. "Mornin'." Shaniqua was making protein waffles while Vik was playing on his phone.

Vik slipped his phone into his pocket. "I never realized how passive aggressive you could be. You didn't say a word yesterday."

"I choose to be aggressive instead," I said. "Remember that time I got assaulted at Payless with a flip flop? That little girl didn't see the swing of my purse coming at her."

Vik laughed, looking around at the others. "Guys, Viola is back."

Remy sat down beside me. "Have we heard back from the funeral home yet?"

Shaniqua turned around, sliding waffles onto my well-used plate. "Not yet, they're searching."

Confused, I asked, "What's this now?"

Vik got up to fetch a bottle of Protein Power. "Barbara-Anne wanted her burial to be next to her husband."

"That's great. What's the issue?"

"We don't where he was laid to rest," said Shaniqua.

"Has anyone tried Google Maps?" asked Remy. "I once forgot where I parked my car and it helped me locate it."

"Umm, Remy, you do know that there is a time lapse, right?" said Vik.

Remy's mouth hung open. "Ohh! That explains why my house had a for sale sign on it."

Vik turned to me. "Anyways, we still have a lot of work to do, and that marathon that Christos signed us up for is right around the corner."

With some delicious waffle scooped into my, I asked, "Are we still doing that?"

Shaniqua paced around the kitchen, shaking her protein shake. "Hell yeah! We haven't been working out this hard and eating this clean for nothing."

She wasn't wrong, the marathon was the motivation we needed to keep us consistent with our intense six days a week workout program.

Raising up off my seat, I gently touched Shaniqua's shoulder. "Thanks for knocking some sense into me last night. I haven't cried that much since Will's death on *The Good Wife*."

"Girl, you know I got you. Should you ever need a smack, I'm here."

I smiled warmly. "Aww, that's so sweet."

"Where is Christos?" asked Remy. "I haven't heard from him since Thanksgiving."

Vik puckered his lips and looked in my direction. "Maybe seeing Viola naked scared him off."

I quickly stuck my finger in Vik's face. "Hey! I once posted a bikini photo to Facebook that got 600 likes."

Shaniqua grabbed my empty plate. "Wasn't that a nip slip photo?"

I rolled my eyes. "You're so missing the point."

When I arrived at the gym after eating Shaniqua's delicious waffles, I was surprised to see the group huddled around Janette instead of on the treadmills. Something was clearly wrong and I was moments away from finding out.

"What do you mean he *quit*?" Shaniqua said, dropping her bag onto the floor as if she was ready for battle.

"Okay you guys need to open your ears and listen carefully cause I'm only saying this once." She took a deep breath. "He came in one day, grabbed his things, and vanished. At the moment, we don't have a replacement trainer and I'm not sure how refunds will work under new management."

"Wait," I said, "what about new management?"

Janette huffed. "Ugh, don't you guys read your e-mails? The gym was sold. Rumor has it that it's going full closure." She looked at me condescendingly. "Look on the bright side, Viola, with unemployment you can focus on making money from your little YouTube videos."

With my hands tightly on my hips, I said, "Okay, first of all, your attitude is more disgusting than a plate of Denny's sliders. And second of all, the joke's on you cause I don't make any money from my videos."

She flipped her hair and walked away from the desk.

Vik rubbed his forehead anxiously. "Guys, what are we going to do?"

That was clearly the million-dollar question as we had no trainer, a funeral to plan, the gym was soon to be closed, and we had a marathon to run. Was there something else I was forgetting? Oh yeah! I was getting married to Franklin and had a wedding to plan.

I guess that slipped my mind.

We carried on with our planned HIIT cardio workout, but a lack of motivation was looming above our treadmills. Well, that and a rickety ceiling fan that we bet would fall on somebody's head at some point during the year. My guess was December.

During my mid-morning snack, I was summoned to the training room.

Chewing a protein bar, I walked into the room. "What's up? Remy said you guys were looking for me."

"Not sure myself," said Vik. "Shaniqua just grabbed me."

Shaniqua stretched out her neck. "We have a serious issue that needs to be addressed."

"If you're referring to Viola's broccoli farts," said Vik. "I agree."

"Umm, how can any reminder to eat your veggies be an issue?" I asked.

"Shut it, you two!" said Shaniqua. "We are not ready for the marathon and without a trainer we won't make it past the halfway point. I suggest we drop out."

"I can lick my elbow," offered Remy.

Vik turned to Remy in confusion. "That comment was as pointless as an Arby's sandwich, but I agree that we aren't ready."

Shaniqua looked at me, anticipating my thoughts. "Do you have anything to add, Viola?"

I inhaled deeply and looked up at the ceiling. "I've seen Remy lick his elbow, it's very impressive."

"Viola!"

"Fine. Let's quit."

The word disappointed could have easily been tattooed on my forehead. The truth was that I was still up for running the marathon, but I couldn't have done it without them and their support.

That evening Shaniqua had a date—her first date since she and Shamar broke up, which left me and Vik left to entertain ourselves. Unfortunately, my movie choice on Netflix made Vik pass out on the couch.

Feeling distraught about the guild's unanimous decision to quit the marathon, I tiptoed to my bedroom to make a phone call, holding tightly onto my extremely loose pajamas.

"Come on, pick up… pick up," I whispered to myself, pacing back and forth in front of my unmade bed. There was no surprise when the call went to voicemail.

"Hey, you've reached Christos, leave a message and I'll get back to you... thanks." That was clearly a lie, as I'd left more messages on his phone than Taylor Swift's last stalker.

"Christos, it's Viola again for like the thousandth time... I don't even know if you're checking these messages, but if you are, right now the guild needs you... I need you. I'm not the same person I was before Barbara-Anne's death. Well, that's not true... I still re-use my underwear for more than a few days. Seriously, though, if you still love me I want you to call me. I'll be waiting."

"What if he doesn't call?" Vik asked, startling me half to death. His hair was a disaster from brushing it against the couch arm.

I tossed my phone onto the bed. "He'll call."

"Well, I'm going to bed. Do you need to borrow a pair of pajamas? Those are starting to look like clown pants. I have some blue ones you can borrow."

"Thanks, Vik, but I'm good. Besides, blue doesn't really suit me. I'm more of a vomit green or mucous yellow kind of girl."

Feeling a bit tired, I plugged in my phone, eagerly awaiting Christos's call, and went to bed.

Loud noises in the living room woke me up. It was Shaniqua stumbling into the apartment in the middle of the night. Dying to know how her date went, I dragged myself out of bed and moseyed over to her.

Shaniqua saw me and immediately gave her assessment. "What a loser!"

Plopping myself on the couch, I started to pry, "Not a good date?"

"The foo didn't even have a car. He picked me up in an Uber."

I chuckled. "Did dinner go okay, at least? I'm sure you had a delicious gourmet meal at a fancy restaurant, no?"

"Viola, he took me to Burger King."

I laughed even harder. "So I take it he didn't get lucky tonight."

"Viola, I haven't been with a guy in a long ass time. He got lucky twice."

Chapter Eighteen

❶❽⓪ Lbs

November 28, 2016

The following morning Shaniqua whipped out one of her magical meals as her cell phone rang loudly, interrupting an intellectual conversation I was having with Vik about the impact of human evolution on the environment and the consumption of natural resources and minerals.

Okay, that was a lie. We were arguing over whose butt was curvier: Kim Kardashian or Nicki Minaj.

Shaniqua grabbed our attention with an announcement. "That was the funeral home. They found a burial spot for Barbara-Anne and it's next to her husband."

I clapped joyously. "That's great news!"

Vik looked at Shaniqua. "So when is the funeral?"

Shaniqua tossed her phone onto the counter. "Today."

"*Today*?" I shouted. "I'm not ready! I'm still working on my photo collage and I've only barely started on my PowerPoint slideshow."

Vik rolled his eyes. "Viola, that collage is ugly."

I scoffed. "Hey, ugly can be turned beautiful."

"Viola, ugly can't be turned beautiful. This isn't Instagram."

"Has anyone heard from Christos?" Shaniqua asked.

I waved my phone in the air. "He hasn't called yet."

Shaniqua stuck her finger in my face. "You're going to be there, right?"

I made a face at her, completely offended. "Of course I am. Why on earth would you think that I wouldn't?"

"Didn't you once skip a funeral for a McDonald's breakfast special?"

"Okay, first of all, it was a wedding. And second of all, the coupon I was planning to use expired that morning."

Vik slid his phone out of his pocket. "I'll let Remy know."

The funeral was held mid-afternoon, in a beautiful and lush cemetery. I arrived to join the guild, who were standing by a large pile of dirt next to the casket, which hadn't been lowered yet.

"Is it just us?" I asked, scanning the busy cemetery. A lot of visitors tended to their deceased loved ones that day, but we were the only ones burying someone.

"It's just the four of us," Shaniqua replied.

Unfamiliar with funeral services, I could only recall what I had learned from movies and television shows. Typically, they would include a priest or somebody to officiate among a group of attendees and assigned pallbearers. Then came eulogies, prayers, poems, songs. But this was reality, and what it came down to was staring at a coffin, a pile of dirt, and the few people who truly loved you. It was perfect.

The guild quietly stared at her casket for a few minutes, absorbing the remaining energy and aura that had surrounded Barbara-Anne.

Walking over to the tall pile, Vik grabbed a handful of dirt and faced the casket. "I know you thought that the makeover I gave you made you look like a whore, but you will always be beautiful to me regardless of how whorish you look." Tearing up a little, he tossed the dirt onto the casket.

Remy was next up. "You were the only one who didn't think I was dumb, even when I led you in the wrong direction when we first met in Central Park... and that other time when we somehow ended up on the subway tracks and almost got hit by a train."

It wasn't until I saw Remy tear up that I felt a lump in my throat. Up until then I was feeling strong. Taking a deep breath, I looked over at Shaniqua and whispered, "Can you go next?"

Shaniqua walked up to the casket and gently placed her hand on it. "One day at work there was a customer giving me lip for a cold panini. I wasn't feeling good and didn't have the energy to fight back. For the first time in my life I was about to lose a battle, then suddenly a water bottle came out flying out of nowhere and hit her right in the back of the head, knocking her out cold. I never properly thanked you for doing that." She removed her hand from the casket.

It was my turn.

"Hi, Barbara-Anne, it's Viola." My mouth started to quiver, "This wasn't supposed to happen. You were supposed to play with my future kids, spoil them with birthday and Christmas gifts, and tell them all the embarrassing things her mother did, like the time I flushed my hair down the toilet, or the time I took selfies with a fedora I found on the subway and got lice."

Shaniqua walked up behind me and rubbed my shoulders. "Anyways... thanks for being a motherly figure. We know that you will continue looking down over us." Wiping tears away, I grabbed a clump of dirt and tossed it at the casket. "Goodbye, Barbara-Anne."

I grabbed Shaniqua's arm tightly, and the four of us walked away from the casket. I couldn't help but envision how disappointed Barbara-Anne would be if she found out we were dropping out of the marathon. Luckily there was still time to convince the guild to re-think their decision.

After the funeral, Remy, Vik, and myself gathered in the living room for some group bonding, which basically meant that we were each sitting apart, quietly glued to our cell phones. Shaniqua was the most productive out of all of us, as she was busy cooking up a storm in the kitchen.

"Did anyone hear anything about The Fitness Hut?" Vik mumbled.

I placed my feet up on the couch. "Nope. Let's hope the new owners keep it open."

"Oh, I just remembered something important about the gym!" said Remy.

Vik and I stared at each other for a second before I spoke. "Did you hear something?"

"No," he said. "I just remembered that I hid some chocolate bars in the toilet tank."

Vik scrunched up his face. "Why?"

"They were melting in my shoe."

I hopped off the couch. "I have an announcement to make."

"Is it that you shout out Harry Potter spells during sex?" Vik asked.

"Hey, those spells were hard to memorize! But no. I don't think we should drop out of the marathon." Shaniqua took a deep breath, holding air in her mouth. "Hear me out! Look how far we've come. Our weight loss speaks for itself. Who cares about making others proud? Let's do it for ourselves.

Vik stood up. "I don't agree with Viola's choice of hair, clothing, or shoes, but I agree with her on this. Let's do it."

Jumping up and down cheerfully, I looked at Remy. "Rem? Are you in?"

"Wait, what? We weren't planning to do the marathon?"

I quickly raced over to Shaniqua, wrapping my arms around her tightly. "Please say you're in! Please say you're in! Please say you're in!"

"Girl, get off me!" Shaniqua said, pushing me away. "And why do you smell like cheese?"

"Oh, I rubbed some gouda under my armpits this morning. It's supposed to bring luck or something. So are you in?"

"Since when are you spiritual?"

"I'm very spiritual. I take the advice of my Magic 8-Ball very seriously. So are you in?"

Shaniqua glanced at Vik and Remy. "If we do this, we are going to train our asses off, cause hell or high water, we are crossing that finish line together."

I leaped onto Shaniqua, "Thank you! Thank you! Thank you!" I turned around and addressed the group. "You know, I read that family and fulfillment are the two finest things in life."

Vik rolled his eyes. "Honey, please, the two finest things in life are Prada bags and Prince Harry."

The stage was set and all that remained was for the actors to rehearse for the big day, I for one had no doubt in my mind that we were about to achieve the biggest milestone in our lives. Was I forgetting something? Oh yeah, I suppose marrying Franklin would be another milestone too.

After creating room in his busy schedule, Franklin reserved us a table at the smuggest restaurant in Manhattan. Elements of smugness included being e-mailed instructions on how to address your waiter, table rules such as no reading off the menu, and a pronunciation guide of international foods and wines.

To help me prepare, I dragged Vik into my bedroom to make me look elegant. I was going for a cross between Julia Roberts in *Pretty Woman* and Alexis, a high-class prostitute that hung out in our back alley.

"How does this look?" I said, twirling in my off-the-rack black cocktail dress.

Vik looked with a look of horror. "Honestly, Viola, I don't think formal wear is your thing."

"Hey! I look good in formal wear. All eyes are on me when I wear my monocle and top hat on the subway."

"All I'm saying is that I don't think you will be making any best-dressed lists in that outfit."

Turning around, I modeled for the mirror. "I have potential. Did you know Viola made *People*'s Top Fifty Sexiest Names list?"

"Viola is also the name of a high-end vibrator."

I slid my phone off my dresser. "Ugh... still no call or even text message."

"Relax. Franklin will call you when he's on his way."

I bit my lip and stared at Vik for a few seconds in hopes that he could read my mind. "I'm talking about Christos."

"Christos hasn't replied to any of us. Just forget about him."

I exhaled and sat on the edge of the bed. "I've tried... I can't". I fell back into the bed. "I think I'm in love with him."

"You can't just drop a bombshell like that out of nowhere," said Vik. "You're not Beyoncé."

Covering my face with clammy hands, I asked, "What do I do?"

"Don't marry Franklin, that's what you do."

I removed my hands from my face and turned onto my side. "You don't get what it's like to be a woman. People place this pressure on you to get married, have kids, live happily ever after. And then there is this biological clock that's ticking down. I have to marry Franklin. I mean, who knows if Christos even still feels the same way anymore?"

"Viola, like that hairdo and choice of shoes, you're being ridiculous."

I leaped off the bed. "I'm being serious, Vik. I once thought I was having hot flashes. Thankfully it turned out to be food poisoning."

"Hey, Cinderella," said Shaniqua. "Your Prince Charming just arrived."

"Hey, Shan, how do I look?" I spun around like a princess.

She looked me up and down. "You look like Alexis."

"I'll take it," I said cheerfully and ran out of the room.

The second we entered the French doors, we were whisked away to our table, which was in the center of a dimly lit room. Ten wooden tables surrounded us, each of them occupied with a mix of well-dressed, middle-aged, thirty-something couples. One woman even wore a tiara, which made me a bit jealous as Vik had stopped me from wearing mine.

After we sat down, it didn't take me long to make the first mistake of the night. "Wow, this place is beautiful!" I said, grabbing a swan-folded napkin off the table.

Suddenly a tall man dressed in black swiped the napkin out of my hand and laid it down on my lap. "Good evening. Welcome to Russian Roulette. My name is Rene, and I will be your waiter this evening. Can I interest you in a bottle of wine?"

Franklin smiled. "Thank you. We'll have a bottle of your finest red." I couldn't take my eyes off Franklin's outfit.

"I love your suit. Is that the one I spilled cheesecake on?"

"No, I got this one at Bloomingdale's a while back."

Tilting my head, I smiled flirtatiously. "Well, it really brings out your eyes. So when do they bring out the menu? I'm craving chicken right now."

Franklin furrowed his brow. "There's no menu. They bring out a random dish for each person."

Confused, I looked around at the other patrons. "But what if somebody is allergic to something?"

"They have EpiPens on hand… Didn't you read the e-mail?"

I bit my lip. "I started reading it, but then it disappeared into another folder, and then I got distracted by a viral video of a seagull taking a crap on a sunbather."

"Where did it go?" Franklin asked, a bit annoyed.

"It went in her mouth; it was disgusting… you have to watch it."

"No, Viola, where did the e-mail go? Actually, never mind. So how are the wedding arrangements coming along?"

Looking away, I quickly tried to change the subject. "Oh, I think I went to school with that girl over there. Yeah! She was a cheerleader!" I threw my hands in the air. "Mel! It's me, Viola! Hey, Mel!"

Franklin turned around to examine the girl in question. "Viola, that woman is in her eighties. You haven't done any planning, have you?" He took a deep breath and leaned in. "Viola, I'm going to be out of town a lot. I don't have time to babysit you."

Rene returned to the table with the bottle of wine. As he poured it, I slid my phone out of my pocket to see if there were any missed calls or text messages. Nothing.

Taking a sip of the wine, Franklin looked at Rene and said, "It's good, thank you." He nodded his head politely, poured me a glass, and walked away.

"You're right," I said, taking a long sip. "I need to focus on wedding planning. I'll do it after the marathon, how does that sound?"

"Wait a minute, I thought you quit?"

I gasped cheerfully. "Didn't I tell you? I convinced the guild to stay in the marathon. We start training tomorrow."

"That doesn't sound like you, you always quit. You're a quitter. I don't even think you will make it to the end of the finish line unless there is a food truck." Franklin snickered, feeling proud of his insult. I quickly checked my phone again for any missed calls. Still nothing.

Rene brought two plates to the table, placing one down in front of me. "For the lady, we have pan-seared pork tenderloin in a caramelized apple, pear, and onion glaze. And for the gentleman, we have a seasonal vegetable medley in a medium red curry and coconut milk sauce, pecan soup, sweet jasmine coconut rice, and scallions. Bon appétit!"

It's a well-known fact that I wasn't a fan of pork. There's something about the texture and taste that turned me off. But being polite, I took a small bite of the tenderloin.

Franklin took a bite of his green dish. "Oh, delicious... am I right?"

I wanted to say it smelled like a dirty gym sock and tasted like a foot. Trying not to gag, I said, "Oh, so good."

"Do I know how to pick the best restaurants or what?"

"Mmm hmmm." Stealthily, I lifted the napkin up to my mouth and spit into it. Thankfully Franklin was too into his meal to notice.

Suddenly Rene popped up behind me. "Ahem, miss, you have a piece of tenderloin on your dress." I looked down at my knees, quickly realizing I'd missed the napkin.

Franklin rolled his eyes. "Viola, you're so embarrassing."

"This is nothing. I once hid discarded food in my bra."

Franklin shook his head. "Okay, well, back to the wedding, I have a date in mind."

"Wait, you already decided on a date?" I could feel my pulse racing as anxiety kicked in. "Two years from now? Two and a half?"

Franklin cleaned off what was left in his plate. "Let's get this problem out of the way as soon as possible. Let's shoot for a couple months from now."

Trying to remain calm I said, "Get this *problem* out of the way? We're not talking about a fungal infection here."

Franklin took a deep breath and leaned back into his chair. "We have no choice. I only have one free day available."

"Day? When will we have the honeymoon? I had plans to grope Goofy at Disney World."

"Oh, that's not going to happen. Viola, you need to grow up and learn to make sacrifices. I'm a doctor now. I don't expect you to understand, so its OK."

"It's not OK," I replied. "You're being disrespectful to me."

Franklin looked at me, completely stunned. "Calm down Viola, it's fine."

"You know what?" I stood up and replied in utter disgust, "It's really not. You had no right to call that radio station and insult me the way you did."

He quickly got defensive. "Just sit down! People are staring."

"I don't care!" I said, looking quickly at the other tables. "Franklin, how you treat me and others is cruel. It's not all your fault though, I blame myself for being so pathetic and blind. But no more."

Franklin scoffed. "What are you saying?"

Looking down at Franklin, I lifted up my cellphone up to my mouth like a mic. "We're done *bitch*!" I stretched my arm out and dropped the 'mic'. Unfortunately, I didn't account for the bowl of soup below it, which made a messy splash all over the table. Biting my lips, I quickly grabbed my wet phone from the scalding hot soup and marched out of the restaurant with my head held high.

Like Cinderella, I arrived home just after midnight, and similarly to her losing her shoe, I accidentally lost an earring.

"Hey, Viola, how was dinner?" Vik asked as he mixed a protein shake.

Exhausted, I collapsed on the couch. "We went to Russian Roulette."

"Isn't that the place that sent three people into anaphylactic shock?"

"Yeah, and after I left, a woman with a peanut allergy was carried away on a stretcher."

"All right, I'm headed to bed. Don't forget we start training for the marathon tomorrow."

Covering my mouth for a lengthy yawn, I said, "Can't wait… Oh and I dumped Franklin."

Stunned by my announcement, Vik choked on his protein shake.

After I answered all his questions, I was finally free to jump into bed. I passed out while obsessively scrolling through old text messages between me and Christos.

Chapter Nineteen

178 Lbs

November 29, 2016

The next morning, I woke up in a panic as I completely forgot to set my alarm and was late for training. My backup alarm would typically be Shaniqua's shrieking, but she'd spent the night at her new boyfriend's place, and Vik must have had an errand to run as he was nowhere to be seen.

Despite having to run around the apartment like a child with uncontrollable diarrhea, I felt really excited to get to the gym. Not only did the guild have a new goal in reach, but we were also starting a new journey. I had no doubt in my mind that we were going to cross that finish line. A whole new chapter of my life was about to begin, filled with wedding parties, birthdays, and, of course, unplanned pregnancies.

Grabbing my gym bag and cell phone, I stumbled out the door and ran to the car. I really didn't need to rush, but I was driven by excitement and I didn't want to miss a moment. I tossed my cell phone onto the passenger seat and drove off.

Five minutes into the drive, I realized I was speeding after a car honked at me. I slowed down a little, then my phone rang loudly, causing a lot of intrigue.

I took my eyes off the road for a second to peek over at the phone—it was an incoming call from Christos!

While keeping one shaky hand on the steering wheel, I reached over to grab the phone, clumsily tipping it onto the ground.

Realizing that I could lose my only opportunity to hear his voice, I quickly took my eyes off the road and dove for the cell phone. After a few bounces, I was able to grab it and answer the call in time.

"I love you!" I shouted just as a large blue truck barreled into the driver's side of my car, causing my vehicle to roll over several times.

While upside down, I heard people shouting from all directions, but all I could see was gray smoke, shards of glass, and an airbag covered in white powder. Trying desperately to unlock my seat belt, I was unsuccessful and eventually passed out.

Unaware of the date, time, or place, I woke up surrounded by beeping machines, a short woman, and a long breathing tube that was inserted into my mouth.

"Welcome back, sleepyhead. I'm Betty, one of the nurses here in the ICU. You have been asleep for a very long time. Can you hear me okay?"

I tried speaking before realizing that the tube was not going to allow it.

"Oh, don't speak, dear. We don't want to bruise your throat. A simple nod will do."

I nodded, quickly realizing that my hands were roped to the rails of the bed. Naturally I tried to escape from them.

"Relax, sweetie, the restraints are there to ensure you don't pull out the breathing tube. Oh! I almost forgot, there's somebody here to see you. Are you okay for a visitor?"

I nodded, trying to push myself up higher against my pillow as the visitor entered. Feeling chilly and groggy, I didn't recognize the mysterious man until he grabbed onto my restrained hand.

"Viola, it's Christos." I barely recognized him as his iconic beard was shaven off.

Although I was warned, I tried talking but was instantly blocked by the pressure of the breathing tube.

"Shh… it's okay." Christos gently lifted the blanket over my shaky legs.

Nurse Betty came back in. "I'm going to give you something to help you relax." She looked at Christos and said, "A breathing tube can be traumatic for some people."

As Betty injected the painkiller into my IV, Christos leaned in, kissed my forehead, and whispered, "I love you, too."

I must have passed out from the medication because I don't remember what happened after that.

I was awoken by loud conversations surrounding my hospital bed. Several men and women in white coats chatted amongst themselves while I was trying to comprehend the big medical words they were throwing around.

Things were looking brighter—the breathing tube and restraints had been removed.

"Viola, I'm Dr. Rotenberg and behind me is the medical team. Do you know where you are?"

I swallowed intensely and replied with a raspy voice, "Who's Viola?"

The doctors immediately started panicking and flipping through their clipboards.

"There was nothing indicating amnesia," said a woman.

Dr. Rotenberg turned around. "Let's run another MRI."

"I'm just messing with you guys."

He breathed a huge sigh of relief. "We are making arrangements to move you to the general ward."

Clearing my throat, I asked, "So am I good to go home, then? Cause I have a marathon to train for, and nothing is going to get in my way."

The doctors quietly glanced at each other for a few seconds before Dr. Rotenberg spoke. "Ms. Ginamero, your legs sustained extensive trauma from the accident. We can try physical therapy, but even with a lot of hard work, there is a good chance that you will never walk again."

Chapter Twenty

❶❼⓪ Lbs

December 6, 2016

After I was moved to the general ward, the guild was allowed to visit me all at once. I learned from Betty that they'd taken turns sitting with me while I was in the ICU, but I was asleep whenever they came in. I hadn't seen them since before the accident and was excited to see all of them. And Christos.

Staring at my shiny new wheelchair, I was nestled in my new bed when Shaniqua burst into the room, followed by the rest of the guild. I clapped in excitement as I saw each of their beautiful faces.

"I missed you guys so much!" I said, trying not to tear up. "Where is Christos? Actually, wait, let me apply some lipstick before he enters."

"Honey," said Vik, "lipstick isn't going to help. You look like you were transferred from the psych ward."

I reached into the wooden bedside drawer, where the contents of my purse were dumped. "Trust me, it's no ordinary lipstick. It's a beautiful lusty red color that I discovered off the rim of a used Starbucks cup."

Vik gave me a look of disgust. "Eww... Viola."

"Relax, it was in a Ziploc bag."

"Ziploc bags are very tough," said Remy. "You would be surprised to see how much pee they can hold."

I puckered my lips, gliding the lipstick along my chapped mouth. "Okay, go get him. I'm ready!"

Vik shook his head in confusion. "Get who?"

"Christos, of course!" I said, tilting my head flirtatiously for his arrival.

"Okay, first of all, when you tilt your head like that you look like a constipated chicken. Second of all, Christos isn't here. He's still MIA."

"Huh? What are you talking about? He came to see me in the ICU. He told me he loved me. Wait a minute." I grinned devilishly. "Are you guys playing a joke on me? Is he hiding in my bathroom? I hope not, cause let's just say this hospital food is not making my bowels smell like potpourri."

"Viola, we guarded the ICU the whole time," said Vik. "Christos never came. You must have been delirious."

My eyes widened in shock. "No, he was there. I remember because his face was fully shaved, too."

"Okay, now I know you were hallucinating for sure," he said. "Christos would never in a million years shave his beard; that thing took forever to grow."

I looked over at Shaniqua, who was quietly staring out the window with her arms crossed against her chest. "Shan, aren't you happy to see me?"

She slowly turned around, revealing fire in her eyes. "I need a minute alone with Viola." The boys quickly scurried out of the room.

Smiling, I teased, "Are you coming over to give me a big hug and kiss?"

"Bitch, have you lost your *mind*?" I forgot how loud Shaniqua could get when she was furious. "Viola, you nearly died."

"That wasn't my first near-death experience. I once choked on a strawberry during food sex."

"Girl, I'm not in the mood for your jokes right now." Shaniqua took a deep breath and sat down next to me. "If I ever catch you texting and driving again, I'm going to snatch your phone and smash it into pieces on the pavement at the next red light." She gave me a stern look and said, "You got it?"

"Got it."

"Good," she said, leaning in to hug me tightly. "If you need anything, I'm here for you. We're all here to get you through this." Shaniqua yelled into my ear, "Boys, you can come back!"

Remy and Vik entered with a large tote bag, pulling out the second most important item in my life, the first being a roll of toilet paper.

"My laptop!" I cheered with excitement. "This is perfect! my cell phone got busted in the accident and I'm behind on my Facebook stalking." Vik passed it to me. "Actually, can you put it on the wheelchair?"

An awkward pause filled the room.

"Okay, let's address the elephant in the room. I have a wheelchair now. It's not a big deal. I'm looking forward to accidentally running over Janette's toe."

Remy whispered to Vik, "I don't see any elephant…"

Shaniqua grabbed the bag from Vik. "We have more for you." She dug into the bag and pulled out several bottles of supplements, including the sweetest nectar of them all.

"Aminos! Oh my God, I think I just had a mini orgasm." Hugging the bottle like a newborn child, I asked, "So how's the marathon training going? Isn't it tomorrow?"

"Like the state of your hair, it's a disaster," said Vik.

Shaniqua added, "Vik is right, at this point we just hope we can make it to the finish line. We can only last three of the seven miles on a treadmill.

"I had to run to the bathroom multiple times," said Remy.

"To puke?" I asked, feeling concerned.

"No, I had diarrhea."

Setting down the bottle, I said, "You guys got this. I know you will make it to the finish line. I'll be cheering you from here."

"When are they releasing you?" Vik asked.

"No clue. They have to make sure the apartment is wheelchair accessible. I don't even think there's a ramp outside of the building. I may have to move."

Shaniqua grabbed my hand. "Girl, if we have to carry your ass in through the front door, we will."

A short woman in scrubs popped her head into the room. "Sorry, guys, visiting hours are up."

Vik waved. "All right, Viola, we'll see you tomorrow. Enjoy the laptop, and please run a comb through that hair."

"Don't worry, I have a plastic fork I saved from dinner that's perfect for the job."

Shaniqua gently touched my shoulder. "I left my number with the nurse. If you need anything, you let her know."

"Can she bring my dignity back? Cause the doctors saw my goods in the ICU, and let's just say I'm not expecting any positive Yelp reviews."

Remy was the last to exit the room. Before leaving, he asked a profound question, taking me completely by surprise. "Hey… how come you don't make anymore videos? I miss them."

I pondered the question, sitting alone in the room. Was it time to return to the online world? I'd abandoned my YouTube star status as it had become too distracting, but really, my fans were the ones who had given me the initial motivation to lose the weight.

The night nurse was kind enough to bring me my laptop, and I felt a little guilty, as she was busy with a rotation switch. I felt even more guilty after I brought her back a second time to plug it in. I told her I owed her a coffee after I brought her in a third time to turn on all the lights in the room.

After a few minutes, I was all set for my big return. "Hey, guys, it's Viola." I waved cheerfully with both hands. "It's been a long time since I posted my last video, but I'm here now and I have a lot to share."

I gently slapped my cheeks. "As you can see, I lost a ton of fat off my face and body—the entire guild did. I look and feel incredible, and I have you guys to thank as one of my motivators."

Tilting my engagement ring in front of the camera, I shrugged my shoulders. "Franklin finally proposed! Look how pretty it is! And the diamond is real, trust me. I Googled how to spot a fake. But this ring is going back, I dumped him. Ladies and gents, don't be afraid to be in control, nobody has the right to mistreat you. Learn to value your life, value the ones around you, and most importantly, value yourself."

I took a deep breath. "Life is full of ups and downs. We lost a member of the guild and I was recently in a car accident. Actually I'm still in the hospital and will be here for a long time, as I was told that there is a good chance I will never walk again. That kinda sucks, cause I was supposed to run in a marathon tomorrow with the guild."

Pulling my long hair over my shoulder, I puckered my lips. "That's okay, though, you know why? Because I know I will walk again. Don't let people tell you what you can't do. Work hard, stay motivated, be consistent, and you will achieve everything."

Suddenly, I was interrupted by a repulsive smell. "Eww… I smell sewage. I think my toilet is backing up… Oh, wait, never mind, it's just my hair. I can't remember the last time it was washed."

I tossed my hair behind my head. "I have one more thing I wanted to say before I go to bed. Working out and watching what you eat isn't about becoming thin or muscular; it's about making an investment in yourself. Look around at all your loved ones and family members. How many of them have some sort of health issue that could have easily been prevented with a healthy diet and activity? My message to all of you is: Start now. Invest in yourself for the future. I promise it will pay off."

"Okay, my hair is now making me gag, so I'm going to have to buzz the nurse to help me Febreze it or something. Anyways, feel free to leave a comment below. Oh, and please remember to click like before you leave. I'm not sure how many people follow this channel as I don't pay attention to the counter, but I wish you all the best and once again, I thank you for your inspiration and motivation."

I tucked the laptop between my legs and closed my eyes, but after half an hour of tossing and turning I gave up and decided to stare at the ceiling. I couldn't help but think about Christos. Was I really hallucinating that he was in the ICU? I mean, it wouldn't have been the first time my eyes played tricks on me. I once thought I saw Mel Gibson at Walmart, but it ended up being a random bearded man who came in to steal produce.

Chapter Twenty-One

❶❻❾ Lbs

Marathon Day – December 7, 2016

I woke up feeling like I'd just given birth to a watermelon, mainly because I was exhausted from the night nurse who was forced to interrupt my sleep constantly to take blood, empty my catheter, and take vitals. I didn't show one ounce of annoyance, though, as she was just doing her job and she worked incredibly hard. In fact, I had nothing but respect for her. If I was in her shoes, I would have been passed out on the floor in front of the patient.

The marathon was about to start and I was thinking about the gong show that was probably occurring over at the apartment right at that second. Shaniqua and Vik were probably fighting over the bathroom, while Remy was searching for the biggest Ziploc bag he could find.

I wished I'd had the chance to wish them good luck in person—the marathon was a milestone. Sure, to most people it was just a run/walk from point A to point B, but to the guild it was the final piece in the jigsaw puzzle of our big goal, and I would be lying if I said I wasn't disappointed in myself. I was sad that I wasn't able to complete the final goal, but like my monthly cold sores, I'd learn to live with it.

Covering my face with the bedsheet, I tried to get a few more minutes of shut eye when I heard a familiar voice.

"Girl, are you still sleeping?" The sheets were ripped off my face to reveal Shaniqua, Vik, and Remy standing next to my bed.

"What are you guys doing here?" I said, using the bedside rails to pull myself up. "The marathon is about to start! You're going to miss it."

"We had a pit stop to make," said Vik.

I cringed. "Does Remy have the runs again?"

Shaniqua sternly looked at me. "You didn't think we were going to do this thing without you, did you?"

Confused, I asked, "What are you talking about?"

"We are running out of time. Remy, grab her and put her in the chair."

I never realized how muscular Remy was until he lifted me up and gently placed me in my wheelchair.

"Guys, as much as I would love to do the marathon with all of you, I can't push myself alone for seven miles."

Vik looked at Shaniqua. "Should we show her?"

Shaniqua nodded.

Remy wheeled me over to the window where a large white van was waiting at the entrance. The driver of the van waved at me enthusiastically.

"What are you guys up to?" I asked, waving back at the guy.

"No time to explain; we have to leave now. They don't allow late entries."

"We have like fifteen minutes to get there," said Vik. "We better move!"

Remy quickly spun me around.

Exiting the room, I asked, "How can I leave? Isn't there a protocol or something?"

"We got you a day pass," said Shaniqua. "That's why there's a van waiting for us downstairs. I told you, girl, we got you… always."

"Good luck, Viola!" shouted a male voice behind me.

"You can do it! We all believe in you!" yelled a female voice.

As Remy wheeled me down the corridors of the hospital, several nurses and doctors wished me luck.

Vik shouted, "We have twelve minutes!"

"There is the elevator!" yelled Shaniqua. "Quick, everybody get in!" She frantically pressed the close-door button.

Remy started hopping as the elevator dropped to the main floor. "All this rushing is making me have to pee."

I smiled warmly. "I feel like I'm being kidnapped. This is like a dream come true."

Shaniqua shouted as the door opened. "Okay, we need to run to the entrance!"

My greasy hair started bouncing as Remy raced to the entrance, where the big white van was waiting for us.

"We have 10 minutes!" shouted Vik.

The driver greeted me as Remy parked the wheelchair on the lift. "Hi, I'm Brock. Your friends filled me in. Hold on tight, cause we only have a few minutes to get there. He secured the chair as the guild hopped into the back with me.

Brock hopped into his seat and drove off as if he'd just robbed a 7-Eleven. Remy was forced to grab my chair as it moved constantly with the inertia of the vehicle.

Shaniqua's phone rang, and thinking it was marathon related, she quickly answered it. "Hello?"

Cramped against the metal walls of the van, we all quietly listened to her conversation, but she hung up before anything could be understood.

Holding tightly onto my wheelchair, I asked, "Who was that?"

"Some lawyer guy who has been trying to get a hold of us. I haven't had time to deal with it, so he's just going to have to wait."

"He's probably looking for more of Barbara-Anne's records," said Vik.

Brock shouted from the front of the van. "Hey, do you guys like historical trivia?"

I shook my head. "I'm terrible at anything history. I used to think Lady Marmalade was the Queen of France."

"One minute left, folks!" said Vik. The van took a sharp turn, making Vik fall onto the metal floor.

Feeling a bit scared, I asked, "Should we be praying for our lives back here?"

Shaniqua looked at me. "Girl, since when are you religious?"

"Hey, I have respect for the church."

"Didn't you once skip Christmas mass for all-you-can eat fish tacos?"

"In my defense, guacamole was a free add-on that night."

The van came to an unexpected stop, forcing Shaniqua to fall on top of Vik. Brock turned his head and announced, "We're here!"

The last time I raced against the clock was when I accidentally microwaved a burrito for ten minutes. Thankfully, arriving late for the marathon was not as messy, or so I thought.

Arriving a few minutes after the starting gun went off, we headed straight to the check-in table, hoping it wasn't too late to enter.

Shaniqua shouted, "Move your ass!" The guild, including myself were panting. We were all ready to collapse at the check-in table.

Reaching the table, we all shouted to grab the attention of the woman at the table, who had her back turned.

"*Janette?*" I said as she turned around, holding a clipboard against her chest. "I didn't recognize you in that hat and sunglasses. You are totally rockin' that look. And your tan has this glo—"

"Save it, Viola," she said. "You're not getting in. None of you are."

I rolled myself around the table to get closer to her. "Oh, please, please let us through. It's my fault we were late!" Batting my eyelashes flirtatiously, I said, "I will make you a mango smoothie. On the house, of course. What do you say?"

"With chocolate chips?" she asked cheerfully.

"Sure!" I said, clapping my hands together.

"No!" she replied, clapping mockingly. "You guys have a few minutes to get out of here before I call security. You may be registered, but only participants who have checked in can cross that starting line and that won't be any of you."

I turned around and looked at the guild. "I guess that's it, then."

Shaniqua took a deep breath, walked behind the table, bent down, and whispered a long sentence into Janette's ear. The second she stood back up, Janette starting writing on her clipboard.

Smiling forcibly, she ripped off four pieces of paper and handed them to me. "Here are your marathon numbers. I wish you all the best of luck."

Curious as to what Shaniqua said to her, I grabbed the papers from her hand. "Thanks." Janette grabbed her belongings and quickly ran off like a deer caught in headlights.

Vik looked down at the table. "Umm, I think she forgot her purse."

Handing out the numbers, I bit my lip in excitement. "I'm feeling really nervous. I told you guys, I can't push myself for seven miles."

Shaniqua grabbed the back of my chair and began running to the starting line. "You're not pushing yourself."

To my surprise, hundreds of people were holding motivational signs along the metal barrier gates, cheering and screaming as they saw me roll through the starting line.

I was taken in with surprise. "Oh my God, where did all these people come from?" The signs were heartwarming and humorous. One man held one that said 'Forget Franklin, Marry Me!' while another one said 'Viola gave me a Bubble Butt.' But one sign in particular made me tear up a little: 'We Invest in You.'

"These are the people that saw your video," said Vik. "The ones who want to see you succeed."

I couldn't help but get emotional, as I never realized how much others cared for me. We are usually so busy in our own worlds that we forget about the others around us.

Vik gently pushed Shaniqua out of the way, grabbing the back of the chair. "Okay, it's my turn."

Looking up, I yelled, "We did it, Vik!" The crowd cheered louder with every step we took.

"Yeah, and you're wearing nice socks today, too!"

"Aww, thanks for the compliment."

"Viola, I wasn't complimenting you, I was complimenting the socks." He bent down and took a sniff of my hair. "Okay, I'm out!"

Remy jumped in, grabbing the chair tightly. "Hey, Viola, I have something to confess."

"Hey, Rem! What is it?"

"I once got a distracted-driving ticket."

"Did you get it for texting?" I asked, feeling a little concerned.

"No, I was picking my nose."

Looking up, I smiled warmly at his upside-down face. "Don't ever change, Remy. I love you just the way you are."

"Love you, too, Viola."

The first few miles were a piece of cake to run, as the energy from the crowd pushed us through, but by the final mile we were forced to take many walking breaks due to exhaustion.

"I'm not going to make it!" Vik shouted. "Think anyone will notice if I hopped in an Uber?" We were all panting, including myself as I pushed myself during the final mile.

"Only one more mile, guys," I said. "We can't give up now!" We were dead last, but the crowds had stayed back to cheer us on. Either they were getting louder with each mile or my hearing was getting more sensitive from wax buildup.

Vik looked at me, barely able to stand. "Easy for you to say, you have a catheter."

Barely able to speak, Shaniqua yelled at us with very supportive advice. "Everybody just shut the hell up and run!" The sweat on her T-shirt was so heavy it looked as if she'd entered a wet T-shirt competition.

Vik pointed at Remy, who impressively was the only one who still had stamina and was running with consistent speed. "What's his secret?"

"Oh, I'm imagining that I'm being chased by a bear," said Remy.

"There it is!" I shouted, spotting the finish line. "Whoa, look at all the people."

"Ugh, I just got a bad taste in my mouth," said Vik.

"Me, too. I think I just rolled into someone's fart cloud."

The crowd roared as we approached the finish line. I should have been excited, but my stomach was in knots. I was about to complete a milestone, and the one person I wanted to be at the finish line was missing.

Several people were at the finish line preparing to take photos of the guild.

Looking to my left at Shaniqua and Remy, then to my right at Vik, I took a deep breath and said, "When we cross that line, we're no longer a guild." I smiled warmly. "We're family." Like the sudden leak in my catheter bag, we were about to make a big splash.

The crowd rushed us as we crossed the finish line.

"Good job!" shouted another female participant, patting my shoulder. Every person there was shouting some sort of supportive comment, but we were too exhausted to comprehend anything.

Vik collapsed on a group of sweaty male participants, and to this day he still denies that it was intentional. Shaniqua grabbed onto a nearby tree like King Kong, smacking cell phones out of her face. Remy, with a miraculous amount of energy, utilized it by taking selfies with a group of screaming girls.

Surrounded by swarms of people all around my chair, I couldn't move or see anything but crotches. After a few minutes, a gap was created, allowing me to see into the distance.

I caught sight of a recognizable figure. I wheeled myself closer, gently pushing people aside.

"Christos?" I whispered to myself. Like the time a Pinkberry opened nearby, my bladder was about to burst with excitement.

Standing a short way's away stood Christos, wearing a black sports jacket, white button-up shirt, and black dress pants. His clean-shaven face proved that I was not hallucinating his ICU visit.

We stared at each other for several seconds, frozen like statues ten meters apart. It wasn't until I spotted a carry-on suitcase hiding behind him that I started moving closer.

I looked nervously at Christos, "Is it really you?"

Christos nodded, "It's me."

Tearing up, I reached out to him, "I'm so sorry for everything, I've been a complete idiot, can you please forgive me?"

Christos walked towards me, and kneeled down to hold my hands. "I'm still madly in love with you, Viola."

I wrapped my fingers tightly around his. "I love you too!"

Christos lifted me into the air, and spun around while we kissed passionately. The crowd, quickly taking notice, clapped and cheered. I was turning red in the cheek, and not because the back of my hospital gown was untied and showing my bare ass, but because he still gave me butterflies.

My eyes widened as I took notice of the carry-on again. "Are you going somewhere?"

Christos gently lowered me back down into the wheelchair. "I've learned that until I receive closure, I won't be able to move on. I have to find Helena."

"You're leaving me?" I asked, confused.

"I'll never leave you," Christos replied, kissing my forehead. "Remember this moment, but not as a memory of me leaving, but as the start of a new journey. Our journey."

With his eyes locked onto mine, he slowly took a few steps back and turned around. Feeling a panic that I was never going to see him again, I called out to him, but within seconds he was engulfed by a swarm of people and disappeared.

After the crowds cleared and all the participants went home, the four of us sat down on the finish line, staring into the distance.

Vik looked at me. "You've been quiet. What's up?"

"I'm just tired," I said. The truth was that I couldn't stop thinking about Christos. Where was he going? Was he planning on coming back?

"Hey, did anyone else see Christos earlier?" said Remy.

"Nope," I said nervously. "Don't think so, Rem." It felt wrong to lie, but until I knew more, there was no point in telling the guild anything.

"You're probably right," he said. "I also thought I saw Jesus hiding in the bushes."

Suddenly Shaniqua stood up to read an e-mail. It was the announcement we were expecting, and the most important event to kick off the next big challenge in our lives. Losing the weight was only the start—more on that later—I wouldn't want to jump ahead.

Clearing her throat, Shaniqua announced, "Hey, guys, effective immediately, The Fitness Hut is permanently closed."

I exhaled deeply. "Well, looks like we are unemployed, Shan. It's been a good run. What are you going to do now?"

"Viola, I'm moving to Chicago to manage my cousin's hair salon."

"*What?*" I shouted, almost falling out of my chair. "When were you going to tell me?"

"After you got out of the hospital." I was speechless and sick to my stomach. "Girl, you know I love you, but I have a mountain of debt to pay off and the job in Chicago pays good money."

Resting my cheek on my hand, I said, "Well, at least I still have Vik."

Vik bit his lip. "Actually, I was thinking of traveling around the world for a year... I have to spend the balance in my trust fund before my parents take it away."

I looked over at Remy anxiously. "Rem, please tell me you're not going anywhere."

"No... but all these girls gave me tiny pieces of paper with numbers on them. I think it's a code."

I took a deep breath, looking at the blue sky. "Maybe I'll get a dog."

"Viola," said Shaniqua. "You're the last person who should be taking care of a dog."

"Hey, I can take care of a dog. My Tamagotchi lasted one full year before it starved to death."

Vik stood up. "The sun's starting to set. Maybe we should get back to the hospital."

Shaniqua dug into her pocket and pulled out a set of door keys. "Not without saying goodbye to a friend first."

Although he was going against protocol, Brock was kind enough to make a pit stop at The Fitness Hut before taking us back to the hospital.

Unlocking the front door, Shaniqua was the first to enter. "Viola, can you lock up? I'll grab the lights."

"Don't worry, I'm on it," I replied, closing the door.

It was a surreal feeling, being the only ones in the gym. On a normal day you could hear the humming of treadmills and the continuous clanging of dumbbells hitting the floor.

The first stop we made was to The Protein Hut, where my eleven-year employment had officially come to an end.

Shaniqua looked at me. "You know what I'm not going to miss about working here?"

I wheeled over to her. "Watching me eat fallen fruit off the floor?"

"No, cleaning those nasty-ass bathrooms. Hey, did you lock the door?"

"Of course. Shan, you need to have faith in me."

"Really, Viola? Do I have to remind you of the time you thought you locked the apartment door, and we returned to find Mormons in our living room?"

"Hey, I became really good Facebook friends with two of them. Trust me, it's locked and nobody is getting in."

After reminiscing about all the good and bad times behind that counter, we eventually made our way to where our fitness journey began—the training room.

Remy entered the dark room. "Hey, where are the lights?"

"Right here," said Vik, and the training room lit up with memories.

I rolled over to a corner of the room. "Aww, this is where I first projectile vomited."

Suddenly a man holding a briefcase walked into the training room. "Hello?" He was a clean-cut, middle-aged man dressed in a suit, complemented by black square-framed glasses.

Shaniqua looked at the man. "How the hell did you get in here?"

"I let myself in, the door was unlocked."

She turned around and gave me a dirty look. "You said you locked the door."

"The door must be broken. Shan, I'm tired of not being trusted. I promise you that I locked it. It really hurts that you don't belie—"

"Actually, the keys were left in the door," the man said. He pulled them out of his pocket and handed them over to Shaniqua.

Quickly changing the subject, I wheeled over to the man. "The gym is closed, sir, but we can let you out."

"Actually, I've been trying to get a hold of you guys," he said. "I left several messages with Shaniqua."

"What are you talking about?" said Vik.

Shaniqua pushed Vik aside. "Oh, you're that lawyer that's been calling me. Listen, we've had a long day. Whatever records you need can wait until tomorrow. Aight?"

He shook his head nervously. "I think there has been a misunderstanding. That's not why I'm here."

"I don't have time for this," Shaniqua barked. "Remy, carry this foo out to the curb." Remy walked up behind the man, lifting him up.

"Wait!" the man shouted. "You guys are in Barbara-Anne's will!"

"Stop!" I shouted. "What did he just say?"

"Did anyone know anything about a will?" said Vik. "I didn't see anything when we cleaned out her house."

"Remy, put him down," said Shaniqua. She crossed her arms. "Okay, you have two minutes to explain why you're here."

He quickly kneeled, unlocked his briefcase, and pulled out a stapled document. "Before Barbara-Anne died, she amended her last will and testament to add you five individuals."

"Oh my galoshes… Us?" said Vik.

"Are you sure there isn't some sort of mistake?" I said.

Remy raised his hand. "My parents told me I was a mistake."

Shaniqua shook her head. "Viola's right. Barbara-Anne only had the house, and the bank took that. As far as I know there is nothing else in her name."

The man flipped through the will. "Actually, she and her late husband owned a few businesses, but after his death she sold the majority of them and kept only one, The Fitness Hut. And according to her will, you five are now the owners."

The four of us quietly glanced at each other before Vik spoke up. "So you're telling me that the four of us own this gym?"

"No, that's incorrect," he said. "Five of you own this business."

Confused, I asked, "Who's the fifth member?"

He flipped through the pages. "Let's see, the five listed are Viola, Shaniqua, Remy, Vik, and Christos." He slipped the will back into the briefcase, locking it tightly. "I have to get going, but I'll be in touch for the full turnover. Oh, and I will need all five of you available for signing. He took a quick glance at the gym. "I have to be honest, it might be in your best interest to sell this business as soon as possible. It's been performing at a loss for a while now." With those final words, he opened the training room door and slipped out, leaving us with a thousand unanswered questions.

Shaniqua looked me. "What just happened?"

I smiled. "I think our next challenge just happened."

"Should we sell?" asked Vik. "We know nothing about running a business."

Feeling nervous and anxious, I grabbed my hair. "Okay, let's deal with the elephant in the room. Who knows when I will be discharged from the hospital, plus Shan's moving to Chicago and Vik is travelling abroad for a year."

Shaniqua grabbed onto the back of my chair. "Girl, I have told you a dozen times. I got you, always. I ain't going anywhere now. Are you forgetting we didn't know a thing about weight loss and fitness? Now look at us."

"Shan is right," added Vik. "We can do this. And I can use my trust fund for start-up expenses."

I nudged him. "Are you sure? What about your travel plans?"

"I'm sure. Besides, somebody needs to make sure you look like an owner, and not a troll doll."

Remy whispered to Vik, "I still don't see this elephant."

Taking a deep breath, I looked out the window, "We still have one loose end to tie up."

"What's that?" Shaniqua asked.

"I don't know where he went, or why, but all I know is that we have to find Christos."

Epilogue

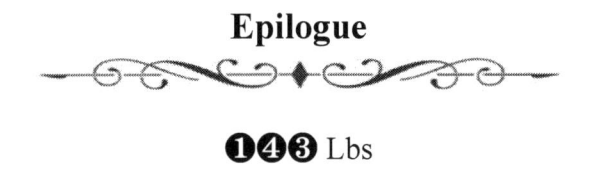

❶❹❸ Lbs

Thanksgiving Day – November 22, 2018

"I can't believe that was two years ago. It feels like the marathon was yesterday." I leaned over the white cradle and placed Anne gently down. "Newborns are supposed to be sleeping. You are clearly a night owl like your mom."

Leaning against the rails, it was hard to peel myself away from Anne, being fully mesmerized by each little kick from her tiny foot and squeal out of her soft baby lips.

Anne started crying. I gently picked her back up and held her tightly, rocking her back and forth. "Sweetie, I know you want to know the rest of the story, but Mommy has to get downstairs, your aunt and uncles have been waiting."

Swinging back and forth, I heard the door open behind me. "Oh, honey, if that's you, can you please grab her bottle? Maybe she's hungry."

Warm hands wrapped around my body, pulling me in tightly. "She's beautiful, just like her mother. She's also a poop machine, also like her mother."

I turned around and gently kicked his shin. "Christos!"

"Are you still telling Anne stories? Ooh, did you get to the part with Helena?"

"God, no! I'm gonna need a glass of wine for that one."

Christos kissed my forehead, scratching my nose with his fully grown beard. "It's been one hell of a journey, my beautiful wife, I'm sure Anne will look forward to the finale in the sequel."

I raised my eyebrows and looked at Christos. "Oh, it's definitely going to have to be a trilogy."

Looking down, I noticed that Anne had fallen asleep. We ever so quietly lowered her into the crib, turned on the baby monitor, and tiptoed out of the room.

Christos closed the door and followed me down the stairs towards a commotion of laughter and loud chattering.

"Viola!" screamed Shaniqua, barely able to move, as she was as pregnant as she could be, due any day now. "Girl, come sit down, you've been up there forever. We had to send Christos up to get you." She was sitting next to Remy, holding his hand.

I sat down at the table next to Remy and Shaniqua. "Did you and Remy narrow down baby names?"

"We are trying not to choose a silly name like celebrities do," said Remy.

Shaniqua smiled at Remy. "Yeah, so we are going to go with Quinoa for a girl and Kale for a boy."

"Shan," said Vik, "I still can't believe you two are having a baby. It feels like it was just yesterday when Remy was getting on your nerves."

Christos sat down next to me, rubbing my shoulder. "A lot has happened in the last two years, but here the five of us are." He grabbed the turkey slicer off the table. "Are we all set to eat?"

"Wait!" I leaped out of my chair and ran to the kitchen. I returned with a single white glass plate and placed it down on the table next to Vik. "A plate for Barbara-Anne."

Christos squeezed my hand. "Would you like some coffee, dear?"

I nodded.

Christos poured scalding hot coffee into my cup, forcing me to bring it up to my chin to blow on it for several seconds.

Suddenly Vik leaped up off his chair as if he'd sat on a tack. "My shoes!"

Shaniqua looked down at the floor. "Umm, Viola, I think my water just broke."

The flavor of that coffee became unforgettable to me, and not because it was a reminder of the day Shaniqua went into labor, but because I spilled half of it down my blouse.

Losing the weight was just the start, the guild will return in…

THE FAT BITCH BUSINESS

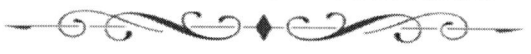

Printed in Great Britain
by Amazon